Missing

and a collection of other thought-provoking short stories

Chris Boult

Published by New Generation Publishing in 2020

First Edition

ISBN 978-1-80031-789-5

www.newgeneration-publishing.com

New Generation Publishing

Previous titles

In The Shadow of the Bayonet

Out of the Shadow

Recovery

Green Terror

Identity

The Welsh Boys

An Island Life

About the Author

Chris studied in Nottingham in the late 1970s. He joined the OTC and the TA and later served as a short service officer in the regular army before joining the probation service in 1986. He served as a probation officer and a manager in various setting and at different levels, working mostly with high risk offenders and often closely with both the police and the prison service. He retired from service in 2015. He started writing novels in 2013.This is a departure from the norm and his first publication of a series of short stories. It represents his eighth book.

Website : www.chrisboultauthor.co.uk

Chris is available to give talks to local groups on his experience of writing your own books.

Acknowledgements

Thanks to the large number of people who have helped me with this book. A particular thanks to all those family and friends involved in initial proof reading and advice.

Thanks to my publisher and Titanic Brewery for their assistance. Also thanks to Sheila King of Chapters bookshop in Stafford, Sam Littlemore of The Words Worth bookshop in Eccleshall for their support for local authors and to all other venues that continue to stock the books. Thanks to Lin Philips for her energy in organising local events for authors to share their work.

Thanks also to retired colleagues and those still working in criminal justice for their help with accuracy and in trying to keep me up to date with developments at work.

Author's note

Short stories present a different and interesting challenge. There is no scope for the level of character development and detail associated with full length stories. The narrative has to attract the reader and move the story on at a pace. I have deliberately written stories with a range of topics, albeit with some similar and overlapping themes. The common theme running through all my writing stems from my life and work experience. As such I have opened the book with a preface offering some personal reflections on criminal justice.

This is a different venture, one that I have enjoyed writing and hope you enjoy reading.

Please note that all these stories were written in the context of a world before Covid-19.

To all my family and friends

"A short story is a love affair. A novel is a marriage. A short story is a photograph; a novel is a film."

Lorrie Moore

"Short stories are tiny windows into other worlds and other minds and dreams. They are journeys you can make to the far side of the universe and still be back for dinner."

Neil Gaiman

Contents

PREFACE:

Don't worry, you'll only get five years. Reflections on criminal justice.

Introduction

Where to start? At the beginning, I suppose. Why take up a career in criminal justice? Well, believe it or not, when I first showed an interest in becoming a probation officer I was fascinated by notions of law and justice and, put simply, I wanted to help people with their problems; Naive of course, but true! So I wasn't motivated by catching people or punishment as aims in themselves, as others might be, but accepted these as inevitable features of 'the system.'

In my era, I was advised to complete the two years training (Certificate of Qualification in Social Work) and a degree, as that was the way the profession was going; all graduate entry. Also to get some 'life experience' to be able to present myself to join the service by the age of twenty seven, all a bit of a mouthful for a callow youth of sixteen!

Then it was possible to sign up to do a four year course that combined a degree and the CQSW, run by the polytechnics, in the 1970's. So that's what I did at Trent Polytechnic in Nottingham.

I also joined the University's Officer Training Corps, the OTC, a branch of the Territorial Army. This was great fun and good experience, in general, although at times it felt like being type cast as the Genghis Khan of social work and the wet woolly liberal of the army!

I completed the training in both fields, gained a Territorial Army commission, and passed selection for Sandhurst to join the regular army on a Short Service engagement. This would just about add up the years to reach twenty seven, allowing me to be eligible for the probation service. So what direct relevance did the army have for someone wishing to work in criminal justice, other than gaining 'life experience', as I'd been advised? Well, perhaps not a lot, I was to discover later, but it was a worthwhile experience in itself. Patrolling the streets and countryside of Northern Ireland was a sort of criminal justice; a peacekeeping role in support of the civil powers. Experience of a uniformed organisation, security and intelligence would also become useful later, as I would discover working both in the prisons and with the police.

In fact, had I have known at the time that, after completing my qualifications and having completed a short service commission, I would then be eligible for direct entry into the prison service as a junior Governor, my career might have taken a different course.

So, from starting training in 1977 to joining Staffordshire Probation Service in 1986, to retiring early due to ill health in 2015, what did I learn about criminal justice? What were my reflections on that experience?

I learnt early on that things changed constantly. By the time I joined the service at, as it happened, the age of twenty seven, eligibility had been reduced to twenty two!

This is the subject of this preface to my collection of short stories, not fiction this time, nor an autobiography, but a few thoughts on criminal justice in general. Others have written about their experience of being vets or doctors, for example, this is a personal view of life as a probation officer. Some names and details have been changed to protect the individuals.

Guilt & innocence.

Do we ever convict the innocent or let the guilty go free? Of course we do, no system is perfect. The question is to what extent does this happen and I expect that the honest answer to that is that we really don't know.

I certainly dealt with many offenders who claimed not to have committed or directly committed the offences they were currently serving a sentence for. This can take many forms. For those who complained bitterly about the injustice of perhaps being present at the time of the offence but not delivering the fatal blow, it was a relative view of culpability. I found myself saying that if you adopt a criminal lifestyle, the chances are that eventually you will get caught. You can hardly complain about being hard done by on one occasion if you take no account of the many other times when you committed offences but were never caught. It must be tempting for the police to seek to prosecute on the margins, taking a wider view than simple culpability for individual offences. It's not right, however, in principle, to target the 'innocent' for our own convenience, but I'm sure it happens.

For example, there was a young man that I met in prison at the start of a life sentence for murder. He had been active as part of a gang involved in dealing drugs, amongst other criminal activity. It was an entrenched lifestyle and he had an established and extensive criminal record, but did he commit this particular offence? He claimed not. His gang had targeted and shot dead the leader of a rival gang in a pub car park over a dispute about 'territory'; the claimed ownership of exclusive trading rights in a given area. His defence was simple; that, on that occasion, he simply wasn't there. He could not provide a reliable alibi and other members of the gang, reluctant to inform the police of any incriminating details of the incident, made no attempt to verify his story. So the police simply rounded up the whole gang, who they were already monitoring, and charged them all collectively with murder.

He might have been right, but as I explained, as a probation officer, it was not my role to make that judgement. Also, the official account of events and associated evidence could well be incomplete. The police could be aware of further information that was not admissible in court and not readily available to me, so I had to work with what I'd got: a murderer. A man prepared to kill to protect his own criminal activities. In this case, the offender was philosophical and accepted his lot without undue complaint. He focused on doing his time and preparing for demonstrating his suitability for release at some point in the future.

There were also those who claimed to have had no connection with the offence at all – the completely innocent. I met plenty of those, particularly in prison. Again, sometimes the system will get it wrong, but the difficulty for the practitioner is that far too many people claim to be innocent to be tenable, so which offenders, if any, are genuine? It was not my direct concern. The conversation I had regularly with prisoners was along these lines:

It's not my role to consider your guilt or innocence. I have to work on the basis that the system has got it right, whilst knowing that is not always true. You were there, I wasn't. You know what actually happened in your case and, if you genuinely believe that you didn't commit the offence, then I can't help you, your only recourse is to appeal. If you are right, I wish you luck. If you are simply trying to avoid the issue, then that won't help you.

Early release from a custodial sentence depends to a large extent on a calculation of risk to the public based on admission of guilt, acceptance of responsibility, some notion of regret and/or remorse and satisfactory completion of some work to address underlying factors contributing to offending. These could be, for example, substance abuse, poor thinking skills and decision making or unemployment or homelessness. It follows therefore that presenting your case to the parole board for consideration for release will not be well received if you simply state that 'you didn't do it' and have not addressed any of these factors. For some offenders, this is a device to avoid difficult issues and they effectively elect to prolong their own incarceration. For the genuine, however, it did seem harsh to me that adopting a stance of principle should result in a stalemate.

I certainly met several life sentence prisoners serving time for murder who I felt at least had a plausible case for appeal but, for various reasons, were either unable to bring their case to the relevant authority or were unsuccessful. Navigating your way through the rigours of a life sentence is no simple task, even for the most able and well balanced of people, which of course most prisoners aren't. Unlike the popular conception 'life does mean life', as even if and when they are released from prison, supervision on life licence is permanent, with the ever present possibility of immediate recall to prison without necessarily committing any further offence. Degrees of non-compliance or deterioration in circumstances leading to reasonable concern about escalation of risk to the public are sufficient grounds, in themselves, for the probation officer to request immediate recall, and it happens regularly.

Two cases come to mind of those serving a life sentence who I met in prison whose convictions seemed to me to be questionable. Neither had a prior criminal record and neither demonstrated the sort of behaviour in custody that would cause concern. For one, the crucial piece of evidence central to his conviction was the finding of a single finger print where the victim was murdered. This did seem a little too convenient. The other was subject to what he claimed was a false confession under duress from the police. He had no obvious motive to kill the elderly couple who had been targeted for a burglary. He was also a most unlikely burglar.

By way of perspective, however, in the vast majority of cases attracting a life sentence that I met, and there were many, the evidence tended to be compelling or overwhelming, leaving no doubt about culpability. In most cases, the prisoner accepted this, albeit uncomfortably or reluctantly. Breaking down those layers of self justifications and excuses can be a very long, painful but necessary process.

Whatever stance a prisoner takes about culpability, there is a period of adjustment following sentence. Prior to conviction and sentence, the concentration is all about organising your defence, honestly and realistically or not, as the case may be. Post-sentence the concentration needs to change and this can happen soon or, for some prisoners, it takes considerably longer, or indeed for others is a point that is never reached.

If an appeal is unrealistic or not, under consideration, post-sentence, the prisoner needs to change their perspective to an honest and open-minded reflective approach to their own failings and limitations. This is not something that many offenders find easy, but it is a necessary part of any attempt at rehabilitation. If the person has already come to the realisation that they have to change their destructive lifestyle then capturing the moment can be energising and therapeutic. This is a theme we shall come back to later.

One memory remains with me. Having just started as the manager of the probation team of one particular prison, I received an early invitation to attend and speak to 'the lifers group.' A mutual support group started by a colleague, this was a self-help exercise recognising the particular needs of this group of prisoners. It was an odd feeling, sitting alone as a member of staff in a smoke-filled room, as they were then, with twenty convicted murderers and rapists. Not an experience that many people have. It was an early attempt, of course, to weigh me up and to intimidate a new arrival who would have an impact on their future sentence management, all part of the game.

Does either prison or rehabilitation 'work'?

This is the big question – are any of our efforts to divert people from crime and reform offenders effective? If not, why do we spend huge amounts of money on potentially making 'bad people' no better or even worse?

The answers to these questions are inevitably not entirely straight forward. The history of this debate in essence has moved from 'nothing works' to 'prison works' to 'what works' and beyond.

Prior to the 1970's, these questions largely weren't being asked in any systematic way. When they were, the initial response from the academic community, from analysis of worldwide research, was that 'Nothing works'. This was often cited as a council of despair and misused to discredit worthy attempts at progress and reform. What was actually meant by the phrase was that no one method is consistently clearly more effective than any other. In other words, there was no magic single solution to addressing crime. This, of course, is hardly a surprise. More about the development of ideas will come later.

As a response, right wing thinkers used this mantra to bang the drum for punishment and deterrence. Never mind 'trendy' attempts at reform, the over-simplistic dictum was that if you treat offenders harshly enough not only will they cease their activities, i.e. not reoffend, but it will deter others from doing so to. That was effectively an appeal to popularism. It was a simple justification for a self-perpetuating system and the recasting of the mantra by Michael Howard as home secretary to 'Prison works' with a massive investment in prison building and the lengthening of sentences in general.

In the same way as you can't build your way out of congestion by simply making more roads, the same can be said of dealing with crime; that you can't solve crime by simply building more prisons. The facts were that a doubling of the prison population over several decades produced little or no discernable improvement in reconviction rates.

That has been the main measure over time of 'effectiveness'; what proportion of those released from prison go on to reoffend within two years? The figure has stubbornly remained at around 60%. How does this compare with results from community sentences, you might ask? This is much more difficult to answer. You are not comparing like groups for a start.

It is easy to get lost in semantics here, but I always felt that a 60% 'failure rate' exclusively from a group who had already failed actually represented a 40% success rate, which wasn't bad!

The search for properly evaluated programmes to address offending behaviour continued worldwide from the 1980's onwards. Some themes started to emerge, indicating a more rational approach to criminal justice policy. General programmes, aimed at improving offenders' thinking skills and decision making, emerged and there were specific programmes to address different types of offending, the most prominent being those to address the worrying growth in sexual offending. Hence the further revision of the mantra to 'What works', i.e. a far more rigorous attempt at identifying effective methods and approaches and applying them across the spectrum of the criminal justice system more consistently.

This was the main driving force during most of my career spanning the end of the twentieth century and the beginning of the twenty first. By the time I retired in 2015, the tide had turned again with the re-emergence of scepticism about the impact of established programmes and the opening up of the market to the private sector.

So, to return to the question, what does work and are our endeavours effective? Undoubtedly, different approaches work better for different people, so you need skilled, well-motivated and well-supported people to assess each individual. Community sentences can be effective, cheaper and less damaging than prison. Prison is nevertheless a necessary institution to hold particularly those who present the greatest risk of harm to the community, potentially until they are deemed to be safe to release. I have no problem with that in principle, however we imprison far more people than is strictly necessary under that definition and often for far too long, which is incredibly expensive. The average cost of a prison place per year is in the region of at least £30,000, roughly comparable to the fees of our top public schools!

Perhaps a more realistic and humble aspiration would be to at least do no harm in criminal justice responses to crime, but we don't even meet that test. People regularly die in custody, and in prison they are brutalised and become drug addicted, or more sophisticated offenders. In other words, we can make things worse.

Can I point to any successes?

From my experience, did I manage to do any good in helping people turn their lives around and what made the difference?

I can honestly say that, of all the many offenders I met and worked with over more than thirty years, very few were beyond redemption. Very few really made the hairs on the back of my neck stand up. Very few could be said to be essentially 'evil'.

Most were more inept and misguided than dangerous. A respected colleague used to prescribe more to what he described as 'the cock up theory' than any notion of intrinsic badness, i.e. that so often offenders just got it wrong, mishandled situations, failed to make sound decisions and failed to learn from experience.

Having said that, even the most dangerous and intransigent offenders, when placed in a one-to-one situation in an interview room, are usually capable of some reflection and insight into their own behaviour. Movement towards an honest acceptance of events, responsibility and acknowledgement of harm caused is an essential stage in rehabilitation.

Two young men I worked with who did particularly well happened to share the same first name. Let's call them John, not a very scientific predictor of success but there you are. One settled in my home town after residence in the hostel that I was managing at the time. He broke away from destructive influences from his family life in the city. He still works here and I still see him from time to time. The other went on to get married, find employment and kept in touch, sending me Christmas cards for many years.

Another got into trouble in business and I employed him in the service after his release from prison and he was able to give back some of his valuable experience to the community.

My overriding view of prison remains that, for many offenders, it does at least break the pattern of their offending and provide a breathing space to reflect and a chance to change, if they decide to do so. That being a central point – you can't force people to reform, you have to take them with you. Recognising the point at which someone is ready to change is key.

For example, a young offender who I dealt with as a juvenile and whose family I got to know, seemed set on the path to self destruction. Let's call him Darren. I happened to meet him years later outside the local hospital with his father. I asked him how he was and whether he was still getting into trouble and he assured me that he wasn't. He said he was in fact waiting for his wife to deliver their latest child. What made the difference? I enquired. Not holding any real hope of the likelihood of a reply that the critical factor was my expert advice and guidance.

He got fed up of forever looking over his shoulder, he told me. Offending became too much hassle. In other words, he grew out of it; classic. There's something to be said for sticking with them from an early age in the hope that they burn out before causing too much harm.

Another overriding positive memory is the power of multi-agency work, i.e. simply working better together. At its worst, agencies can work in glorious isolation and actually undermine each other. There were many attempts in my time at coordinating actions more effectively. By far the most successful was MAPPA; Multi Agency Public Protection Arrangements. Little known to the general public, this is an approach of nearly twenty years standing to bring information and action planning together in the interests of protecting the public from the most risky and dangerous offenders. Managing this process was the culmination of my career and a great privilege, although it had its costs. It often saddened me when, inevitably dealing with high-risk situations, sometimes things went wrong, but there was little media appetite to share and celebrate the things that went well and I can assure you that there were many.

How did the probation service and criminal justice develop over my time?

When I joined the service in 1986, there was a legacy of enthusiastic amateurism; an encouraging belief in humanity and a strong ethos of 'care'. This sounds strange now with the far greater emphasis on control and punishment, but care and compassion were far more dominant notions then, if a little paternalistic.

The hope and, indeed, trust was that if you selected the right people and trained them well to understand, to empathise, to encourage, guide and support individuals, they could prosper. No serious consideration was given to discernible, measurable 'outcomes', the attempt at reform and rehabilitation was considered sufficiently worthy in itself.

This began to change in the 1980's with the early advent of a more questioning stance from government with the emergence of the mantra of 'Efficiency, Economy and Effectiveness'; challenging public services to justify their roles and question their value for money. In many ways, this was not an unreasonable response to attempting to better target and allocate public resources to addressing crime, and we were found wanting.

Our amateurism was exposed. The faith in individual autonomy and 'professional judgement' was difficult to justify and defend against a more discerning political stance. On inspection, yes, there were some great initiatives and individual efforts in different parts of the country, but we couldn't present a well-argued and evidenced, coherent response to what probation supervision entailed. It varied, and it varied enormously. Neither was cost consciousness, even in our thinking. We needed to change.

Psychology, on the other hand, with a much more scientific background and evidence-based approach, was far better placed as a profession to gain government support and to offer to spearhead the development of 'programmes' to address offending.

We did change and start to ask interesting questions about how things were organised and resources allocated to be more cost conscious and efficient. However, there was a trap here; like many public services during this period, the more efficient we became, the more was demanded and expected, and cuts went far beyond eliminating waste and far too deep into core services. This was neither efficient nor effective.

From perhaps an unsustainable position of expectation of continual expansion and annual rise in budget and pay, the complete opposite emerged as the new way forward. Budgets, pay and conditions of service only ever deteriorated for far too long. It became the self-justifying and perpetuating political dogma of the time.

Team sizes shrunk, leaving no spare capacity. Localism was abandoned in favour of large 'shed-like' open plan centralised offices, resources shrunk and initiatives became only ever top down from career-minded politicians with questionable understanding or commitment to sustained real improvement. The best innovations usually came from the bottom of the organisation, not the top, from the people actually doing the job. They knew what worked but were increasingly ignored, until the will to challenge anything evaporated and fatalism, apathy and stress became established and entrenched.

Then there were two even worse trends to come; austerity and obsession with privatisation. Rather than invest our way out of economic recession towards prosperity the blind dogma of the time, led by George Osbourne as the chancellor, was to cut every public service budget by unprecedented levels. I believe that this was deliberately intended to break public service in an attempt to discredit it and hand it over to the private sector whole sale, in the questionable belief that the market would automatically deliver simpler, cheaper and better outcomes. This was always a far too simplistic assumption, utterly biased in its perspective and completely at odds with any rational or evidence-based assessment.

Strong words, I appreciate, but government set itself on a path to destroy many of the valuable tenets of civil society, preferring self-interest and greed to notions of service and community. Criminal justice has been diminished beyond recognition, with the abandonment of local courts, access to credible police services and meaningful community rehabilitation. The prisons have been allowed to sink into desperate states of violence, depravity and shame, even to the admission of government itself.

The involvement of the private sector can play a part. There is a good tradition of work from the charitable and voluntary sector, partnership can work but wholesale movement of work to the lowest bidder does not.

The reform of the probation service under Chris Grayling has been accepted to have been a disaster. Breaking up an integrated national network of probation provision in favour of twenty one separate private contracts was never going to improve cooperation, efficiency and deliver better outcomes for victims, the community and offenders alike.

In practice, the new private companies discovered that this enterprise wasn't as easy as they first envisaged and more to the point was difficult to make money out of. Once they concluded that there were two predictable outcomes. Firstly, to want to walk away, the initial enthusiasm, such as it was, for taking on these contracts diminished. Secondly, a tendency to manipulate the figures to ensure 'success' and therefore payment for services not delivered. At worst, this led to some gross abuses of the system, with private firms being caught out claiming payment for non-existent offenders and for pressurising staff to make the records fit the narrative. The reality was very different with poor and distant levels of contact between workers and offenders.

Thankfully, at last this decision has been reversed, but has wasted millions of pounds of public money and caused pain and anguish in the process.

It is not overstating the case, nor being unduly dramatic, to say that our whole criminal justice system has been driven to near the point of collapse.

We have to do better.

It's easy to criticise but so much needs and could be done to improve things.

So, for what it's worth, here are my top ten suggestions of how we could improve criminal justice provision in this country, across the board.

1.   Start young.

Prevention is better than cure.

Early investment and intervention can save considerable pain and cost later.

Initiatives like nursery provision and sure start help set the agenda and save money later down the line.

Diversion schemes, mass investment in sport and leisure activity helps prevent hopelessness and drift into crime.

2.   Speedy meaningful justice.

Police intervention, prosecution and impact need to be quick and responsive to have a positive deterrent effect. Schemes like mediation and community justice panels can deliver a response rapidly to reflect both the public's displeasure and the need to redress and compensate both the victim and the community. If someone steals something, wouldn't it be helpful to return it plus work to refund its value direct to the victim?

3.   Assumption of a community sentence first.

Reduce immediate imprisonment to only apply to the most serious offences and establish community penalties as the norm for most offences, in the form of rehabilitation programmes and community service. The latter needs to be visible to ensure public support and respect, and I don't mean offenders wearing 'prison-like uniform' or labelled high visibility jackets, but by plaques on sites to draw the attention to the good given back to the community, like clearing church yards, canal paths, gardening for the elderly, rubbish clearance, making and repairing things for community groups, assistance with green projects, like recycling; things that the community identify with and benefit from.

4.   Prison at its best.

Many prison staff are dedicated to the task of attempting to turn prisoners' lives around, but this needs imagination and investment. A high proportion of the twenty-four hour days spent in confinement in a small cell does not deliver rehabilitation. Meaningful education, employment, opportunities to demonstrate responsible behaviour and good health provision are all worthy of investment.

The role of prisons could be recast to reception, training, industrial, resettlement and residual. Reception prisons would receive all new arrivals, induct, assess and allocate them to the most appropriate provision. Training prisons would concentrate on rehabilitation and programmes for those motivated and assessed suitable to engage with and respond to such a regime. Industrial prisons would concentrate on meaningful reparation with participants 'earning' their release literally by reaching some work-related financial target as compensation to the community for those not motivated or suitable for the training regime. Resettlement prisons would concentrate on preparing prisoners for release by practical training in essential life skills and establishing viable release plans. There would need to be a 'residual sector' that dealt with those who, for one reason or another, did not comply. Elements of this already exist and transitioning to such a model would, in my view, be feasible.

5.   Restoration of a meaningful parole process.

An incentive to behave in prison is effective at attempting to undermine the counter culture of hopelessness, violence and drug abuse. In my time, the parole board had become so risk averse that the whole process became meaningless. I remember one case of a young man caught up in gang crime in London. His behaviour in custody was exemplary and his proposed release plan was sound; resettlement with his sister in Scotland with the offer of a job locally. This was a dead cert bet for parole, if anyone was ever going to qualify for it, he was – but this young offender was refused. I couldn't believe it. It seemed a ridiculous decision, a wasted opportunity.

6.   The best release and support planning.

At its best, this already exists, or at least it did in my day. Prisoners need to be released to viable accommodation and employment. At Drake Hall women's prison, at the point that I retired, some excellent schemes were being developed with the realistic prospect of employment training in the prison leading to a real job on the outside. This coupled with real community support can give prisoners a realistic chance of making a successful transition from prison to the community. Some employers, like Timpsons the shoe repair chain, have seen the potential of employing ex-offenders. Initiatives like 'The Clink Restaurant', staffed by prisoners and open to the community, can offer good food and service at a cut price with real training and experience and the prospect of transfer to a real restaurant in the community on release. Offenders then potentially have a stake in the community and could value it rather than seek to exploit it.

7.   A review of legislation.

As ever more activity becomes designated as 'criminal', it is inevitable that more and more offences become committed. A suitable response could be a rigorous review of existing legislation with a view to eliminating outmoded and irrelevant offences from the statute book.

8.   Greater support on release.

If we are serious about rehabilitation support in the community, particularly post-release from custody, is vital. This is nothing new and actually I think we were quite good at it, but there is scope for improvement. Better coordination between the prison and probation elements regarding particularly employment and accommodation would help here.

Schemes exist to show the way to link employment and training with a direct transfer into the community. This is a positive and imaginative partnership with the private sector. Links with accommodation can mean return to family, which is not always for the best, or more often to probation hostels. These have become more like mini open prisons in the community and moving on for the most risky, particularly sex offenders, is always difficult and contentious. What is needed is a greater supply of secondary, affordable accommodation without the 'label of criminality.'

9. Greater community involvement in rehabilitation.

But there is more to support than this. The Americans have a different approach with open disclosure to communities about individual offender's resettlement plans, with obvious repercussions. However, at the same time, they have tried to develop what they call 'circles of support', i.e. volunteers in the community who are prepared to befriend ex-offenders and attempt to directly reintegrate them back into the community with positive role models. This would be contentious, but it could well be effective.

10. A realistic conversation with the public about what is achievable with managed levels of risk.

This is perhaps the key. Politicians expect high standards of both prevention and prediction from those working in criminal justice, but it is not an exact science. We need to be honest with the public about this. No system is ever going to be perfect. Some offenders will go on to reoffend regardless. It is better to be aware of that than feign shock and horror when it happens and further the myth of infallibility and regard the system as having failed. At the extremes there is a choice – do we imprison everybody who might cause us harm forever, just in case, at astronomical cost? Or do we accept a certain level of disruption and reoffending and use those funds for more pro-social purposes, like health, education and social care? In this regard, we need, I think, to be bold and send less people to prison and be more prepared to release those already there.

I could go on, but this would be a start. We also need to do more to address the imbalance of black, Asian and ethnic minority people being over-represented in the offender and prison population. This is not an after-thought or a desirable add-on, but an essential prerequisite. Women offenders need a different approach by a system largely designed by men for men. In most cases, the imprisonment of women, I would argue, is unnecessary and the development of women's centres in the community offers a better prospect. Having said that, as gender equality develops, some of the negative behaviours previously associated only with men become more obvious and prevalent in female offenders too. For example, the use of violence and maybe the last taboo; female sexual offending.

Something also needs to be done about the obsession with measurement and monitoring and the unrealistic expectations it encourages. It needs to be simple, realistic and honest.

Finally, I acknowledge that no doubt the debate has moved on since I retired and my observations need to be seen in that light. The task goes on; rebuilding criminal justice, terrorism, knife crime, international and organised crime, as well as low-level offending, are all challenges for the next generation working in this field.

It's been a fascinating journey, but not without its costs. Stress levels are too high, with serious health implications. I worry about those embarking on their careers and wonder how sustainable their futures might be?

SHORTS

1. Missing

Chapter 1

It was the not knowing, she thought. The constant wondering – what had really happened? She asked herself that question over and over again.

Richie seemed OK. Nothing obvious appeared to be bothering him. He shouted goodbye as usual as he left the house for a walk. He loved walking. He walked miles, sometimes with others but often alone, usually directly from the house into the local area. That day was no different, except on that particular day Richie didn't return.

Life had been so difficult without him. What do you tell people? How long do you hang on to the hope that he might yet return? At what point do you try to accept it, stop obsessing about what might have happened. None of the answers were forthcoming.

People had been very kind, at least initially. When the police got involved, the media took an interest but despite all their best efforts – nothing. No sight, no sound, no sign of what may have happened, where he went to or where he might be now. To all intents and purposes, Richie Dolman, Angie's much loved husband, had simply disappeared without trace that day. None of his mates had gone with him. He only had his usual day sack over his shoulder with basic essentials; a set of waterproofs, some lunch, a spare fleece, some safety kit, probably a little money, a light sleeping bag, just in case. He hadn't taken either his wallet or his phone that day. Surely he couldn't survive very long with just those meagre possessions, she pondered.

There were so many loose ends – his diary with some appointments and commitments, his post, bills to be paid, emails to answer. He was still receiving his pay, but she wondered at what point his employer would assume the worst and what would happen then? Would she receive his pension? None of these things were clear and Angie didn't have the energy to seek answers, at least not yet. She felt so alone. They had never had children and she was an only child, both of her parents had died and she was left to bare all the aftermath of Richie's disappearance herself.

When would this nightmare end? she asked herself.

Chapter 2

At first Angie had prepared dinner for two, as usual, then sat and stared at the full plate opposite her as she tried to eat hers. Sharing conversation with a memory, as if he was still there, even asking him questions like 'have you put the bins out?' as if she were expecting answers.

As the years passed, and still struggling to come to terms with events, the fear grew that there may never be a knock on the door, a call, a message of any kind. There had been nothing. Birthdays, wedding anniversaries, Christmases had come and gone with no contact and no new information.

Some of Richie's affairs did eventually reach some form of resolution with various agencies and organisations closing contact with him, but the reminders were still there; his spare walking boots in the utility room, his clothes in the bedroom; the very sense of him in the house. *At least after a proper bereavement there is an end*, she thought. But in these circumstances reaching an end point seemed impossible. Friends took different views, from advising her to clear him out of her life, consider moving house and trying to make a new start to maintaining the sanctuary and the hope (or delusion) indefinitely. Angie never felt comfortable with either approach so avoided making any decision. She couldn't rest but neither could she close this chapter of her life without knowing something, anything about what had really happened.

There were organisations, websites, many approaches to finding the missing, but Angie was reluctant to invest too much emotional energy in the pursuit of an answer by any of these means. She had tried initially but found nothing. Richie was fit and healthy. He was a confident navigator in all weathers. He knew the local mountains well; there was no obvious reason why he should have got into difficulty or not be able to resolve most situations himself. Had he been in an accident, was anyone else involved? No one had come forward, there were no witnesses and of course a body had never been found.

Richie Dolman, WHERE ARE YOU? she would cry out at night…

Of course there was no answer. Sorrow was the overriding emotion initially. Her poor love, whatever happened to him? Friends generally took the same view. However, after a while with no resolution, other thoughts plagued her mind. *What other possible scenarios could have taken place?* she wondered. At times sadness could turn to anger, bitterness, regret, even blame. Then she would feel guilty.

It was torment. It was never ending. It was unfair. It was unreasonable. It was many things, but it was real. He was not here, he was not confirmed dead and the circumstances of his disappearance remained unknown. All that she was sure of was that he was 'missing'.

Angie discovered that 'the missing' are actually quite a large number of unaccounted for people, some cases going back many years. No one really knew the true figure. The actual number was, of course, no comfort to those left behind, only that is the sparse reassurance that you are not alone in this harrowing situation. You are not unique, you are a recognised minority. Recognised in the sense of not being invisible, but recognition was only ever tacit. Platitudes were offered but no real impetus to secure resolution was ever fully addressed. The not knowing remained. It was ever present, haunting, unresolved.

Chapter 3

Richie had left the house early that day, content with his apparently perfect life, but was it? Richie had always been troubled about his poor relationship with his twin brother, Jack, and his ambivalence towards their parents. *Had this adversely affected my relationship with Angie*? he often wondered. He tried to dismiss such thoughts.

The light was poor, but it was a crisp cold winter's morning, his preferred winter conditions. He stepped out confidently along the lane to the first stile and onto the familiar path that would take him far into the hills and mountains that he loved so much. Snow was on the ground and Richie enjoyed laying down the first footsteps on the virgin white surface. He was suitably dressed for the conditions and was carrying enough equipment to survive most eventualities. Walking in winter presented its own particular risks, he considered, and walking alone even more so. Nevertheless, he felt confident and looked forward to the challenge.

He carried a map of course, the laminated 1:50,000 version, the walkers preference, with sufficient detail to facilitate accurate navigation in the hands of an experienced mountaineer. With his level of familiarity, however, the map often remained in his pack and only tended to be consulted in the more difficult or extreme of conditions where visibility was poor or accuracy was required to ensure safety. Although both fit and experienced, Richie was never reckless or complacent; he maintained a healthy respect for the mountain environment.

As usual, Richie made good progress over familiar territory as he climbed out of the village and ever higher into the hills. He was unsure of his eventual destination. He had all day after all and only needed to be back by around six o'clock as it was his turn to make the tea. He had decided to cook one of their favourites. At this time of year it was dark certainly by four o'clock, with fading light often being a feature from much earlier, so aiming to be safely back home by six wasn't any impediment and he expected to be coming down well before that.

There were, of course, many possibilities for the route that day but Richie had two or three options uppermost in his mind, depending on his progress and the weather. He had checked the forecast before leaving but was only too well aware of how quickly mountain conditions can change. There was a significant level of snow still on the ground from the previous night and it was deeper in places than he expected.

Progress slowed as Richie climbed higher and up onto the ridge that would be the main feature of his walk. With clear blue skies visibility was good as he stopped to admire one of his favourite views. The hills were quiet that day. Richie had only seen two other walkers and they were some distance away. He felt like he had the hills to himself.

He loved the solitude, the fact that the same walk was never the same walk – different conditions, light, time of year, all had a part to play in making each experience unique. Today was no exception; he loved the wind in his face, the distance he covered, the wonderful views, the sheer drama of the rugged environment.

By early afternoon the light was beginning to fade. As he had anticipated, by the time Richie found the route he was looking for off the mountain and back down to safety, darkness was setting in. He had enjoyed his walk, but thoughts turned to home.

Chapter 4

Angie glanced at the clock without concern, looking forward to hearing Richie's enthusiastic voice herald his return with tales of hardship and adventure. He had always been an outgoing sort of man and had long enjoyed a love of the great outdoors and the local area. That was one of the reasons why they had chosen to settle where they did – to be in the heart of the mountains.

She looked at the pile of food left on the kitchen surface ready for him to make their dinner and felt secure and contented. Richie would soon return and they could settle down for a cosy evening at home.

It was half past four as she envisaged Richie making good progress down the mountain and heading confidently for home. She made some tea and started the daily crossword in the paper as she waited. Five o'clock passed and it was approaching six as feelings of doubt started to intrude on her usual confidence in Richie's plans. She quickly dismissed such thoughts and got up to check that there was a cold beer in the fridge. The log fire was lit and the house felt warm as she awaited the arrival of her energetic partner.

Ten to six. Cutting it fine, she thought.

Five past six.

Twenty passed six. Maybe he'd called in for a pint at the local pub on the way back?

It was unusual for Richie to be late. Although he gave an impression of being casual, he was actually meticulous about his planning and well known for good navigational skills and sound judgment on the hills. Although snow had started falling again, and conditions certainly were cold, Angie was not worried about his ability to cope in such circumstances. She poured herself a large glass of wine as she tried to discard any negative thoughts from her mind. He would be safe. He would be here soon, she kept telling herself.

***

Richie had taken a break half way down the mountain on his return leg and was sitting on a rock drinking coffee from his flask. It was three o'clock. Snow had just started falling and he was keen not to hang about, instead focusing on getting back down. As he started to pack up his day sack Richie suddenly felt a little strange. Unusual feelings – he felt slightly dizzy, a little numb and even confused. He was not sure what was happening but was certain that he didn't feel right. There was no one else in immediate view as he tried to retrieve his phone from its usual pocket in the top of the rucksack, only to remember putting it on charge in the house. He must have left it. Strange, he wasn't usually so careless. *What to do next?* he considered. Only one thing was certain in his mind; it made no sense to take another step until he felt OK.

Chapter 5

By seven o'clock, back in the house, Angie was starting to feel really concerned. She rang a couple of their friends to check whether any of them had set off with Richie, but no one had or knew of any plans for Richie to be in a group. *What shall I do?* she thought. Rosemary, one of her friends, came round to comfort her. By seven thirty they agreed that it was probably sensible to ring the local mountain rescue, if only to share the situation with a friendly voice. They both knew many of the team and Richie was well known to all of them.

Angie rang the police and they put her through to mountain rescue.

'Mountain rescue. How can we help?' came the reply from Craig the team leader.

'Hi Craig, it's Angie Dolman here. I hope I'm not over reacting but Richie went out walking this morning and was expected back by six at the very latest and he still hasn't returned.'

'OK Angie' replied Craig, immediately feeling concerned as he glanced at the clock. 'Seven-ten and you would have expected him back by four or five, before it got too dark?' said Craig knowing Richie's routines.

'Yes, that's right.'

'Who is with him, Angie? And what route was he planning?' asked Craig, trying to establish some basic facts.

'I'm not entirely sure, Craig. I think he's on his own, none of our friends have said anyone was due to go with him this morning. As for the route, well, as you're aware, he knows this area well so tends not to tell me in detail about routes or plans. He walked from the house, as usual, so you probably know his likely routes. It's been a good winter's day and he will have taken all his usual kit, I'm sure.'

'Can you just check that? Has he got his day sack? The blue and grey one. I know what scale of equipment he usually carries in that.'

Becoming increasingly concerned, Angie checked and was able to confirm that the blue and grey sack was missing, so as far as she could tell Craig was right and that would be what Richie had taken with him. She mentioned that he left his phone at home on charge, which was unusual and had left his wallet.

'Angie, I'm concerned. This isn't at all like, Richie. I'm not going to mess about here, I'm going to call out a full team and set off to look for him as soon as possible. It will be no problem getting volunteers in the circumstances; Richie is well liked and respected here.'

'OK,' said Angie meekly, starting to feel a mild sense of panic as Rosemary, her friend tried to reassure her.

'Angie, there's probably a quite simple explanation here. Let's not jump to conclusions – he's a very experienced walker. I'll ring the pub just to check if they have seen him.'

'Hi, it's Rosemary, I'm with Angie Dolman. Richie hasn't returned home. He's not there with you, is he?' she asked earnestly.

The landlord sensed that she was concerned so thought better of making a joke about wives chasing up their errant husbands, but was able to tell her honestly that Richie had not been in the pub and no one had seen him that day.

Meanwhile, Craig was collecting together a suitable team and liaising with the police to put out a message to local patrols so they could keep an eye out for him. Richie would be immediately recognisable to any of the local officers.

Members of the team were well prepared and ready to respond quickly in such circumstances and Craig soon had enough experienced members to form two teams and start searching from two different directions. Snow was falling heavily by now and it was a very cold and dark night, far less than ideal to start such a search. Craig consulted the others and, on balance, concluded that Richie had probably set off on one of his favourite ridge walks, given the clear conditions at the time. If so, they could approach the most likely ridge from either side and aim to meet in the middle.

It was just after nine o'clock by the time the teams set off. Craig had promised to keep Angie informed of any developments. In the circumstances, they made good progress to the foot of the ridge simultaneously from both directions. The teams remained in touch by radio and all used powerful head torches, both to find their way and to scan the area for any signs of activity. Unfortunately, it became immediately apparent that the evening snow fall would have covered most foot prints left during the day, which was not going to help them track or find Richie. Both teams were well motivated and determined to find their man. Janice led the sub team.

As they expected, with little or no foot prints left in the snow the chances of finding anyone seemed remote, especially as they were not sure of Richie's route. Although they felt quite confident that they would be in the right area, it was speculation after all and they could be completely misguided and therefore searching in the wrong place.

Neither team were surprised to find no one else out on the hill at this time and in these conditions, so they did not have the advantage of being able to question other walkers. As the conditions deteriorated, Craig began to accept that realistically their chances of finding anyone that night were deteriorating rapidly.

Craig stopped to confer with Janice. She agreed. When the chances of success are so remote and the risks to your own party relatively high, there is realistically only one possible rational choice. Craig agreed to call off the search for the night and to start again in the morning. If Richie was a casualty, if he'd had an accident, for example, he had the knowledge and skills to survive in such conditions, but his equipment was limited. To the best of their knowledge, he had a bivvy bag but without a good winter sleeping bag the chances of survival reduced significantly. Surely he would have taken a sleeping bag, they thought. He was certainty capable of preparing a snow hole to make camp over night, assuming he wasn't injured, but realistically they all knew that his chances weren't looking good. If Richie was to survive, they would hope to find him quickly the following morning.

Cold, disappointed and frustrated, the rescue teams returned to their base without success.

The following day the police received several sightings of lone walkers on the hill but none could be confirmed as definitely Richie Dolman. No one else was reported missing and there were no grounds to believe anyone else may have been involved in any form of mountain accident. Although Richie was deemed to be fit and healthy, alone in those circumstances difficulties could arise from medical conditions without the complication of an accident. Mountain walkers, like the general population, could be subject to heart attacks or strokes, although most rescues involved navigation errors, poor preparation or equipment or combinations of these factors. After that, accidents were the next most common reason for a call out; often sprained or broken joints, slips or falls.

On return, Craig rang Angie and could sense her unease and fear of a tragic outcome. Sadly, they were both all too aware of the risk of fatality on the local mountains, particularly in winter. Mountain folklore was rich in tales of heroic survival against the odds, but harsh reality was less romantic.

Chapter 6

By four o'clock, Richie found himself still sitting on the rock with his sack in front of him. He must have nodded off and by now was cold and covered in freshly falling snow. He stood up and shook himself down. Whatever he was feeling, he knew at that point that he had to move. He looked around him, but there was no one in sight, light was fading and he was still quite high with some distance to go to safety. His thoughts were blurred, he felt confused and uncertain.

Richie lifted his sack and started to move. Slowly at first, he continued along the route he had intended but soon began to drift. Following a route in snow can be extremely hard. A vast snow field all looks the same, paths and navigation features can be covered leaving little indication of either route or direction. Accurate navigation becomes essential in such circumstances, either by compass bearing, timing or pacing, or indeed all three. Progress inevitably is slow.

Richie stumbled, falling occasionally, and was increasingly losing a sense of direction. Falling on high ground in some places can lead to sheer drops with little chance of survival. Richie felt strangely detached from the situation, quite relaxed and underestimating the danger he faced. Richie had never experienced such feelings and found himself in new and very unfamiliar circumstances. Time seemed to stand still as he stumbled on.

Some sense of reality returned in moments of relative alertness when Richie could rationalise the situation he now faced, but they were short lived before a return to confusion and a dangerous sense of complacency. It was now approaching five o'clock. Richie had been out on the hill all day and would have expected to feel jaded by this time, but in the moment he felt detached, distant from the world and all that was familiar to him. Disorientated and confused, he stumbled on until a glimmer of recognition ran through his mind. A wall, a stile, a path junction ahead looked familiar. Richie stopped and shook himself again, trying to regain some composure. He glanced at his watch. He tried hard to concentrate. Did he recognise this place?

Slowly, he became more confident. Yes, this was familiar, he considered. Yes, he felt confident. He stopped and sat by the wall to catch his breath and to consult his map. Yes, he was sure. *This is where I am.*

His thoughts became a little clearer. He remembered something about dinner and knew that he should be home by now and that he wasn't. He had drifted quite some distance away from his destination and away from the route he had planned. Richie began to reason that it was now unrealistic to reach home that night and that he needed to stop and make camp. A good rule of thumb on the mountains he always thought was to be prepared to spend a night out if necessary. He was glad that he had actually packed a warm, light sleeping bag and felt confident that he could survive a night out on the hill. It had been some time since he had practiced digging a snow hole and making such a shelter for the night, but the technique was familiar to him. The snow, he reasoned, was both deep and firm enough to do the job.

Richie looked about, trying to make out the ground immediately around him in the gloom of fading light. The snow had stopped falling, the sky was clear and the moon was out. He recognised a spot just ahead that would make a suitable camp; a dip in the ground, out of the wind and where the snow had drifted against a section of high wall, making enough space to be able to burrow into.

With renewed determination, he approached the chosen site and, using his ice axe and a piece of broken fence post as an improvised shovel, he started to clear a space in the snow. The temperature, he judged, must have fallen several degrees below freezing, making the snow hard enough to create an opening that would enable him to clear enough space to sleep in. Out of the wind and under cover a snow hole can be surprisingly hospitable, but he reminded himself that it was about survival not comfort.

After an hour or so, Richie had made a reasonable snow hole shelter to be able to survive the night. He drank his last coffee from his flask and crawled into his sleeping bag, wearing all his available clothes, and into his waterproof bivvy bag. Lying on his insulated mat, the ground was firm and stable. He had lit a candle and glanced at his watch before trying to get some sleep. It was just past eight o'clock.

Richie endured a fitful sleep. He was reasonably dry and not too cold or uncomfortable. When glanced at his watch, it was now six o'clock in the morning and he felt it was time to move. As he stretched and clambered out of his snow hole, Richie tried to make sense of the previous day's events.

He tried to remember how he had ended up there, some distance away from his original route. He still felt strange and uneasy. In the early morning darkness Richie endeavoured to orientate himself. Using his head torch, he found a place to sit and check the map before packing up, ready to move on. Yes, he felt confident that he was where he thought he was the previous day.

Once packed, Richie felt driven to break up and disguise his snow hole before moving off, as if he actually didn't want to be found. He was cold and running short of food but at least he was dry. He walked on with no plan or aim in mind for several hours in the dull morning mist, travelling in the opposite direction to his home and his original route.

After a while he stopped and tried to gather his thoughts. *What am I doing?* he asked himself. The answer was that he really didn't know. He felt detached from his ordinary life, distant and alone, but despite that he felt calm and not troubled by it. *Had my life really been so contented?* he pondered. *Was my marriage really that good?* he speculated. Posing far more questions than answers, Richie pressed on as the light improved and the prospects of a clear crisp day emerged.

He tried to establish how he actually felt now. He was still confused, and still he felt strange, light headed, a little dizzy and was increasingly aware of feeling hungry, having not eaten a proper meal for over twenty four hours.

As he covered the ground, Richie saw no one and pressed on… to where exactly? Well, he was not sure, but nor did he seem to care. This seemed to be more about the journey than the destination. It occurred to him as he stopped to catch his breath, *why am I not feeling compelled to return home?* Why was he embarking on this journey in the opposite direction? Was he trying to escape something? Nothing seemed clear, only an increasing sense of certainty that he should continue.

One thing was becoming clear, however; Richie Dolman felt certain that he was not going home.

Chapter 7

It was six am as Craig rang Angie to tell her that the two rescue teams were about to set out again along the ridge in an attempt to find Richie. The teams were up for it and Angie was excited, hoping that they would find her man alive and well.

In the early morning, the teams deployed with resolution and determination. The snow was crisp and the moon was bright as they headed for the familiar ridge that they had attempted to search the previous evening in the dark. In the emerging light, prospects of success were much better. They stepped forward with conviction, determined to find a fellow mountaineer and a friend in difficulty; it was the very ethos of the mountain rescue volunteer service.

Diligently, the two teams scoured the area for any indication of human activity, but to no avail. There was nothing; no footprints, no people, no sign whatsoever of human activity. The area seemed totally deserted. Where was he?

After several hours of searching, the two teams converged and sat down to share their findings.

'Odd, isn't it?' remarked Janice. 'No indications at all.'

'Yes, I agree, although new snow fall will have obscured or covered prints, I would have expected to find something, but there's nothing,' responded Craig.

'You're right, I feel uneasy. Something is wrong here. It's as if he didn't set out at all yesterday, or he walked somewhere else.'

'You mean, we are looking in the wrong place?'

'Quite possibly.'

'Well, if you are right, Janice, it only begs the question: where did he go? And where is he now?'

The teams gathered round and consulted their maps, trying to make a best guess of other possible routes. There were, of course, many potential options. They checked with the police but no reports had been received from their officers, the public, other walkers or local farmers.

'If we are going to extend the search, we're going to need more help. The area is vast,' pronounced Janice as others nodded in agreement.

*****

Richie continued in the same direction. At times he felt relaxed and self assured but at other times he was still confused and disorientated. What was happening to him? He was not sure. The only thing he seemed sure about was that he needed to eat, to take on some fuel.

As he stumbled on, Richie caught the smell of bacon cooking and looked round to identify any likely source. There was a bothy ahead – a small mountain shelter, usually an ex-Shepherd's hut – free and available for mountaineers to use, either routinely or in an emergency. As he approached, the smell of food cooking became stronger.

As he entered the hut, Richie found an older man busily cooking up a large breakfast on a small gas stove. Hot tea was also in his mug. The man looked up and smiled.

'Good morning! I come up here often. I drive as far as I can up the old track then walk the last stage to the hut for a late breakfast before settling down in a hide and trying to photograph the wildlife. It's my hobby.'

'Sounds fun to me!' Richie replied, trying hard not to look too enviously at the breakfast.

'And you?'

'Oh, I'm just walking…' replied Richie limply.

'Want to join me? I always cook plenty and usually someone like you rolls up who looks like they could eat a horse or two.'

With a mixture of sheer relief and excitement, Richie gratefully accepted the offer and joined the man for a hearty breakfast. After which he felt really tied. Day two since he had left home, he reflected. *What next?* he thought. Rest seemed the first priority so Richie rolled out his mat and his sleeping bag and soon fell asleep.

The weather had improved slightly, still very cold, but clear skies were overhead indicating no immediate threat of more snow.

As he woke, the man was standing next to him offering him tea.

'What's your story?' he asked gently.

'Story? Well, nothing really. I set out for a walk and here I am.'

'You look troubled, my friend,' the man perceived.

'Do I? Well, yesterday I didn't feel too well, but I'm feeling a bit better now.'

'Modern life – too much stress. It's not good for you. We need to learn to relax more. You look like you need some time to yourself. You can stay here as long as you like. I'll be going shortly, but I am happy to leave you the rest of my food; you obviously need it more than I do.'

'That's very kind.'

'No bother. I hope you resolve whatever is troubling you.'

'Thank you,' responded Richie, feeling quite emotional.

Chapter 8

Media coverage started to mention that Richie Dolman, well known local mountaineer, was missing and was last seen two days ago. Photographs were displayed and requests for help and information broadcast.

The police started to help in the search and recruited local people to cover as much of the surrounding area as possible. Hospitals in the region were all contacted and traffic cameras scrutinised for any sightings. People did come forward to describe where they had been on that day, which was some help in a process of elimination, but the search realistically continued with no clear idea where Richie had walked at that time.

Despite their best efforts, the authorities were unable to trace Richie and by day three hope was beginning to fade of finding him alive. The weather continued to be very cold and the snow persisted on the ground, hampering both tracking and the pace of any search in the difficult conditions. The rescuers knew that he was reasonably well equipped and Angie did seem to remember him referring to carrying a sleeping bag before he left. They were all aware, however, that he had little food and no means of cooking anything.

As the search widened, it was still some considerable distance away from where Richie had ended up and no one had checked the bothy. Angie's precious husband still seemed to have effectively disappeared and suspicions were starting to arise that all was not what it might seem. What were his plans and intentions that day? Had he really gone walking at all? Different scenarios and possibilities were considered and largely rejected. In the absence of known facts, media speculation was not constructive or effective in determining his whereabouts.

Angie rang friends and family to see if Richie had been in touch, or if they had any idea what might have been on his mind. His GP and his employer were consulted but no real firm indications of anything critical emerged. He appeared to be a stable, contented man with no obvious problems or concerns on his mind. On the contrary, he presented himself as being confident and as having managed to achieve that illusive 'work/life balance' rather well, many of his associates considered. Angie searched the depths of her mind and memory, trying to find any clue that might help. She fluctuated between pity, concern, desperation and doubt, scepticism and suspicion.

Richie did spend much of his time 'alone', or at least out of the house either at work or following his hobby of walking in the mountains. He always had done. *Was there someone else?* she wondered. Was he, in fact, not always on the hills when he had said that he was? Angie fought back the tears as she felt so sad, interspersed with fear, regret, mistrust, anger and then guilt. How could she doubt him? Yet how could she account for his disappearance?

The police investigation continued, with several scenarios being considered. Was it abduction, or violence or robbery of some sort? Did he have any enemies or anyone that might want to kill him? Did he lead a double life? What did they not know about him?

No one line of enquiry was looking at least possible. Attention shifted to Angie herself. Did she know more than she was telling? Was she, in fact, responsible? Had they planned this together? Was it some sort of insurance scam?

In the days following his disappearance, more questions than answers emerged and the commitment to finding Richie risked losing momentum. They desperately need a break, a lead of some sort, to restore faith and conviction.

***

Back in the bothy, Richie was facing his third night alone. The previous day was a blur, with moments of consciousness in between periods of sleep and exhaustion. The food supply the old man had left was generous and he had lent him his gas stove. Richie tried to gather his thoughts. It was as if his life had suddenly stopped and was about to start again. Not to erase the past but to leave it behind – it seemed no longer to be relevant. He seemed strangely detached from it. Most of all, Richie just wanted time alone to think, to reflect and to reassess.

The following morning, at the start of day four, the older man came back to take more photographs and brought more supplies. He asked no questions. After a while, he set off again and left Richie in peace.

Back home, the man did see a newspaper headline in a shop as he called in for bread and milk, but he chose to ignore it. 'Man still lost on the hill,' he considered – what's new about that? *Why can't they just leave people alone?* he thought. Anyway, it wasn't his area they were searching.

Richie considered that it was time to make his next move. He still needed more time away and did not feel ready to consider any plan to return home. Remaining blissfully ignorant of the efforts to find him, neither did he consider any need to present himself to the authorities. Confusion had clouded his judgement. What to do next?

He knew his food supply would expire. He had no wallet, no means of payment and no form of identification. He was effectively anonymous.

Where could he go? Who could he turn too? Both his parents had died and his family was never particularly close, but he could, he supposed, contact his twin brother. They had never really got on. They used to fight constantly as children and were eventually brought up separately, with his brother Jack moving to his grandparents. Richie always felt a sense of resentment that Jack had been given the better deal. Jack lived alone and not too far away. To get to Jack's was at least a realistic target, Richie considered.

Chapter 9

After walking for several hours, Richie reached a minor road. He walked to the next junction where he saw a lorry pull over onto a lay by. The driver had got out. Richie approached him and asked casually if there was any chance of a lift.

'Where are you heading ?' enquired the driver.

'South of here, not far,' Richie replied.

'You look a bit rough, mate. Been on some sort of expedition, have you?' he asked.

'Something like that.'

'OK, jump in. I'm heading south and could drop you off at the next town.'

'That sounds perfect,' Richie replied.

The lorry driver talked through the whole journey about his exploits and adventures on the road, whilst Richie made polite but disinterested acknowledgement of his host's story.

When they reached the next town, they pulled in at a cafe.

'I expect you're ready for a bite to eat,' remarked the driver as they said their goodbyes and he strode off to the cafe.

The thought did occur to Richie that maybe he ought to maintain a low profile and sitting in a large transport cafe wasn't such a good idea, even though he remembered he did keep an emergency tenner in a dry bag in the top of his sack. It had been there for years so he could have bought some food.

As he walked away, he saw a few taxis lined up ready to take passengers and reckoned that he was within a ten pound range of his brother's house, so he opened the rear door and climbed into the first taxi. Richie gave his brother's address and sat back in silence as he tried to remember anything about the town.

Richie definitely recalled using the Black Horse pub as they passed it on the left and approached his brother's house. *Will he be in?* he wondered.

Richie paid his fare and walked up to the house. His brother opened the door.

'Where the fuck have you been?' he exclaimed.

'You have half the world looking for you and you just wander up my drive as calm as you like!'

'What do you mean?' asked Richie meekly, not surprised by his brother's less than warm welcome.

'What do I mean? You've been missing for nearly a week now. The police, mountain rescue, local people have all been out searching the hills for you. What have you been doing? Why didn't you get in touch?' Jack shouted at him on the doorstep.

'Can we just go inside, Jack? I need to sit down.'

'So it's all about you, as usual…' Jack spat back as he led the way into the house. 'What about those you have left behind? What about your poor wife, Richie? Remember her? That lovely woman that I never thought you deserved. How do you think she is feeling not knowing what happened, where you're been, whether you are even still alive?'

Richie spluttered as he fell into the sofa. Some sense of realisation seemed to penetrate his confusion.

'I've not been well, Jack…'

'Oh, all about you again, you selfish inconsiderate bastard. You always were, even as a child,' Jack interjected.

'No Jack, listen. On the hill, I became unwell. I felt confused, exhausted, and I don't recognise these feelings. I don't know what's happening. I've been drifting for days, then I thought of you, that you might help. You are my brother, Jack!'

'Help, help now? Why should I? I wouldn't care if you had died on that fucking mountain, Richie, for all you're worth. We hate each other, remember? We always did.'

The brothers continued to trade insults and shout at each other as they had done many times before over the years. As they stumbled into the back garden they started to grapple with each other. After one insult too many, Richie pushed Jack away from him. Jack stepped back and tripped, falling down the garden steps and banging his head hard as he landed in the rockery.

Richie tried to help but Jack was unconscious. He couldn't revive him. Even in his confused state of mind, Richie knew that Jack was dead or dying. He panicked – what to do now? Jack had fallen, he considered, but who would believe him? Everyone knew the two brothers were always at loggerheads. No one would accept this was an accident. Richie feared that he could be blamed for his death.

In the moment, Richie felt his head start to clear. He had to act fast. A plan emerged in his mind. Without any documents, Richie had no identity and he needed one. His identical twin brother had a complete identity and now didn't need it. The solution was obvious.

Richie moved quickly to check through the house. He packed a suitcase of Jack's things, found his wallet, his passport and his birth certificate – all he need to create a new beginning. The search on the mountain was looking for a body, now he had one. He just had to get it there.

Richie dressed his brother in his clothes and wrapped him tight in several blankets and a plastic sheet. He washed down the garden steps and the blood on the rockery. Jack was cold by now and his head injury, Richie considered, was consistent with a fall and the sort of impact you would find from a climbing accident. He just had to transport it to a suitable site and leave him for the authorities to find in due course.

Maybe that would even go some way to help his wife deal with the situation, he considered after the barbed comments from his brother. He was right, of course, albeit none too subtle; he had left his wife in a terrible situation. Sudden death was bad enough, but not knowing, being missing was worse. This could provide her with that relief and him with the new start that all his instincts were telling him that he needed.

Richie managed to wheelbarrow his brother's body towards his estate car and to bundle him in the back. The keys had been hanging on the hook in the kitchen. A road map was in the car. Richie took his day sack with him, thinking he might leave it with the body to help identify it as him. He left the drive steadily and headed back towards the mountains. He would need to be careful at this stage, he thought. He couldn't afford to be stopped on the way with a body in the back, nor to come across any of the search parties, if indeed they were still active.

Feeling tense and shocked, Richie was trying to keep calm, which was of course impossible. He had never liked his brother but never envisaged actually killing him and taking his place. Thoughts ran through is mind of how he would have to become him. Contact his employer, perhaps report sick, find his diary. Leave the country…

Richie chose minor roads and country lanes to avoid any police cameras spotting the car. Apart from the risk of being stopped, time was on his side. The body was securely wrapped, he considered, and the car he hoped would have no trace present once the body had been removed. As he got closer to the area where he was walking that day, Richie remembered a particular view from the ridge with a potentially dangerous narrow path overlooking a sheer drop. It would have been easy to have slipped on such a path or found the snow collapsing beneath him, sending him down the sheer face to his death. If he could hide the body somewhere below that ridge, as if it had fallen, it seemed to him that anyone finding it would reach the obvious and plausible conclusion.

Richie was able to drive quite close to the site that he had identified. However, there remained the problem of how he was going to be able to move a body on foot, on his own, over some distance, over rough ground to the place he wanted to leave it. There was no alternative. Even a quad bike would have struggled on this terrain, so the only option was to carry his brothers body. He hadn't thought of that. No rucksack would have accommodated him any way, but carrying a dead weight over his shoulder was going to be difficult and obviously hard to explain if he came across any other walkers. By now, he looked really rough, unshaven and dirty. It would be obvious that he'd been out for some time and carrying such a parcel would be impossible to disguise. It would inevitably arouse suspicion.

As he tried to lift the body out of the car he heard voices and quickly placed it back inside and closed the rear hatchback. Richie managed to avoid contact with the passing walkers but was beginning to panic. Maybe it would not be possible to carry the body as far as he had planned. What if he hadn't fallen from where he had planned but had slipped at a lower level and banged his head but been able to carry on some distance before collapsing and going into a coma? That was feasible, he considered. He looked around – where would you head for if injured and looking for help?

There was nowhere obvious. Maybe he would have just crawled into another snow hole? Then he remembered a cave not far from here. Could he conceivably reach the cave with Jack's body? Quickly, he got back into the driving seat and drove off towards the area of the cave. He could just about drive to within a mile of the site he had identified. He needed to check out the cave first – it might be occupied.

Parking as best as he could and trying to disguise the body in the back of the car, Richie set off at speed to check the cave. There was no one in the immediate area and it was how he remembered it: deep, dark and wet. He set off back to the vehicle but as he approached a group of youngsters had stopped for a brew within sight of the car. He paused, heart pounding as he waited for them to move on. Quickly, he lifted Jack out of the boot and, together with his day sack, set off as best as he could to carry him to the cave. Going was slow. He was exhausted, but it was too late now to do anything other than to continue. It took him two hours over the rough ground to carry his brother to his resting place. Once in the cave, Richie used things from his sack to try to make it look like Jack had made camp. He unpacked the plastic sheet and the blankets and placed him in his sleeping bag with other items left around as if Jack had tried to settle for the night. The head injury looked convincing and Richie felt confident that the scene was plausible. There was still snow on the ground and the cave was deep enough to make the body difficult to find without detailed inspection. As snow began to fall again outside the cave, Richie speculated that it could be some time before Jack would be found.

Worried but relieved, he made his way back down the track to the car. Whatever happened now, he considered, he had made his plan and there was no turning back. He couldn't reappear as Richie, for better or for worse, he was now Jack Dolman and that was it.

As he drove back to Jack's house, Richie did begin to think for the first time about the impact on his wife and began to feel a sense of guilt, even regret, but it was too late for that now. He had no choice but to see his plan through. Richie Dolman was dead and, as Jack Dolman, he was now on his way to Jack's house and a new future.

Chapter 10

The police had called. Rosemary had just come round to offer support. Angie sat quietly in tears after the distressing news that the authorities were about to call off the search for Richie. It was a devastating moment. Any prospect of discovering what might have happened had been taken away. She was in despair.

***

It was several years later that the police received a report that a group of climbers had come across a body in a cave. A rock fall at the back of the cave had kept it hidden for all this time, but a recent earth tremor had moved sufficient rocks to expose what turned out to be a body. The police had informed Angie that the body of a walker had been found in a cave near to the area that Richie was believed to have gone missing. What could be identified from the clothing and personal possessions found at the scene was consistent with the description of Richie when he set off from home. No suspicious circumstances were suspected and it was felt highly likely that the body found was that of Richie Dolman.

Rosemary just sat and held her.

'At least it's over now, Angie. You know that he's been found and what happened,' she said, trying to be helpful.

'I need to see him to be sure Rosemary, and no we still don't really know what happened,' Angie replied, tears running down her cheeks.

'It was an accident, wasn't it? That's what the police officer said. The body was found with a head injury, assumed to be from a fall. It seemed likely that he had made it as far as the cave, probably looking for shelter, but he then died from his injuries.'

'Yes, but all that is speculation and assumption. I need to know, Rosemary. I need to how my husband died. I'll need to wait for the post mortem. Now, are you up to coming with me to identify the body?'

Rosemary spluttered but felt obliged. 'Yes, of course, Angie. I'll come with you.'

Rosemary drove – the mortuary wasn't far away. Angie tried to keep calm as she walked into the building with her friend at her side. A member of staff and a police representative were present as they followed inside and were shown a covered body. The sheet was pulled back to reveal the familiar shape of a face of a man they both knew and they felt was recognisable, despite the trauma to the head and obvious signs of decay. Cold conditions sometimes slowed down the natural process of decay considerably, which seemed to be the case in this instance.

'Yes, that must be Richie,' declared Angie faintly as she turned to go outside for some fresh air. Rosemary comforted her as the police officer sought her confirmation of identity – she nodded.

The post-mortem report would be ready in a few weeks, they were told.

The news was announced in the media and the final pieces of evidence were gathered by the authorities.

The post-mortem report concluded that Richie Dolman had died following a blunt trauma injury consistent with a fall onto a rocky surface. The local mountain rescue team confirmed that there had been several similar accidents in that area over the years and that what was known about Richie's death was consistent with such an explanation. The coroner recorded a verdict of accidental death.

Jack, as Richie, was laid to rest in the local church yard. Some family members, friends and representatives from the rescue teams and the police attended the proceedings. Afterwards, Rosemary led Angie away from the grave side.

Chapter 11

Richie woke up in his brother's bed to start a new life. He couldn't face attempting to act like his brother in a work setting so rang in sick and followed it up with a letter of resignation due to a change of circumstances. The employer was sympathetic to Richie's claim that the loss of his brother had prompted him to sell up and move abroad.

Richie tied up his and his brother's affairs as best he could. Ironically, after years of feeling resentful of his brother, he found that Jack had done better than him out of the inheritance from both their parents and grandparents. Once the house was sold, he found that he had a sizeable pot to begin again and decided to move abroad. At first, he went to Spain to relax by the coast for a while and considered moving on to Australia or New Zealand. In any of those places, he had no need to constantly think how Jack would have handled a situation. He could now relax and be himself under a new name. No one he met in Spain had any prior knowledge of either Jack or Richie, so they would suspect nothing. He found some casual work in a bar and rented a small apartment. Life seemed good.

Richie hadn't yet sought any medical investigation following his disappearance, so he hadn't really explored what had been the cause of his malaise in the mountains. In layman's terms, it seemed that he had something of 'a funny turn', followed by exhaustion probably linked to mild hyperthermia and possibly indicative of an early warning of the need to take stock of his health. Or had it been more than that? Perhaps it was a mild heart or angina attack, or indicative of some sort of mental breakdown? He wasn't sure.

Spain did him good and he felt relaxed. From time to time, he did still feel guilty and a sense of regret about what had happened, but he tried not to dwell on it. He had been successful in breaking free from what he perceived had become a suffocating lifestyle and to have made a completely new start. He was more settled, he was content. Or so he liked to think.

***

Angie struggled to settle or find contentment. She was still in emotional turmoil years later. Still half wondering whether Richie might yet walk back through her door. Still wondering exactly what happened that day he had gone missing. Feelings of sadness, disappointment, regret, anger and guilt still plagued her almost daily. She couldn't rest – the explanation was still incomplete. Although she had identified the body at the time, she never felt completely sure. Was he really dead?

Ten years later, sitting in her garden with Rosemary, the topic of Richie's disappearance came into the conversation. Over all that time, no new information had ever emerged.

Rosemary reflected, 'Jack, Richie's brother, didn't come to the funeral, did he, Angie?'

'No.'

'A little odd, don't you think?'

'I suppose so,' Angie replied.

'Have you ever thought of trying to contact him directly, to ask him what he think happened?'

'No.'

'Do you think you should? Do you think it might help?' Rosemary asked.

'They never got on, you know, Richie and his brother, they hated each other. I don't suppose Jack would miss him, maybe that's why he didn't come to the funeral?'

The idea had been planted. Angie decided to follow her friend's advice. Maybe Jack would have a view on his brother's disappearance? She hired the services of a private investigator. He was able to confirm that, after Richie's death, his brother Jack had sold up and moved to Spain. The case interested the investigator, as an ex-police man. As he was planning to go on holiday himself to Spain, he offered to make some enquiries to see if he could trace Jack and therefore arrange the possibility of Angie making contact and seeking his opinion.

In the event, it didn't take much time to identity several Jack Dolmans, but only one of the relevant age who was registered under a Spanish address. The investigator stayed in the next resort to where Jack lived and, armed with a photo of Jack, set out one evening to trawl the local sea front in the hope of maybe finding him. On his third outing, sitting at a table on a restaurant on the front and looking out to sea was a man who looked very much like Jack and, therefore, like how he imagined his identical twin Richie would have looked some years on from the photo.

He sat across the road from him for a while and managed to sneak several photographs before going across to speak to him.

'Excuse me, sir,' he asked. 'Are you a holiday maker or an ex-pat?'

'Why do you ask?'

'I just wondered if you could recommend any of these restaurants along the front, if you are familiar with the area?

'Sure,' the man replied, 'take a seat. In my view, this one is far and away the best in town. Jack Dolman, by the way,' he said, offering his hand to shake.

'Thank you. Simon Jones,' he replied, using a false name. Engineering a coincidence by claiming to come from the town in the UK that Jack had left, Simon easily struck up a conversation.

'Hey, my friend, let me buy you a drink,' said Jack. Looking around for a waiter but seeing none, he left to go to the bar himself.

After a glass of Sam Miguel the investigator offered to exchange phone numbers. He then made his excuses and promised to book in to eat at the restaurant the following evening. He thanked Jack and left.

Back home in the UK, the investigator contacted Angie to share his findings.

'Good to hear from you. I hope you had a nice holiday. It was so kind of you to offer to make some enquiries. I hope it didn't spoil your time there?'

'No, not at all!'

When the investigator described what he had found, Angie couldn't believe it. She started breathing heavily and wasn't sure whether to laugh or cry. The investigator was also able to tell her that he had seen Jack again before he left Spain and he had told him that he was planning to return briefly to the

UK the following week. So, if she wanted to speak to him, she should be able to make contact now!

With very mixed emotions, Angie took deep breaths and phoned the number her investigator had given her.

'Hi Jack Dolman…'

'Jack, it's Angie. Remember me? Richie's wife.'

'Yes, of course. What a nice surprise. What can I do for you?'

She knew instantly but wanted to make sure.

'Could we meet? I'd like to ask you some questions about Richie's disappearance?'

The reply became tense.

'Oh, it's been a long time ago now, Angie. I'm not sure I can help.'

She was persuasive and talked him into meeting for coffee the following day. Jack had come back home for a short time to see his solicitor and to tie up some loose ends from the various family estates. Meeting would be easy.

Chapter 12

Angie was up early, keen to meet for coffee as arranged. She tried to keep calm. She had waited a long time for this opportunity.

Jack arrived late and seemed uncomfortable. Angie sat patiently at the table as arranged then she caught sight of a man entering the cafe. Yes, the brothers were identical twins but, even with the passage of time, she was sure. The man before her was Richie, not Jack. Her mind went back to identifying the body in the mortuary. She had always felt a niggle of doubt. Seeing someone you love in those circumstances wasn't the time to differentiate between twins, she reflected.

They talked politely before Angie made her apologies and she said that she had to leave. Jack had been careful. He gave nothing away. He was deliberately vague. No new information emerged, as she suspected.

They parted with a reserved handshake and Angie got up to walk out of his life, as he had walked out of hers all those years ago. Yes, she was in no doubt that the man she had just met was Richie, but equally that the man she had married had effectively died in the hills that day, whatever the precise circumstances, and that now she could begin to move on.

She had one last duty to perform.

As Jack remained at the table, having ordered some lunch, a tall man in plain clothes appeared in front of him.

'Richie Dolman, I am arresting you for the murder of Jack Dolman…'

2. INVASION

Author's note.

Please note that this story was written in Autumn 2019 before the general election and of course the advent of Covid-19. It was written as a story, and an attempt at a plausible future history. As events have unfolded in reality, the world has faced a very different challenge, but it might not have been so....

Chapter 1

25th December 2019

On Christmas Day the world awoke in anticipation of feasting and opening presents. The breaking news that greeted them that morning, however, was totally unexpected.

At midnight on Christmas Eve a substantial Russian force had invaded Finland. The advance had been dramatic and decisive. No real resistance was mounted in time to slow down or halt the inevitable. By dawn on Christmas Day the invasion was all but over. Finland had returned to Russian hands.

There had been tensions but the world intelligence community was not expecting this outcome. There was no plan in place for this eventually, not in detail anyway. Nothing was there to be dusted off, revisited, researched, updated and distributed to all who needed to know. Nothing was ready to be implemented quickly and at short notice.

For the West this was a disaster. After the Russian intervention in the Crimea, the West's reluctance to intervene in Syria, and the generally dire state of British political leadership, Mr Putin was feeling confident, buoyant and bullish.

While the West was in chaos he had taken his chances, assuming that beyond bluster and posturing any reaction to his invasion of a sovereign state would be lack lustre and ineffective.

Large numbers of Russian tanks had been on exercise during December without attracting too much attention from the West. They had then turned towards Finland and raced to the border before anyone had noted its potential significance. The Finish authorities were caught totally off guard as early reports started to emerge of tanks moving on all major routes. By the early hours of the morning on Christmas Day the capital, Helsinki, was surrounded, the parliament building and state media secured. Ports, airports, motorway intersections, major bridges and many other infrastructure key points were in Russian hands.

As families awoke and children eagerly awaited the start of Christmas festivities the country's political leaders were preparing to formally concede control back to the Russians who had ruled Finland before independence was secured in 1917 and again in 1940 after a further Russian invasion in 1939. Russia had been in full control from 1809 before conceding autonomy in 1917 with the Finnish declaration of independence. Russian interest, domination and annexation had therefore been a significant feature of Finnish existence for a considerable time. Sweden also had similar ambitions, and Denmark too had hoped to dominate this strategically important territory. A greater sense of stable independence had effectively only been secured since the end of the Second World War.

Whilst the world watched in horror, a major independent nation occupying a vital strategic position fell into the hands of a potential adversary. For the Russians, the regaining of control over Finland had been a low key long term aim for many years. It provided a foothold on the northern flank of Europe. For the West, Finland's occupation posed a direct threat to both Europe and America.

Finland had always been a key buffer state between East and West, not formerly part of NATO but on cooperative terms and not allied to Russia. Its loss was significant. Whilst no blood had been shed, this was a dangerous precedent and a major humiliation.

The West needed to respond. It was then that the horse trading started.

Chapter 2

President Trump was said to be incandescent, storming around the white house shouting at officials, issuing wild dictums and seeking someone to blame for this intelligence failure. How did we not expect this? He wanted answers. Who had missed it? Who was responsible? He called for an urgent meeting with his closest advisors and military chiefs.

In Westminster, this was a most unwelcome challenge to a tentative fledgling government. After the chaos of BREXIT, the general election in 2019 had delivered an indecisive response to the incumbent government's BREXIT strategy under the new Tory leadership of Boris Johnson.

As anticipated, the results for the Conservative party were disappointing as an angry public was desperate to have their say over the miserable conduct of government by an administration that had plumbed new depths of incompetence, indecision and intransigence. Labour had done little better as the electorate delivered its verdict on an unclear and fractured stance of 'constructive ambiguity'. The winners were, as expected, the Liberal Democrats, the Greens and the Independents. The much talked up Brexit party expectations failed to materialise after their initial victories in the European elections in May 2019. In the final result they were tactically wrong footed, in many constituencies achieving second or third place but not gaining many seats. The Change UK party failed to fire the public's imagination and were forced into a humiliating post-election merger with the Liberal Democrats. Had they done the sensible thing and joined them in the first place they could have secured an overall majority, but they hadn't chosen that option.

The numbers were interesting but only really left scope for one viable alliance; a Liberal Democrat pact with Labour, the Greens and most of the Independents, leaving the Tory's to lick their wounds and exposing Nigel Farage's flamboyant claims as wildly over optimistic.

Whilst Jo Swinson had won the Liberal Democrats' leadership contest, given her inexperience, Sir Vince Cable was persuaded to stay on as Prime Minister with Emily Thornberry as deputy. Both Jeremy Corbyn and Tom Watson had lost their seats.

The prospect of Vince Cable working effectively with Donald Trump to create a coherent strategy was not a scenario that filled anyone in power with confidence, including Vladimir Putin.

Across Europe heads of state were making their protests in response to the Russian action, lead by Emmanuel Macron and Angela Merkel. Heads of state in the other Scandinavian countries were especially nervous and only too conscious of how easy it would be for Russia to continue and roll across open borders into Sweden and Norway. There was no history of Russian invasion that far west and annexation of Finland had been a dormant Russian objective since the end of the Second World War.

A showdown had been coming for some time. Western countries had been very reluctant to allow themselves to be drawn into another campaign after the experience of Iraq and Afghanistan. The first Iraq war had much clearer objectives than the later campaigns. To overturn an unheralded invasion of

Kuwait was a much more realistic, distinct and justifiable aim that the more nebulous aspiration of creating 'a free and democratic Iraq', in the famous words of George W. Bush, in a country with no democratic traditions. Stated aims in Afghanistan were often even more obtuse with the concern from the military about the dangers of 'mission creep'.

The history of foreign intervention in Afghanistan has been a chequered one to say the least. No one nation had ever succeeded in securing domination over such difficult terrain against a determined indigenous force, for whom defending their homeland had become a way of life for generations.

Initial western objectives were somewhat vague and confused. Over time, and certainly after the 9/11 attacks on America, the identification and destruction of alleged terrorist training camps seemed to become the primary objective. Though arguably justified and well intended, the realistic chances of success, let alone of establishing another western-inspired stable democracy, seemed remote indeed.

The whole series of events in The Middle East and North Africa from the beginning of the twenty first century had presented the West with real dilemmas in the context of their experience in Iraq and Afghanistan. Diplomats would freely admit that – had those campaigns run differently – the West, led by Barack Obama at the time, could well have intervened far earlier and more effectively in Syria. The opportunity was lost for the European Union to demonstrate leadership and coordinate an effective plan to secure the lives and resettlement of refuges. The void had of course been taken up by Russia, seeking to extend her influence in that part of the world, and they were assisted by Iran and some of the other Arab states. Other than the deniable deployment of special forces, the response from the West was pitifully inadequate, according to many commentators, giving the initiative almost wholly to Russia and her allies.

Any analysis of the outcome of military intervention over the preceding years following The Second World War was bound to draw mixed conclusions about its effectiveness and wisdom. The public appetite to deploy troops, with the consequent loss of 'blood and treasure', was lacking, given the many competing priorities for funds on the domestic agenda.

Of course some argued that inaction only changes the focus and that we paid the cost anyway in the consequent growth of Islamic fundamentalism and ISIS in particular. Resentment was left to fester inside some of the nations more directly involved that they had been left to shoulder the burden of defending democratic principles against a brutal and callous enemy. The impact on Lebanon, Jordan, Turkey, Greece and Italy, for example, not to mention the Kurdish people, was far more severe than that experienced by the rest of Europe or America.

How far the West had laid the foundations for the creation of Islamic terrorism was still an open question. Was there any legitimacy to claims of discrimination and animosity against Muslims in general? Could the West have handled things differently and avoided some of the worst consequences of allowing the popularisation of hate to grow?

This was the context in which Western leaders would need to decide what approach, and what action, if any, they would be prepared to take to defend Finland.

Mr Putin had been right to anticipate a bluster and flourish of diplomatic anguish and condemnation, but little immediate prospect of action.

Of course, military chiefs were instructed to prepare plans for various scenarios, from outright counter invasion and liberation to bolstering the defence along the northern edge of Western Europe. Familiar though they were with the inevitable tensions surrounding their relationships with their political masters, it was clear from the start that this was a major crisis which would need careful, resolute and clear consideration. It was a legitimate concern from commentators that such a reaction was unlikely to be forthcoming. Russian intervention in Hungary and Czechoslovakia in 1956 and 1968 caused serious concern in the West, but they were interventions further from home in areas of Eastern Europe that had traditionally been considered to be within the Russian sphere of influence, so Finland represented a significant escalation in the perception of the threat posed by Russian expansion.

Chapter 3

Tensions were immediately apparent at the first meeting of the United Nations Security Council after the invasion where hostile exchanges were evident between Russia and most other members, with China taking serious note of developments.

Similarly, within NATO the discussions were animated. Condemnation was universal and action of some sort seemed inevitable. A diplomatic delegation of the most senior representatives was immediately dispatched to express outrage and opposition in the gravest of terms. Sanctions were rapidly applied, whilst Donald Trump fumed and berated the assembled members for their timidity as if his finger was already on the button.

Diplomats perceived that Mr Putin could not have been surprised by this level of reaction and that steady nerve was required to face him down. No one wanted a war but this situation could not be allowed to stand.

Russia stood stoically by, refusing to consider their action as anything other than a realignment with the full consent of the Finnish people to offer them security and solidarity in the face of constant Western aggression.

The situation quickly deteriorated and by early 2020 NATO troops were deployed along the borders between Norway and Sweden and Sweden and Finland. Norway and Sweden had already established close ties with NATO and had held joint exercises. British Royal Marine Commandos had a long history of familiarity with Norway and had developed considerable expertise in the tactics of arctic warfare. In short, alliances and common understanding was already well established between Scandinavia and Western Europe.

An American General was appointed as overall Allied Commander and formations were established to defend the remainder of Scandinavia and Northern Europe. 1st (UK) Div was deployed in Norway in a long defensive formation with the Marines conducting long range patrols. 1st US Corps was deployed in Sweden, supported by the French and elements of the Lithuanian and Estonian armies.

The strategic approach was one of mobile defence, in the hope of holding the line against any further encroachment, supported by the quick reaction offensive capability of Marines and Airborne forces, who would be ready to counter attack.

In North West Europe, the Danes, the Germans, the Belgians and the Poles formed defensive positions and work was underway to secure the cooperation of other Baltic states to provide their own defence from the eastern border of Poland to the eastern border of Estonia, facing St Petersburg and the Russian mainland. Not since the height of the cold war, and possibly the Cuban missile crisis, had relations been so strained and so tense between East and West.

Chapter 4

In Finland attitudes were polarising between those in support of the Russian initiative and those opposed to it. Supporters accepted the propaganda that their Russian brothers had come to their aid to deter any further Western encroachment into their domain and cheered in the streets, celebrating their liberation, whilst the opposition grew angry, so tension rose and armed resistance was actively planned and prepared. Finland lent itself to the prospect of guerrilla warfare, with its large areas of rugged and challenging terrain.

For many Finns the blatant spin of Russian propaganda held no reassurance and a sense of inevitability grew that it wouldn't be long before someone fired the first shot. As opposition politicians, activists, intellectuals and trade unionists were rounded up and interned, street protests spread across the country.

At a rally in Helsinki on 1st of March 2020 Russian troops opened fire on a crowd of angry protesters and riots in the streets ensued until the early hours. Countless numbers of people had been killed or injured and by morning the streets were heavily patrolled by tanks with ground troops in close support.

Over the following days, numerous incidents of the attempted abduction of Russian troops occurred, with ambushes and selective attacks on strategic targets. The Russian response was swift and brutal. Any known state security personnel were interned and any open resistance met with immediate military action. The country was fast descending into chaos as large numbers of civilians started to move towards the Swedish border. Camps were rapidly assembled in the Swedish interior to receive these people with full UN support. All Western troops deployed in the area were on high alert and limited air strikes were being planned to degrade key Russian installations.

Diplomatic efforts continued to attempt to calm the situation but Russia maintained her stance of defiantly rejecting international pressure. Foreign diplomats and embassy staff were being ordered to leave and trade in anything of essential strategic significance was being restricted or stopped altogether. The threat to oil and gas supply was evident.

Concerns in the West about fuel security had already provided some impetus to expand green energy facilities rapidly. Production had been stepped up of bio fuel across Scandinavia, North America and Canada. The West was less than ready but not completely exposed.

The consequences of delay in implementing plans to speed up the transition to a greener world were cruelly exposed. Questions had been raised many times in the West about our vulnerability and the limitations of our secure independent energy supplies. Now was not the time to be reminded of the utter inadequacy of those arrangements, but that was the inevitable reality.

Chapter 5

As the situation in Finland unfolded, China watched.

Such a degree of insecurity on the world stage was not desirable, the authorities concluded, but it might provide some opportunity. Whilst the Western powers were distracted, China made plans to invade North and South Korea and Taiwan; three states that caused concern and threatened Chinese power and security on their southern borders. Invasion in these circumstances, they reasoned, would gain little attention from the rest of the world, but to threaten Russia directly in Finland would.

China had been quiet whilst sitting on the security council up until now, but it felt that it was time to make their presence felt. Plans were made and troops identified and made ready for deployment to threaten the very border between China and Russia unless Russia was prepared to back down and withdraw from Finland. They calculated that there was some scope for leverage.

Border disputes and treaties between the two super states had been a constant feature over centuries, from at least 1689. Six treaties were signed between then and 1881before the major conflicts of the twentieth century ensued. Tensions, however, had eased in recent years along the contentious border, with both sides reducing force levels considerably from 2015.

Whilst Russia was distracted, China saw her best chance in generations to secure expansion along her eastern and north eastern borders. The country's leadership were buoyant and confident that, even if that objective in itself proved eventually to be unsuccessful, it would provide sufficient incentive to persuade Russia that it was not in her best interests to expand any further west and to consequently withdraw from Finland.

There was another possible scenario, however. America had long feared the remote possibility of a Russian-Chinese pact, which could introduce such a powerful force in world affairs as to seriously threaten America's dominance. Should that ever occur, the impact would be much more serious than what was unfolding in a side show like Finland.

However, on balance, China felt that it was more in her immediate interest to take advantage of the situation and resolve the long term problems of Korea and Taiwan on her southern borders, opening the prospect of expansion into the north at Russia's expense. Such a course of action, if it resulted in forcing the liberation of Finland, could reassure the West to some extent in regards to their intentions towards world peace and security, whilst reserving China's option of a future pact with Russia to dominate the West as a potential longer-term strategy. The various options and scenarios were looking positive.

China was ready to make her move.

Chapter 6

At the following meeting of the security council, actions by China were set to dominate the agenda.

Concerns about escalation and the risks of a nuclear component in this growing conflict heightened as Chinese tanks rolled into North Korea and airborne troops landed along the South Korean border to reassure South Koreans that no further incursions were intended. A frenzied political and diplomatic reaction ensued. Taiwan fell almost immediately after a short naval bombardment.

Kim Jong un, the North Korean leader, had been taken completely by surprise and was unable to respond quickly enough to effectively resist the Chinese onslaught, so any nuclear threat or deployment was avoided. From a Western perspective, this was not all bad news. The North Korean threat had been subdued after all; the only concern was the increase in power and influence of China itself and the uneasy position of South Korea which, although not exactly a western state, was certainly more allied to western ideas than to hard-line Chinese authority.

The western contingent eagerly awaited a statement from the Chinese delegate. When forthcoming, it was brief and uncompromising:

'Forces of The Democratic Republic of China have successfully secured control of North Korea and Taiwan in the interests of bringing peace and security to the region.'

Diplomatic questions were asked and notional objections lodged but privately delegates accepted that this was effectively a fait accompli, at least in the short term. Anxiety was clearly evident in the Russian delegation. They were privately quite impressed with China's initiative but were concerned about possible additional motivations, and they didn't want to lose any potential further influence in South East Asia.

The point had been made and the desired impact achieved; the world sat up and took note – China had arrived and signalled the possibility of her future leading status. Russian enthusiasm towards the Finnish campaign had been stalled. Although tensions remained, a full escalation into open conflict had, it seemed, been avoided.

The West were still obviously concerned about instability and the remaining threat to Europe, but China – for better or for worse – had taken the heat out of the European theatre.

***

The Chinese intervention added to the pressure on Russia to pause before making any further incursions into the interior of Finland or beyond. Officially, of course, the move by the Chinese was condemned by the Russians and its impact said to be marginal. For Finnish resistance, it was a sign of hope. Not wanting to provoke the Russian bear, however, some reduction in counter offensive activity did seem to be taking place. The UN were desperately keen to move ahead with negotiations for a cease fire, using the impasse as a window of opportunity.

Defensive preparations in Sweden and Norway, however, continued with intensity. Supply lines were established, stockpiles concealed and detailed plans for their aggressive defence refined and confirmed.

For the troops on the ground, a winter in Northern Europe was not what they had been expecting. Christmas had been disrupted and deployment hastily arranged. Maintaining discipline and morale in a tense potential prelude to war presented its own significant challenges. The more experienced campaigners quickly realised that this could all come to nothing, escalate very quickly or, more likely, drag on through the winter while political and diplomatic efforts were made to resolve the crisis without resorting to war. War on this scale, of course, could be catastrophic, representing as it would a formal clash between East and West with all the serious implications that the world had lived with and largely avoided since 1945.

The stakes were undoubtedly very high indeed.

Chapter 7

Whilst Russia considered her response to China's initiative in South East Asia, the Chinese were preparing to move large numbers of forces to expand their northern and eastern borders. Any incursion into Russian territory to secure further lands beyond North Korea towards the pacific coast would be attractive to China.

Given the major land grab that had already taken place on their western flank across the Sea of Japan, the Japanese were becoming increasingly nervous and were watching intensely.

***

Diplomatic efforts to explore any possible scope for a settlement over Finland were not going well. Russia had effectively achieved what she had set out to, the annexation of Finland, and she was not about to give it up readily. Russian thinking remained confident that the West would, in the final analysis, be very reluctant to actually commit to war over Finland and, despite their protestations, would be more likely to capitulate and accept what had already taken place.

Sharing the same scepticism the Finnish government in exile, such as it was, tended to take the same view. Neither were they ultimately confident of full NATO support if it came to a position where the only feasible approach would be a full counter invasion. Preparations for such an eventuality were of course being made whilst negotiations continued. However, certainly in the UK political opinion was split on the case for war. President Trump, as expected was talking up the option of full American commitment to reinstating Finland as an independent country regardless of the costs and the risks.

The challenges were considerable and the leading players had probably never been so disunited since 1945. Both the Russians and the Chinese were readily exploiting their weaknesses.

**

Later that day, in a private meeting, the respective leaders of the UK and America sat down together with their most trusted advisers. The atmosphere was grave and intense.

As analysis, interpretation and implications of what they had heard were discussed, it was Donald Trump who eventually broke the paralysis.

'Listen Guys, enough crap – we might have to actually do this!'

The room fell silent as the assembled representatives accepted that for once he might be right. Europe faced its biggest challenge since Hitler invaded Poland in 1939. Now, in 2020, a year after the 75th anniversary of the D-Day landings in Normandy, the same two key allies were sat together planning a response to a new threat to world security. Great Britain, the leader of the greatest empire the world had ever seen, and her allies behind D Day, the greatest ever invasion, could not shirk their responsibility. This unwarranted aggression could not stand. Finland had to be restored as an independent country. Sacrifices would have to be made. Risks would need to be taken but, most of all, the resolve and unity to address this crisis had to emerge from this meeting.

Chapter 8

Meanwhile, Chinese forces were massed along the Chinese-Russian border, north of what was North Korea, ready to launch a major strike north into Russian territory, with the aim of cutting off Khabarovskiy Kray, the peninsula west of Sakhalinskaya Oblast. This would threaten the integrity of the whole of Russia's eastern border towards the Bering Sea.

In the early morning of 5th April 2020, Chinese forces unleashed their attack. Given that it was unexpected, opposition was light and largely ineffective, allowing China to make significant and immediate gains. By the time they consolidated at the end of the first day of the campaign, troops were as far north as the end of the straits alongside Japan's north island, looking out to the Sea of Okhotsk. This was a considerable advance representing a major incursion into Russian territory and a major escalation in world tension. A Russian reaction was inevitable. China hoped that their objective of provoking negotiation rather than further escalation would prove to be successful, but they knew that this was a very high-risk strategy.

***

As the western allies' meeting continued, and plans for war were discussed in greater detail, the momentum for invasion was growing. Drawing on the emotive spirit of 1944, the group continued to plan with focus and urgency. There would need to be a coordinated air, land and sea operation using overwhelming force to secure success. Softening up identified targets would preclude any attack. Intelligence from the Royal Marines' long range patrolling operations, and from Special Forces already deployed directly into Finland, meant details of suitable targets were being confirmed. Discussions continued as collective enthusiasm was only broken by the sudden arrival of tea and sandwiches.

With a suitable pause for thought, one of the politicians praised their collective concentration and success in developing a viable offensive plan when the Senior British Military Advisor added, 'Gentlemen, let us not forgot why we fought the Second World War… what the sacrifice was for…'

'Yes, that same spirit could take us to victory again today, General!' responded the enthusiastic politician.

'Did we fight it so as to be able to sit here again and contemplate repeating the experience in modern times?' the General postulated. 'No, no we didn't. If there was a lesson from both world wars, it was… never again. Lessons learnt at Gallipoli, the Somme, Ypres and Passendale culminated in our success in Normandy. Afterwards, we worked hard to secure a lasting peace, and build international cooperation, institutions and agreements to reinforce that peace. For God's sake, before we unleash the dogs of war let us try every available avenue to reach a negotiated peaceful settlement to this dispute. Let us not forget that since 1945 the world has further developed the capacity for its own destruction. Let's not risk that being the eventual outcome of escalation.'

The room was sombre.

'The General's right,' responded one of the diplomats. 'The D Day proclamation has to mean something in practice. This is our responsibility now.'

The point had been made.

Consideration moved towards reinforcing the leadership of the diplomatic effort to bring about a peaceful solution when the news broke of the Chinese infiltration into Russian territory. With shock and horror, the assembled group heard the details of the Chinese advance deep into Russia – of the loses, the speed and scale of the advance, the sheer audacity. The sentiment of the General's words resounded as fears of a Russian retaliatory response were imagined. The stakes were already high and now they were even higher. The need to remember those involved in those previous campaigns and to commit again to seeking a peaceful resolution was apparent. Success in that regard had largely been achieved in the post-war era but this further challenge to that security needed to be met with the same resolve.

Chapter 9

Rapid efforts were made to secure the attendance of the Security Council members for longer than was originally envisaged in order to address this new development. Frantic diplomatic efforts continued throughout the night in an attempt to persuade Russian not to overreact. The initial message coming from Russia, however, was much more bullish, with threats to respond with attacks directly on Beijing. The stage was set – diplomacy or war.

***

Diplomatic efforts were intense, backed by an increasing consensus of military opinion that a negotiated solution simply had to emerge. The alternative was just too grave to contemplate. Privately, both the Russians and the Chinese delegations probably felt the same but a process of posturing was required to take place.

Frantic movement between private rooms continued, where different interest groups formed proposals and considered counter proposals. The negotiations took all night, with the threat of an imminent nuclear attack on Beijing hanging over them, but a consensus did eventually emerge.

Following a further period of mounting tensions and intensive negotiations, the potential basis for a peaceful agreement was becoming clear.

Russia had been persuaded that there was scope for not losing face and that there were merits to walking away from Finland, on the pretext of needing to reinforce their borders with China to the east. The prospect of avoiding outright disaster seemed to be improving.

Later that day, President Putin duly issued the following statement:

'The heroic forces of Democratic Republic of Russia have succeeded in their quest to establish security in Finland in the face of western aggression, allowing their attention to now focus on the security of our eastern border with China.'

Once more, the world had managed to draw back from the brink, but it had been desperately close.

Postscript

On June 3rd 2020, an agreement was signed between Russia and China to end the conflict. Its principle components were that:

* China were to withdraw from Russian territory and consolidate their position, which would include the occupation of North Korea and Taiwan.

* Russia were to withdraw from Finland and reinstate its full independence.

* China were to continue a different relationship with South Korea, tolerating its autonomy.

* The border between Finland and Russian were to be subject to international monitoring by a peacekeeping force under the UN.

* Negotiations were to be established between Russia and China, aiming to agree a long term settlement to their border disputes. A further international peacekeeping force would oversee its implementation and integrity.

3. Despite the odds

Chapter 1

January 2022

Brussels

After the European elections, the MEPs gathered for the first time in their new configuration. Two conclusions were upper most in their collective thinking. Firstly, the electorate had rejected the drift to extremism (as parties of the far right across Europe had not done so well) and secondly, the winners had been the Greens who had managed to translate the growing level of concern and public unease about the environment into an urgent need for action. Relief and trepidation were therefore the two most prominent and competing emotions in the air that morning; relief that, for now at least, Europe seemed to have saved itself from the dangerous drift further to the far right but also trepidation about the scale of the task ahead.

Marie-Clare Smets, the newly elected European commissioner and a high flying Belgian, looked out at the array of old and new faces in front of her, knowing that an early topic for consideration and debate was the Greens' plan to address climate change. The world had moved on. Most countries expressed a growing acceptance that this was the new world challenge. International terrorism, crime, poverty and inequality remained concerns, of course, fuelling tensions and inhibiting attempts at reaching international consensus. The change in leadership in America had helped, with Donald Trump's narrow defeat in their elections and the dawning of a new era with the arrival on the international stage of Hank Steiner, a much more consensual character than Trump.

Could the international institutions manage to create greater degrees of consensus and cooperation under this renewed drive to address climate change? Had the world ever faced such a set of challenges before? No one underestimated the scale of the difficulties ahead but many tried desperately to remain hopeful.

Chapter 2

The Greens had published their arguments in favour of environmental reform with some practical policy suggestions. The paper had been generally well received but there were of course objectors, both overt and less obvious, to these proposals from various interest groups opposing change and wishing to maintain the cosy status quo. The basic case had already been made and widely accepted: that change was essential to reduce, let alone eliminate, the risk of global catastrophe. It was not too dramatic to postulate that the very future of the planet and humanity itself was at stake. In short, no change was no longer an option.

The growth in the popularity of the Greens and the re-emergence of the liberal centre left had come together to generate momentum for a fairly radical programme of progressive change. The smug conservative blindness to the self-inflicted pain caused through the aftermath of austerity and a botched Brexit was exposed for the hypocrisy that it was. Similarly, outright socialism as an alternative was, it seemed, no more attractive; so centre, coalition, consensus politics emerged as winning the battle for ideas.

The green agenda was simple: a world transformation from carbon-based to green-based energy and a concerted move to greater world equality between the haves and the have nots. This led to the launch of the following policy initiatives:

- A progressive carbon tax on all fossil fuels and carbon-related products, using a sliding scale based on a calculation of relative harm.

- A central drive to invest in green energy sources, including research into: alternative forms of battery power, the issue of safe disposal of used batteries and alternative methods of deflecting the sun's harmful rays.

- The application of a large scale implementation of desalination techniques to ease the coming world shortage of safe drinking water, coupled with methods to radically increase food production.

- Prescribed assistance from the developed world to the less developed to help them apply available technology to their particular circumstances.

- Moves toward the introduction of a Universal Basic Income (UBI), available to all citizens as a basic right, to replace most benefits and enhance social security and cohesion.

- Incentives to travel more by public transport, or walk or cycle as an alternative, together with a greater use of traffic-restricted city centre zones.

- Widespread rejection of plastic packaging, increased capacity for recycling and a drive to clean up the historical world backlog of plastic pollution.

- Initiatives to support the diversity of wildlife and address the growing rate of extinction of many species.

- And, in the longer term, exploration of the feasibility of transporting people to new planets, including Mars.

This was the proposal, this was the manifesto, and this – it was hoped – was the future.

Chapter 3

Subsequent debate was, as expected, both lively and comprehensive. All the predictable objections were registered by those opposed to any tax increases. Questions were raised about the realistic chances of implementation quickly enough to make a difference; scepticism was rife about the feasibility of mass desalination as a means of increasing water supply; and most of all, of course, there was objection to the principal of UBI.

UBI was bound to be controversial. It represented a significant shift in the balance of income and wealth and, according to its supporters, could be funded through the raising of carbon taxes and savings on welfare. For the powerful, this represented a crude money grab to subsidise the poor, even the 'feckless', and was likely to meet with considerable resistance.

For its supporters, the notion of entitlement had an attraction in promoting social cohesion and community. Reducing, or moving towards eliminating, the need for welfare would not only give people a sense of unity, self-esteem and self-reliance but potentially UBI, as an alternative, should be so much cheaper and simpler to administer than welfare. Its benefits could also generate secondary savings across the board in health, education and criminal justice, for example, and therefore provide much needed funds for projects like sure start and nursery provision. Its principle and practicality could potentially appeal to the left and centre of politics and its efficiency and self reliance to the right. As such, the Greens hoped to convince the doubters, but recognised that it was likely to be an up-hill struggle.

Although the debate was impassioned, in many countries the new coalition governments had sufficient majorities to start to implement much of this agenda. Despite objections and opposition, real movement and progress were being made, albeit slowly.

***

For one young man, however, such political consideration was not such a primary issue.

Jaz Rubenstein, born of dual heritage with a Jewish-American father and a black third-generation British mother, at age eighteen was just about to embark on a military career, or so he hoped. He was due to report to the Infantry training depot at Catterick the following day and was feeling a little anxious. Not from a military family, his parents were surprised when he announced at age sixteen that he was going to join the army.

Jaz had left school earlier that year with some reasonable qualifications and had then opted to go to college to start the Public Service Btec level 3 course, which was accepted as a suitable starting point for anyone intending to join any of the uniformed services. He had also joined the local Territorial Army Unit in The West Midlands to get some basic experience. This unit was 3 Mercian. His parents welcomed the idea as a sort of trial period and secretly hoped that it might put him off. They were much more realistic about the risks involved than a young man who, at that point, had never considered himself to be anything other than indestructible.

He stuck to his plans, however, and his parents saw him off at the railway station. He waved nonchalantly as he clambered aboard with what was no doubt far too much kit. Although still a little nervous, Jaz looked forward to the challenge, he took some comfort in the fact that he had taken the trouble to get some military experience through his local TA unit before joining the regular army. He had also received much encouragement from his OC, the Major commanding the company he'd joined, and from his fellow soldiers. Jaz was fit, he was quite bright and he was very determined.

He arrived at Catterick and immediately got stuck into his training. After a haircut and mountains of induction paperwork, the military process got underway with the issue of kit and the first introduction to the drill square. This was all new for many of the recruits, but it was fortunately familiar territory to Jaz, which he found to be a huge advantage.

The other lads were a real mixed bunch. Many from The West Midlands but others from further afield. They were all up for a laugh and friendships were soon established. Jaz found himself to be one of the few recruits with any previous experience and, as such, instantly became the platoon mentor for everything from assembling webbing to learning the basic rank structure and from initial drill moves to correctly wearing the uniform. He liked the role, although he clearly hadn't chosen it. He got on well with their section corporal but was a bit weary of the platoon sergeant at first, anyone further up the line of command after that was to be instantly saluted and listened too intently.

As the course progressed and others found their feet, characters started to emerge and Jaz found that his initial advantage diminished. He felt that he was more than capable of holding his own, however. The course was hard and everyone was struggling to some extent, minor injuries were common and for the most part the lads just tried to rally through. As the season turned to winter, an additional burden was apparent in exposing those who could cope with cold, wet weather and, more to the point, those who could not. By this stage a significant number of recruits had already either opted to leave or been sent home. The relative dreamers and no hopers were soon exposed and rooted out, Jaz felt.

One significant surprise was the relatively new inclusion of female recruits to the infantry. At first the lads were highly sceptical of the three females in the whole company who started with them. Two soon fell by the way side, reinforcing their original scepticism, all but one lass that was: Fiona Hastings from Stoke, who was a real star. Exceptionally fit and strong, the lads warmed to her, admiring her willingness to join in and not shirk any of the tasks that confronted her. It was evident that the instructors were impressed and surprised too by her level of determination and commitment. The military policy was aimed at being more inclusive, recognising the need to boost recruitment levels, but some scepticism was inevitable. Fiona more than held her own and soon gained respect from most instructors and recruits. Boy, she could drink too!

Fiona didn't regard it as her primary task to advance the cause of female emancipation; she simply wanted to be a good soldier. However, the reaction of her male colleagues at times both fascinated and frustrated her. What difference does it make, she postulated, as long as I can do the job? Whilst some soldiers were open minded, old attitudes were well established and, as she was to find out, hard to change. She tried to be relaxed about it, but sometimes that was so hard; she just wanted to be taken seriously. When things were difficult, at least she felt that Jaz understood and respected her and that was a comfort.

Chapter 4

Political progress was encouraging but, to be truly effective, there was still a long way to go to halt the inescapable deterioration in environmental conditions across the world. Populations were still rising rapidly. Temperature rises were only just starting to register a decline in the rate of increase and seas were themselves rising, with the inevitable consequence of significant flooding in many low-lying areas of the world. Any rise in sea levels only added to the pressures man was already imposing on the natural world, by reducing the available inhabitable space and starting to cause, if not panic, a steady movement of peoples. This was predicted to inevitably increase considerably as more and more areas of the world became less and less inhabitable.

Pressures on food production were also a concern. A more unpredictable climate was having a negative impact on food production with greater incidents of failing crops and reduced yields in general. The world was struggling to accept another transition to less emphasis on meat production and more on plant-based sources of food. A run of poor harvests across the world was already leading to limited food supplies on an alarming scale. Chronic food shortage increased pressures and tensions generally and the incidents of mass movements of peoples. Levels of food production in large parts of Africa and the Middle East were increasingly dire, with high levels of suffering, malnutrition and death becoming more widespread.

Under pressure to compete to survive, the new international consensus was struggling to keep a grip on progress. Tensions were mounting and the obvious difficulties were being exploited by the unscrupulous and those wanting to undermine international progress. Incidents of criminal gangs smuggling not only drugs and people but now food too started to emerge. Ownership of the supply of food and water particularly was becoming a key component in the ability to exercise power and influence.

Chapter 5

Africa, as so often before, was perhaps at the centre of both the attempts to thwart reform and of the negative consequences of it. War torn for centuries, subject to strong entrenched tribal rivalries, corruption and abuse of power, in many ways it represented the fight for constructive change versus the defence of entrenched self-interest.

China had invested heavily in supposedly assisting African countries develop their infrastructure, but at a cost. Loans had become millstones round the neck of beleaguered poor countries, driving them into further dependence on their new pseudo-colonial masters. Exploitation of Africa's vast mineral wealth continued aplenty but, as ever, the lion's share of the revenue raised was not spent or reinvested into African coffers but diverted abroad to the already wealthy. This only served to ever widen the gap between rich and poor and not narrow it, as the well-intended international consensus had hoped for.

Under pressure, rival groups turned on each other as sources of further oppression and abuse fuelled hatred, conflict and ultimately war on many small fronts. Nothing was large enough to attract sustained international condemnation, let alone relief, but it was significant enough to further impoverish many, increase suffering, potential starvation and mass migration. Many of the peoples of Africa were on the move, heading north, hoping to reach Europe and perceived salvation.

The sort of chaos and suffering seen in Syria, North Africa and across the Middle East was remerging as the world moved through the 2020's. Although, on the face of it, Syria had been stabilised, any real analysis didn't need to scratch far below the surface to find harsh unpalatable truths. The Assad regime, in their desperation to ensure their own survival, had used every conceivable means to bolster their position throughout the war and the emerging peace. Assisted by Russia for her own ends, the Syrian regime now emerged from the tragedy of recent history in many ways not only a survivor but as having reinforced and strengthened its position and iron grip over a fragile nation.

The aspiration of an 'Arab Spring' – vastly over optimistic western hopes of a self generating democracy blooming over North Africa – were dashed by a very different reality. Rather than true freedom and democracy emerging, more often one form of dictatorship had simply been replaced by another. The colonial sponsors had, in many cases, also simply changed from western to eastern influences.

Senior diplomats and politicians met to consider their responses.

'This is, in many ways, a re-run of the last crisis in North Africa, when a timid West, led by Obama, was so reluctant to commit that it just stood back and we lost considerable credibility and influence,' said one delegate to another.

'Yes, do you mean we should be more proactive this time?' another asked.

'Yes, indeed I do!'

'Despite the risks?'

'There are always risks.'

'What do you think?' they asked as a military senior officer joined them having listened to their discussion.

'These are undoubtedly difficult decisions; there can be a fine balance. I tend to agree with you that we could and should have been more involved in Syria. It's about moral courage, but self-interest plays a part. In the last century we were directly threatened by Germany, making it easier to make a case for intervention than the more recent situation in North Africa. Thankfully, I'm just a soldier; I don't have to make such decisions, just implement them.'

So a pragmatic and somewhat cautious consensus began to emerge in support of limited action to 'stabilise our neighbours in Africa and provide secure safe passage to those fleeing persecution, starvation and death.'

The plan was to conduct a brief bombing campaign to neutralise key targets that helped sustain conflict. Residual elements from ISIS and DASH and other disaffected groups were still present and active in promoting their twisted vision of Islamic rule. These were to be targeted. At the same time, ground troops would be deployed in certain sensitive areas as a peace keeping force and to provide a secure corridor for escaping refugees. Mainland Europe would provide a network of reception camps to process the migrants and attempt to resettle them in areas of relatively low population across the world, free from the threats of rising sea levels, to be deployed as a work force for good.

In 2023 NATO Military chiefs were assembled for an initial briefing in Brussels. A lead commander was appointed and commitment secured to deploy troops from a wide variety of countries. The challenge of integration of such diverse forces would be considerable, but the potential gains in unity of commitment was judged to be worth the endeavour.

The force would be deployed in two large formations. The first would be located across North Africa to establish basic security and peace keeping. The second would be based in Southern Europe, establishing secure corridors and camps to accommodate the refugees fleeing both conflict and the devastating effects of climate change.

Chapter 6

As the military made their plans, the situation they faced was deteriorating. The combination of all the elements of climate change and its consequent pressures were coming to bear with increasing numbers of peoples either directly competing for scarce resources or fleeing areas of habitation that were no longer viable.

In these circumstances, the planners were all too aware of the likelihood of being swamped. The need was clear but the resources to address it were always likely to lag behind and probably remain wholly inadequate. The vision of an orderly transition during this period, they acknowledged privately, could well prove to be a romantic delusion.

So it was with a mixture of hope and fear that troops started to be deployed during the following years. The forward contingent comprising of troops from UK, France, the Baltic states, China and Russia were deployed as intended across North Africa as a stabilisation force. The situation they faced varied largely depending on the local impact of the conflict with ISIS and other associated groups. Parts of Syria, in particular, still showed the devastating impact of war and still required considerable levels of reconstruction.

Movement of peoples from Ethiopia and Sudan was putting pressure of resources in Egypt. Peoples were also arriving from central and east Africa in smaller but significant numbers. Many had been traumatised, were malnourished and exhausted. Many of these people were received by Russian troops. The diversity of language made even basic communication very difficult at times, but a network of locally recruited representatives and interpreters from the peoples themselves was slowly being established. This style of humanitarian mission and peace keeping did not come easily to the Russian troops. Much work needed to be done to attempt to gain sufficient trust between such diverse groups of people to affect any sense of security. The challenge was immense but the potential rewards were considerable.

Chinese troops took the lead in facing the remaining elements of armed opposition from the remnants of ISIS and other disaffected groups. Whilst western commanders did take issue with some of their methods, it could not be denied that they were successful in establishing some order and security from chaos.

The British and French troops were located along the North African coast line and in Southern Europe to receive migrants before any attempts at crossing the Mediterranean and into Europe. Amongst the British contingent were I Mercian, a midlands regiment formed through amalgamation of The Cheshire Regiment, The Worcester and Sherwood Foresters and The Staffordshire Regiment. With considerable experience of recent conflicts, including dealing with similar issues of security and peace keeping, they adapted well to their new circumstances. Their task was to provide sufficient infrastructure to gain the confidence of those approaching them and to deter or detain any fortune seekers who were looking to exploit the vulnerable through unreliable promises of safe passage across the sea.

Once stabilised, an orderly movement of people could be established to travel to the camps, where the second international force were waiting to receive them. Part of that second force led by the Americans was supported by the British and other European armies, together with a contingent from Australia and New Zealand. 2 Mercian were part of this force and were deployed with the Australian and New Zealand troops.

The humanitarian corridors had, for the most part, proved to be effective in channelling people safely to the camps. Initially, the camps were orderly with good standards of basic sanitation, water supply and food but quickly, as anticipated, demand began to overrun supply and circumstances deteriorated. However, with the supreme efforts of the troops involved and the will and determination to make the best of it, the conditions remained at least tolerable. The worst aspects of the strong preying on the weak, exploitation and abuse amongst the assembled peoples, was largely avoided.

Further consideration, however, was required to deal with the growing numbers involved. Although initial attempts at resettlement were largely successful, it became clear that the strategy needed to change to encourage people to stay where they were, if at all possible. To that end a further contingent of African and Indian troops were made available to establish support for migrant people along the main south to north corridors across Africa, with a view to stabilising viable communities wherever possible.

This was proving to be probably the greatest migration of peoples across the world ever. The challenges and implications were considerable but, over time, large numbers of people were resettled in America, Russia and China, in particularly where huge areas of land was previously under-populated. The same issues faced these new communities that the rest of the world was grappling with but at least they were free from the immediate threat of flooding and starvation.

The transition was not without its tensions, however, as many of the peoples being moved, despite best attempts to inform them, were not expecting resettlement in their allocated areas. The numbers soon became too large to offer any form of filtering system to deliver an element of choice over their destiny. Whilst initially this had been attempted, it had proved to be too unwieldy and was discontinued. An unintended consequence was some degree of enforced separation between peoples and communities. It was accepted that this was not ideal but was felt to be unavoidable.

At the same time similar schemes needed to be established in other parts of the world too. The inhabitants of much of South East Asia, for example, faced their island communities disappearing under the rising sea, whilst in the more affluent areas of the northern hemisphere, resentment was growing about the impact of so much effort and resources being deployed to the southern hemisphere when problems were arising nearer to home too.

In Britain, some areas of the coast were under threat of flooding and even the Thames barrier was beginning to struggle to hold back the tide sufficiently to protect London. Politicians and world leaders tried desperately to hang on to a sense of consensus and common purpose. The interconnections inherent in climate change transcended national boundaries and it was abundantly clear that only action on a unilateral level would stand any realistic chance of addressing the current difficulties facing the world community. It was hoped that the experience of the joint struggle would not only prove to have been worth it but to cement better international relationships and cooperation in the future. Some went further and spoke of the emergence of a new mature age of humanity, leaving behind the previous centuries of intertribal conflict. There was no future in war between peoples, common purpose had rendered it obsolete, they argued. Others were less sanguine. Confidence was fragile.

Chapter 7

After Jaz and the successful members of his platoon, including the formidable Fiona Hastings, had passed their initial training, they were posted to their respective Regiments. Most of their group were allocated to 1 Mercian but Jaz and Fiona were sent to the second battalion. They ended up joining the same platoon together. Fiona was the first woman soldier to have got through initial training to join the Mercians and, as such, had to go through the same progress of proving her worth and convincing the sceptics as she had done at Catterick. The other soldiers' reaction to Jaz was at first a little subdued and at times even hostile, as he openly supported Fiona and told the lads honestly how well she had done during training.

The joke going round the company was that "he must be into her pants" to be so loyal. However, it was as mates not lovers that the two new recruits tried to ignore the banter and get on with it. It didn't take long, however, before most of the soldiers came round and accepted her; indeed, after a while almost no one noticed – until of course either someone made some incredibly crass and inappropriate remark, or anything to do with getting changed or toilet arrangements was mentioned.

There were times when dressed in full combat kit that gender became almost invisible, however in everyday barrack dress it was readily apparent and often invoked a range of predictably sexist remarks. Fiona was determined to toughen up, stand her ground and challenge inappropriate behaviour but often it was just easier to let it go. On occasions, sometimes from unexpected quarters, there were those male soldiers who were prepared to confront the worst of male sexist behaviour.

Jaz remained a good friend and they would gravitate towards each other when the opportunity arose to share experiences and reflections on army life.

***

It was some years later that, whilst Jaz and Fiona found themselves on active service with their mates in A company, that they were posted to Turkey. The reaction to the deployment was mixed, Jaz had to say. Whilst most of the guys were enthusiastic and 'up for it', some were sceptical about its real value and whether it was a suitable job for an Infantry Battalion after all. With that in mind, initially the blokes labelled the deployment as 'the pussy tour.'

The label didn't stick for long, however. Soon soldiers were demonstrating praiseworthy degrees of humanity and support for the pitiful specimens of humanity that were arriving at the gates on a daily basis. Even the most hardened could not help but be moved by the heart-rending stories that emerged of suffering. The scale of human determination and the sheer will to survive became apparent. Working long hours with constant demand for assistance was required; this was no soft option.

The ability to relate to people, take change and inspire confidence was vital in building rapport with the refugees. It came easier to some soldiers than others. It was something that Fiona was good at and was able to demonstrate, enhancing her standing with the other soldiers. It was something that Jaz admired about her.

Jaz could remember the CO's address to the whole Battalion before embarkation. His mind flashed back to the speech on the square. The Battalion was formed up ready for the order to move onto the transport to take them to the airfield. The CO indicated to the RSM to break ranks and gather round in a more informal arc.

'Today we, as the 2nd Battalion The Mercian Regiment, deploy to North Africa and Southern Europe on a new kind of mission. Be in no doubt that this is breaking new ground. The world faces a new enemy today, one less tangible than of old but no less deadly and one that we must defeat, if we are to survive. You have all been briefed fully on the challenge presented by climate change and that is our adversary.

'As was said before the British army entered Iraq – we come to liberate, not to conquer. Our task is to help secure the lives of potentially thousands of people who will be displaced by this eventuality. They will come from across Africa; a whole mix of different peoples, with different languages and different cultures. It is not our role to differentiate; in this case people are all just people, all citizens of this planet, just like us. We are going there to give them assistance. Our responsibility will also involve establishing and maintaining basic security and that will at times, I expect, draw us into conflict. We will be tested, we will be challenged, but we will succeed!'

Jaz remembered the CO continuing to reassure and motivate his troops. Morale at that point was high.

The company arrived at the start of the operation and were instrumental in setting up the camps with support from The Royal Engineers who ensured the installation of water, sanitation and basic amenities. These camps were intended as immediate reception centres before onwards movement to more stable arrangements in Southern Europe and then on to permanent relocation. The Mercians set up the tented accommodation and helped with the movement of the vast amount of stores that seemed to just keep on arriving. A more direct infantry role was the regular patrolling necessary to secure the integrity of the perimeter fence around the camp. There was some concern about the risk of incursion from objectors, ISIS supporters or criminal elements just looking to exploit the situation. The soldiers were well briefed on the need to provide safe sanctuary and avoid any abductions, rape or violence against the refugees. It had been made abundantly clear to them that any incidents of soldiers abusing their authority would be dealt with swiftly and severely.

As the refugees started to arrive, the stark contrast between the relatively safe and secure existence of the international military force and their charges was immediately evident. Terrible tales of the worst of inhumanity soon became common place and the desperate level of need these people displayed was plain for all to see. Soldiers would often give up their own rations to feed new arrivals. Medical teams were constantly in demand to deal with everything from dehydration to child birth and dog bites to major surgery. Most of the refugees, of course, dealt with the warm and humid conditions of mid-summer with stoic familiarity. It was the soldiers who struggled, apart from perhaps the Australian contingent who were generally more acclimatised to the conditions.

On the day the CO and the RSM chose to visit A company, the situation that confronted them was fairly typical of what their soldiers had been having to deal with. As they toured round, making an assessment of the state of provision, morale and discipline, they stopped to talk to the soldiers that they encountered.

The CO addressed one young private from Stoke in Staffordshire.

'How are you getting along?' he enquired.

'OK Sir,' came the reply, 'I used to think I'd been hard done by if I missed out on my five pints of Pedigree and a shag on a Saturday night, Sir, but these poor bastards have got fuck all. They haven't got a pot to piss in. They arrive with nothing! Some of them are barely dressed even, all of them hungry and dehydrated. I thought I'd seen a bit of life, Sir, but it was never this bad, even in Tunstall!'

The CO and the RSM couldn't help but smile at the soldier's graphic description before they moved on to another group who were repairing a water tap and asked the same question.

'How are you getting on?'

'OK Sir,' came the consistent reply. 'The tap keeps busting, Sir, coz the folks never stop using it twenty four hours a fucking day. I wouldn't want to pay the water bill!'

'Yes, but you do realise what we doing here and the situations that these people have come from, don't you?' posed the CO.

'Oh yes, Sir. It's all that global warming bollocks, eh Sir?'

'Yes, indeed it is. Do you know what that means?' he enquired expectantly.

'No, not really, Sir. I'm from the Peak District and it's still pissing it down and cold on Kinder Scout, I can assure you!' came the honest soldier-like reply.

'How is our female soldier getting on?' the RSM asked of Private Jaz Rubenstein.

'Oh she's marvellous, Sir!' he replied with enthusiasm, as she appeared next to them. 'Here she is, Sir. She's one of the fittest soldiers in the company, and she's got balls, Sir!' he exclaimed.

'How do you deal with all this sexist banter, my dear? Does it bother you?' enquired the CO, trying to be sensitive.

'No, not at all, Sir. Water off a duck's back as far as I'm concerned. If it gets too much, I simply deck 'em, Sir.'

'I see…' responded the CO smiling. 'Well, I suppose this is the future. I see you have reached Lance Corporal then, my dear? How long before the first woman RSM then, do you think?' he enquired, casting a sarcastic eye over to the current RSM.

'Not in my time, Sir,' came the crisp reply.

Attitudes were changing, but slowly and Fiona still faced an uphill battle, having to continually prove herself, but she was determined not to falter. She would trail-blaze regardless. Fiona reflected; she had just spent an hour with a young woman from Chad who had walked most of the way alone across Africa to reach the camp. If Fiona ever wanted inspiration into female determination she would think back to that young woman.

She remembered when they first met and how desperate the poor woman had appeared. They could only communicate in gestures, initially, but Fiona felt a connection with this woman regardless. In time, Fiona learnt that her name was Kalunga and warmly remembered the look of delight on her face when she first spoke to her by name. It took a while to find a suitable interpreter to allow a more comprehensive explanation of her journey. Fiona found Kalunga's strength and grace so impressive. It reinforced the very nature and purpose of their mission.

Chapter 8

Based on the North African coast, C company 2 Mercian had just returned from a month-long sudden deployment in the heat of central Syria, where elements of opposition fighters still occasionally showed their heads. Most of the soldiers, to the extent that they thought about it, could not understand why people should want to fight those who came to help them – it just didn't make sense.

The deployment was dangerous. The area was still littered with mines and unexploded ordinance of all kinds. Sometimes, for no apparent reason, a bomb would just detonate from nowhere, casting its indiscriminate fragments widely. There had been losses. Only the previous day, one corporal from B company had rushed to help one of his section as he was blown up crossing a road junction, only to tread on an anti-personnel mine himself, resulting in the loss of his lower left leg and the end of a promising career. There were complications too, as the explosion had also damaged his hip and his back. Walking was to prove difficult, even after rehabilitation. The Battalion CO was saddened to see the impact on some of his young soldiers, but also proud of the way most of them had coped with the situation, stayed focused, supported each other and kept their discipline in trying circumstances.

The level of destruction and carnage they had witnessed was horrifying. One platoon had helped in the clearing from one village site of heaps of rubble only to be informed afterwards by the few locals who had remained that what they had been working on used to be a primary school with three hundred and fifty healthy children. None had survived the bomb attack, apparently, and the propaganda war continued with all sides blaming the others for this atrocity.

The enemy was indiscriminate. The enemy was invisible, intangible, unnerving and obtuse. The enemy was not in uniform, did not conform to any preconceived ideas. It was not a nation but an ideology; the enemy was hate, an adversary worth defeating.

And what of the wider Green agenda? Away from the dirty sharp end of a post-war zone, the neat, tidy, intellectualising of radical politics continued its path towards a perceived Nirvana. Would the world community hold together sufficiently to avoid disaster? Would the worst excesses and predictions of the impact of climate change either be avoided or fail to materialise? Would humanity overcome?

The truth, in simple terms at this point, was still hopeful. The battle wasn't over. It would continue, but an admirable start had been secured.

Chapter 9

The troops found that they could deal with the initial numbers of migrants arriving at the coast. However, as numbers grew, their resources soon became stretched. The decision to deploy more troops deeper south into Africa would need time to take effect. This played into the hands of the sceptics who argued that the whole deployment was simply creating its own demand and that the problems were entirely predictable. For the troops, the politics was for others to argue about; they had their orders and were committed to the task in hand.

There was an urgent need to move the first arrivals on from the initial camps in an orderly fashion across the Mediterranean to mainland Europe, to the better resourced holding camps. There was a sense of relief therefore when this started to happen. Some messages back and forth between the two Mercian battalions, for example, helped to motivate the troops and give them confidence that what they were doing was both successful and worthwhile. Modern communication also provided a ready link back home for troops to keep in touch with their families. Support from back home had started to arrive with parcels of toiletries, socks and treats providing some comfort at the sharp end.

When the time came to move the first wave of refugees from their reception, Jaz could sense the tension in the air. Efforts had been made to convince representatives established in the camps that the move was in their best interests, would be conducted responsibly and their destination would continue to offer them hope. It was clear that many were sceptical, fearing a repeat of the previous experiences. Many who had endured countless sufferings before in the days of passage by unscrupulous racketeers, extorting large amounts of money only to deliver perilous journeys in unsuitable crafts to reach a Europe largely unprepared and unwilling to help them. It was clearly going to take more than warm words to reassure people that the troops around them were sincere in their good intentions.

The CO made it clear that he would personally travel on the first convey amongst the refugees as a sign of good faith. Slowly, with the patrolling troops keeping a low profile, the refugees started to move towards the boats. Lance Corporal Fiona Hastings recognised Kalunga, the woman from Chad, held her hand and led her onto the first craft. Others followed. The presence of the women seemed to calm the crowd. Other soldiers followed her lead by informally marshalling people forward, laughing and joking as soldiers do. Those with longer memories may have harked back to the false reassurance of the Nazi deceit in moving vast numbers of displaced people across Europe to 'family camps' that were no more than execution sites on an industrial scale. Scenes more recently in Bosnia would stimulate similar fears. No one was suggesting anything like that, but the presence of scepticism and mistrust was hardly surprising.

In the event, the crossing was safe and uneventful. The reception in Europe was welcoming, efficient and humane. The refugees were able to disembark from the boats, some straight into a camp and others on to trains for a further journey forward into Turkey. At the first centre people were swiftly allocated accommodation and shown the available facilities, including medical care. The base had the appearance of order, nothing like the desperate state of makeshift squalor more usually associated with transit camps. This time the resolve was evident to get it right.

***

Even by the dawn of the first day, the camp was peaceful and Jaz could feel the relief in the air and the apparent relaxation of tension. Words only went so far, even if they overcame the difficulties of translation, but actions spoke much louder. The CO had led his troops, demonstrating his own personal commitment to the safety of these people, and it had worked. Smiles appeared on previously troubled faces. Tents were being personalised and water collected as people quietly joining the queue for instant, free medical attention. This was a real example of what the international community could achieve given the will. Lives would be saved instead of squandered. As he walked around the camp, Jaz thought that he could almost detect a tear in his Commanding Officer's eyes and he too felt proud of what they had achieved.

Later that day, the CO and his party returned across the sea to the North African coast to supervise the next group of migrants making the same crossing. This time both he and the RSM were confident that word would have got back that the crossing was alright and that the soldiers could be trusted.

Back at the reception camp, more people were arriving and a dispute had broken out over the allocation of water between two rival tribal groups. The guard had intervened and restored order without significant injury and elders were summoned to explain what had happened. It became apparent that the two tribes involved had been conducting a low-level war against each other for many years, indeed off and on for centuries. There was no bond of trust between them. Arrangements had to be made quickly to divide the two groups in separate camps and to be aware of the significance to be able to avoid it happening again. The intelligence guys quizzed the elders in an attempt to establish a basic understanding of the situation and of any other rivalries that could cause similar problems.

When the time came to move the second group of migrants, the process proved to be much easier, as the CO and the RSM had expected. Elders had been given time to reassure those who were travelling and confidence was much higher. As they boarded the transport, people waved goodbye to the troops rather than looking on in fear and anticipation of trouble.

Later in the day another dispute erupted in the camp over allocation of tents. This time a serious disturbance broke out, one with fighting and the use of improvised weapons. Troops bravely intervened, risking their own safety to help others. It took some time to restore calm before reinforcements were available to secure the area and ensure the separation of the rival groups.

Once the Company Commander and his Sergeant Major arrived with the elders and translators only one pocket of resistance remained. The two men exchanged glances and forced their way through the crowd to find two soldiers isolated, back to back, facing angry opposition and effectively talking them down whilst holding their weapons ready to use if necessary. At the site of the additional forces, opposition dissipated and order was able to be restored. The two soldiers looked much relieved. The OC, of course, instantly recognised the two as Lance Corporal Fiona Hastings and Private Jaz Rubenstein.

Both were commended for their actions and Private Rubenstein was promoted in the field to Lance Corporal, filling a vacancy left by Lance Corporal Buckley from Chester, who had sadly been killed in a vehicle accident. This meant moving to a new platoon within the same company and, for the first time, breaking up the successful partnership forged between the two suddenly identified "heroes".

Daily routines were established with regular rotation between camp and area patrolling, guard duty and specific task groups. Tasks could vary from conducting targeted searches to longer-range patrols backing up those guarding the secure humanitarian corridors or assisting the engineers with road building and sanitation repairs. Following these early incidents, a detachment of Australian troops were attached to the company and formed a quick reaction force to be able to respond immediately to whatever need arose.

Chapter 10

The journey from North Africa to the European camps was fine but the onward legs across Europe and into China could have still been a relative nightmare. Long hours on over-packed trains did nothing to instil confidence in a nervous group of travellers. Drinking water soon ran out, as did water for the toilets. Nevertheless, the trains rumbled on without a stop.

As the refugees travelled across China in their secure train, conditions deteriorated and tensions were mounting as their anxiety grew about the wisdom and merit of this resettlement plan. The Chinese troops on board were not as friendly or as courteous as the British soldiers had been and, of course, none of the African migrants had any connection with China and mostly little or no knowledge of Chinese affairs, except for a few who had worked with the Chinese on some of their infrastructure funded projects and they were able to offer some reassurance to the group.

By the time the trains arrived at their destination in Far Eastern China, near the coast and the straits across to Japan, the passengers were all tired and hungry; too tired at that point to protest. Their new home was a disused old army camp that had been abandoned after the recent settlement with Russia about their shared border arrangements. The accommodation was basic but adequate. It was a large camp, with the capacity to house at least three times as many as the 2,000 refugees who first arrived.

Near to the camp, a local settlement overlooked a substantial state-run factory complex producing a wide variety of goods for both internal sale and for export. The local town was not able to supply sufficient labour for this level of activity and so the Chinese authorities had been persuaded to take the refugees on the understanding that they would work in the factories and be given opportunities to develop their own ancillary businesses, like restaurants, cafes, taxi services and so on.

The initial response by the group to these new surrounding was mixed and somewhat muted after their long journey. Attempts at relocation on this scale did not enjoy a particularly good history but the international community felt that they were responding appropriately to a crisis and, in that context, the new settlers were expected to largely accept it and get on with it. Not everyone was so accommodating but most did understand that options were limited, and this was a much better prospect than the starvation and drought where they had come from.

The task of integrating an isolated Chinese people with a largely mixed African contingent, with no common language, culture or religion, was clearly going to be interesting to say the least! The international group of observers tasked to monitor their progress were somewhat gobsmacked at the prospect.

A later group, who were resettled in America, had a very different experience; at least for them there were other black faces. Black Americans were interested to meet more recent fellow black immigrants coming to the USA in very different circumstances to their ancestors. There was at least a connection. Considerable effort was made by native Americans to make these new people feel welcome and to use the opportunity to help heal historical wounds of resentment from the white community and anger from the black for their respective experience of the slave trade and the subsequent troubled history of black integration into American society.

Material standards were higher than those experienced by their counterparts arriving in China, but there was less direct access to immediate employment, with migrants expected to more or less make their own way. Some advice and support was available, but the transition from a largely rural, tribal subsistence existence for many migrants to a modern hi-tech industrial context was considerable. Would this help ease America's racial tensions or simply add to them? Vested interests on both sides of the argument were desperate for evidence to emerge to reinforce their respective perspectives. The reality of integration was, as ever, likely to be a difficult and long road, but for many it was worth the endeavour.

Chapter 11

Populations continued to move across continents. A response to the crisis, once started, was likely to continue for a considerable time unless, or until, the whole strategy started to show some positive results. It was becoming increasingly obvious to any serious commentator that this was going to be a very long term project. Global warming had taken centuries to develop and no solution was going to materialise in years or even decades. No, the world was in for a long haul.

In the meantime, concern was evident in some quarters for the security of those migrants allocated to resettle, particularly in China and Russia, given their dubious record on human rights. If the refugees complied then there was the hope of success, but if they didn't there was the real fear of reprisal. In both cases it was quite conceivable to envisage movement from the resettlement camps to the Gulag-style 're-education' centres that, although denied, undoubtedly existed in both countries. In other words, the strategy was not without its risks. Politicians needed to manage such risks responsibly – that being yet another challenge for the new international order.

Progress had no doubt been made, but would it be enough? That was the inevitable question. Equally inevitable was that the answer would remain uncertain. The world had not ended, so much was true, but would it survive, let alone prosper? Real progress had been made, despite the odds, but perhaps the only realistic conclusion was to remain hopeful, to have faith and to continue the journey.

Chapter 12

By the end of their deployment, both lance corporals Jazz and Fiona had acquitted themselves well throughout the tour. Both had more than justified the faith placed in them, represented by their early promotion. They were still in the same company but not in the same platoon, providing only limited scope to meet.

As thoughts moved on to the future, the CO and his command team were busy planning for the next posting and the future deployment of the Battalion. The OC assured both his lance corporals that their concentrated experience in the field counted for much and that he was looking to send both of them to Brecon to complete the section commander's course, with a view to promotion to full corporal in due course. They were both pleased and a little daunted. The OC understood that this could mean posting to a different company for either or both of them but was keen to keep them in A company, if possible.

Jazz had wondered, in his darker moments on the tour, whether his friendship with Fiona might be capable of developing into something more. Obviously, an operational tour did not offer the best context to ask anyone out and, in fact, they had not had any time together to say more than just a few words of very focused 'army speak'. Jazz had to admit that he didn't even know whether Fiona was really "into men", whether she fancied him at all. She might be gay, although he thought probably not, and did in his heart hope for something more between them.

Unbeknown to him, Fiona was having similar thoughts. She too had wondered and indeed dared to hope about a possible future not only in the army but with Jazz. *Might it work out?* she thought. Whilst she loved her job, she did long to get home to take her sweaty uniform off and wear a nice dress, tights and high heels! She longed just to be a woman again for a while. *Might I then have time to spend with Jazz?* she wondered.

What of the refugees? Their story of adjustment and integration into their new surroundings continued. The world would need to accept the inevitability of mass movement of populations and the consequent need for open-mindedness and accommodation. Of course, not everyone was on board, but hope continued.

Kalunga, the young woman from Chad who had so inspired Fiona, was initially resettled in America. Things didn't work out for her there so she applied to move to Britain, where she wanted to find and thank the young lance corporal who had shown her compassion and given her hope.

When she subsequently arrived, she traced 2 Mercian and met up with Fiona again, just in time to help her make plans for a wedding.

4. The Truth

Authors note

This is a sensitive and contentious area. I acknowledge that my perspective is from a professional point of view and no doubt also with an element of male bias. You can 'walk alongside someone but you can't walk in their shoes', so to speak. So let's be clear: this is not written from direct personal experience. It's a story and I acknowledge with humility and humanity it's limitations in that regard, but I hope it throws some light on one of the darker sides of human nature.

Chapter 1

2019

Sitting in the police station, feeling anxious, alone and fearful, Freddy waited to be informed why he had been dragged from his bed at five in the morning and brought there.

He couldn't eat his pre-packed cereal breakfast served in a cardboard dish with a plastic spoon. Trying to regain some composure, Freddy again asked himself whether he could think of any reason why he'd been arrested. He thought of his recent road journeys; there had been no accidents, but had he committed some sort of offence, perhaps been picked up on a camera?

Had I fallen foul of the law at work in some way? he wondered. Again, nothing obvious came to mind. He couldn't think of a single reason why the police would have any interest in him or his activities.

Eventually, the Custody Sergeant opened his cell door and beckoned him to come out. Cautiously, Freddy left his cell and enquired, 'Is that it, can I go home now?'

'You must be joking!' was the crisp reply as the Sergeant directed him towards an interview room.

Freddy entered the empty room, finding just a table and four chairs. He stood momentarily by the blacked-out window, only able to make out a glimpse of the police car park through one scratched corner as he became aware that he had company.

'Sit down please, Mr Wakefield,' instructed the smartly dressed gentlemen, who introduced himself as a Detective Inspector and was accompanied by a younger Sergeant, a woman he guessed to be in her early thirties.

'Mr Wakefield, you have been arrested today in connection with enquiries we are making into allegations of rape and sexual assault.'

Chapter 2

1971 onwards.

The day they got married was such a happy occasion, Freddy remembered. The sun shone all day and much of the time could be spent outside in the grounds of the hotel where the photographs were taken. The occasion was well attended to witness the joining together of Freddy and Jennifer.

Freddy felt so proud of them both but still had to pinch himself and wonder how he, the son of a taxi driver, had bagged the most beautiful girl in the village. She was even the daughter of a prominent local family with links to land and status going back generations. Yes, they could be perceived as an odd couple, but it didn't matter, it shouldn't matter – they were in love and that's what counts, he told himself at the time.

Despite his relative success as a businessman, however, he was always left with the feeling from Jenny's family that he was not good enough. Not when they first got together, not now and there was not any prospect of that ever changing. Jenny's father seemed so hurt that she had rejected all 'the more suitable suitors' that he had suggested to her. She was always something of a rebel, you see, as if taking pleasure in ensuring her father's disapproval. From wearing very short skirts to her first tattoo, from her early experiments with alcohol to her eagerness to date older men when far too young, Jenny was determined to stamp her independence from a family that she perceived would otherwise readily suffocate her.

It came as no surprise, therefore, when she returned home from University and announced her intension to marry Freddy; Freddy who went to a comprehensive school and came from a council estate somewhere in the anonymous north of England. Freddy who slurped his tea, loved fish and chips in the paper, followed the football and drank cheap keg bitter. The same Freddy who had never toured the Scottish Highlands, nor even knew of the existence of malt whiskey.

Having said that, in himself Freddy was a personable and bright, good looking young man, as even Jenny's father had to acknowledge. So, albeit with reluctance, he had been persuaded by his dearest daughter to maintain the family tradition and lay on an extravagant and very expensive wedding. The guest list was extensive, at least on her side. Freddy struggled to name more than half a dozen relatives that his immediate family were in touch with, and only a handful of friends from university. Still, all his friends shared his utter amazement at his success in courting Jenny and the splendour of their wedding.

His business success did at least afford him some credibility in his father-in-law's eyes and it kept him occupied and even away from home for extended periods of travel abroad, allowing Jenny's father to keep his eye on his wayward daughter. By contrast, her brother of course met all the family's expectations by opting to pursue a career in law and progressing steadily to become a barrister, followed by his endorsement as a Queen's Council.

As children came along, looking back on it, Freddy realised that his new family had engineered almost total control over their offspring, by insisting, for example, that they went to the same private schools former family members had attended. Reluctant acknowledgement was the most Freddy ever achieved in their eyes and his own children came to regard him in the same light. His relationship with Charles, or Charlie as Freddy referred to him, knowing how it irritated his in-laws, was far better than anything ever achieved between him and his daughter Abbey, who seemed to hate him intensely from a very young age, eagerly encouraged by the in-laws.

As Freddy's career progressed, he found himself spending more and more time away from home on business – in fact, if he was honest, he preferred it that way. Jenny generally got what she wanted, one way or another, and he became more content not to involve himself too much in family matters. When he was at home in their pretentious, overly large house, uncomfortably close to the family's main residence, which Freddy referred to as 'the stately home', he would regularly get drunk at family gatherings and insult the equally obnoxious guests of his less than beloved in-laws. Jenny's brother even quite admired his candour and how he managed to snipe back just enough to make them notice but not too far as to justify anything more than the mildest of rebukes. And so it became the way Freddy's life with Jennifer had developed.

Chapter 3

2019

After gaining enough composure to insist on having a solicitor present, Freddy had endured the string of accusations levelled against him by no other than his very own daughter, Abbey. They were utterly spurious, of course, he knew that, but equally so he had to acknowledge that they sounded uncomfortably plausible. She had obviously done her homework. The statements and thus the accusations were detailed, comprehensive and even compelling. Taken on face value, they amounted to a long history of classically orchestrated sexual abuse of a daughter by her father from a horrifically young age. As such, of course, there were no witnesses, there would be no forensic evidence – just a comprehensive statement from a daughter now in her thirties and allegedly feeling strong enough to disclose to the police this terrible catalogue of abuse.

With his solicitor's approval, Freddy had either consistently denied the allegations or opted to make no comment. At the conclusion of his interview, Freddy was released on police bail pending further enquiries. He was not permitted to return to the family home or to have any contact with his daughter. However, Freddy had no difficulty in securing satisfactory alternative accommodation with a business friend back in the north of England, well away from the family empire.

He set out for a walk alone in the Pennine hills, trying hard not to feel too sorry for himself. Friends had been shocked and had offered support, but most seemed naively to think that such inconceivable accusations would be quickly dismissed. Freddy himself was not so reassured. He had known work colleagues who had over-stepped the line with women, some of whom had gotten away with it, although others had been absolutely taken to the cleaners. Odd, he thought now, that he had felt the need to hide away some of his business earnings over the years into accounts and investments that his wife had no knowledge of. Financially therefore, he anticipated that he could survive. Neither was he unduly concerned about never seeing this ever more distant family again, nor of losing the family home; a home that, after all, he had never felt had been his. No, the material issues were not his concern, what did concern him deeply was the potential loss of reputation and employment and, of course, the realistic prospect of a lengthy prison sentence. Freddy had no knowledge of the criminal world but certainly couldn't envisage being thrust into the centre of it with anything other than absolute fear and dread.

When he received confirmation from his solicitor that he was ready to go through the papers with him, the first question in his mind to ask was whether he believed him. Freddy couldn't envisage being defended by anyone who regarded him as less than innocent.

At their subsequent meeting, the solicitor was surprised at the question.

'I can assure you that professional advice can be genuinely given in any circumstances. I deal with matters of law, not opinion.'

'So it doesn't matter to you?' Freddy replied.

'No, in most cases it does not.'

'And in my particular case?'

'It's not an issue for me. My role is to offer you impartial legal advice and it is for the prosecuting authorities to bring a case against you. Now, can we proceed?'

As they went through the evidence that the CPS had provided, Freddy became more and more worried. *How can I defend myself against false accusations in these circumstances?* he pondered. His solicitor advised him to keep the faith, but Freddy was less than reassured.

Chapter 4

1970 onwards.

Life for Pony and Ricky had been hard from the outset. They were born into chaos and drug abuse. They came to realise that their life chances had been damned from the start. As two of five children, all of different fathers but born to Sharon, who had all subsequently been taken into care, they were the eldest two, the trailblazers if you like.

Concerns about their welfare and safety had been registered from an early age. Discharging herself early from hospital with Pony, Sharon had failed to cooperate with the follow up postnatal appointments. Pony was consistently not presented for routine inoculations or key checks on her progress. By the time she first went to nursery, her brother, Ricky, had been born at home with minimal oversight and Pony was well behind her early developmental targets.

After a catalogue of reported incidents of Pony either not attending nursery at all, presenting late or in a unkempt and poor physical and or emotional state, Social Services tried their best to support the family, but after numerous attempts with little sustained improvement, proceedings were started to remove both children from their mother on the grounds of safety, neglect and failure to thrive.

When eventually they were taken into care at the age of four and three, debatably the damage had already been irretrievably done. Neglect, poor hygiene, inconsistent feeding arrangements and the constant threat of domestic violence from a succession of violent male partners became too much to tolerate. Once a pattern of drug use had also been verified, the courts had no doubt about the appropriateness of the use of care orders to protect their wellbeing.

Initially, both children were placed with experienced foster parents who all too easily recognised the early impact of deprivation and the symptoms of poor attachment. Sadly, they had seen it too many times before but they stoically persevered in an honest attempt to offer such children love, nurturing, consistency and security. The role of foster parents is as difficult as it is admirable, given the often short notice of arrival and – for the most part – the inevitability of departure, but thankfully some good hearted souls are prepared to offer the service in the interests of the children involved.

At first, the children reacted badly to being moved and struggled to settle but, by the twelve month stage, they were eating well, looking well and were far better cared for than before. Consideration needed to be focused on longer term arrangements. The social worker had been investigating scope for adoption and was reaching the final stages of selecting suitable parents with whom to place Pony and Ricky long term.

The couple who were eventually selected as the most suitable were Anton and Rebecca Pearce. Anton was from a Caribbean background and Rebecca was of Irish decent. As a mixed race couple they had some understanding of the cultural complexities facing mixed race children. Both Pony and Ricky's fathers were of Caribbean decent too, although neither child knew them personally. Initial introductions were made and, over time, familiarity and trust developed sufficiently for them to be confident to move both children on a permanent basis to their new home with Anton and Rebecca in 1976.

Although all involved were very careful to be honest with the children throughout this process, another disruption would often be difficult to manage. Pony and Ricky knew that their mother was not able to look after them and that their foster parents would not represent a permanent placement but nevertheless the adjustment to living with Anton and Rebecca took time to become established. Constant reassurance was offered to the children that this would be a long term arrangement, but the sense of insecurity and lack of self esteem that had set in during their early years left them both with a legacy of difficulty trusting adults and being wary of their own safety and security.

Anton and Rebecca worked hard on attempting to gain their trust and on demonstrating warmth, kindness and active engagement in their lives. Both children subsequently attended the same school, where staff were familiar with the needs of looked after children, and the teachers tried hard to understand them and make allowances for their circumstances. Anton and Rebecca, for their part, made a determined and sustained effort to work closely with the school and to establish a good working relationship.

Their collective efforts paid dividends as, initially, the children thrived in their new surroundings. That is until the abuse started.

Chapter 5

2019

Pony had been married with children of her own. The marriage didn't last and later, as a single parent, she felt that she might be ready to make an official disclosure about her experience of sexual abuse as a child by her adoptive parents. The scars were still raw all those years later, but it felt like the right time.

She tried to remember what had happened, to draw those long buried and forgotten threads of memories together into anything coherent. But once she started, she remembered.

Things with Anton and Rebecca had started well. They were kind and offered sanctuary. Pony was warmer towards them than Ricky, she remembered, as he was always weary of any relationships. It started when she was about twelve, Pony remembered. Ricky was as school, Rebecca was a work and she had stayed at home not feeling well with a poorly tummy. Anton had offered to change his arrangements and to stay with her, saying he could work from home and the firm owed him some time anyway.

She had stayed in bed, as she assumed Anton was working downstairs. After a while, when she had woken not feeling too bad, she remembered him coming into her bedroom with a mug of coffee. He had sat on the bed beside her. This was unusual as both she and Ricky had been keen to avoid any physical contact, or to get too close. He spoke reassuringly to her and asked how her tummy felt now.

She told him that it felt a little better and he put his arm around her shoulder and then moved his other hand under the bed sheets and on to her tummy as if to massage her. Pony remembered clearly being shocked, feeling uncomfortable but somewhat at a loss as to what to say or do. He continued stroking her stomach. She didn't like it and attempted to roll over. He didn't try to stop her and told her that a stomach rub would be good for her. He stayed for a while longer and then returned back down stairs to carry on working. Before he left, he kissed her on the forehead – he'd not done that before.

Pony had never told anyone about this. After he had gone, she remembered distinctly feeling uneasy but not knowing what to do about it. Nothing was said when the others came home later and the following day Pony made sure that she was up early and ready for school regardless of her tummy.

It turned out that the tummy ache had heralded the start of her periods. She had heard 'the talk' at school about all that and knew, or thought she knew, what to expect. It was normal, she had been led to believe.

Nothing occurred between her and Anton for some time until they happened to be in the house on their own again. Over time, a pattern of this type of behaviour emerged with what she now realised was inappropriate touching, becoming more intrusive and more regular as she continued to mature and grow up.

In themselves, each individual incident didn't seem too bad and not really worth making a fuss about, but put altogether it was making her feel more and more uneasy. What could she do? Who, if anyone, could she tell? she wondered. There was no one really. She didn't feel comfortable telling

Rebecca, she certainly wouldn't have shared it with Ricky and hadn't got any friends at school who she could confide in either, so she chose to ignore it, to bury it deep in the back of her mind.

As the intrusion became more personal and intense, Anton started to reward her with little presents – sweets, comics and even a bit of make-up. He told her very clearly that this was just between themselves and that she mustn't tell anyone. Of course, Pony didn't know whether this was just a normal part of 'growing up'. *Did this happen in all families?* she wondered. She didn't know and dared not ask.

This continued for some time – she wasn't sure how long for, but by about the age of fourteen it got worse. Anton would come into her bedroom at different times during the night, get in to bed with her and insist that she took her nightie off and lay next to her.

It wasn't long before he wanted her to touch him too and then he started to have what she realised was sex with her. She didn't like it, didn't want it, but he didn't seem to care or to consider her feelings – it was all about him. He got grumpy if she ever tried to ask him what he was doing or why. He started to threaten her and say that the same would happen to Ricky if she ever told anyone and that she must continue to do as he said. She didn't feel able to challenge that, to put Ricky at risk or to be able to stop him. Pony's only defence was to continue to bury the truth and to ignore it. Until, that was, that she couldn't stand it any longer.

Chapter 6

2019

Freddy was summoned to appear before magistrates for his first hearing. His solicitor had informed him that the hearing would be short, and would result in a committal to Crown Court, the senior court presided over by a Judge.

When his name was called, embarrassed, he stood up and walked into court with as much dignity as he could muster. He was asked to confirm his name and address then invited to sit down whilst some discussion took place between his solicitor, the prosecution and the court clerk, himself a qualified solicitor or barrister, Freddy was informed. For Freddy, the experience almost felt unreal, as if he wasn't actually there. The time seemed to pass him by before his solicitor ushered him outside and informed him that the process was over, at least in this court and for now. Pleas to the charges he faced would not be taken until a later hearing in the Crown Court, by which time the CPS would have provided the remainder of the papers making up the prosecution case.

'Will that be later this week then?' Freddy asked timidly.

'No, no, it all takes a while, I'm afraid. It could be months. You will be informed nearer the time.'

'And in the meantime?'

'You are free to go. Your bail has been extended under the same conditions. You can get on with your life.'

'Really!' Freddy exclaimed. *How would that be possible?* he thought.

***

Jennifer had considered a difficult dilemma. She now recognised that her marriage to Freddy was dead. Her father, she had to admit reluctantly, had been right; she never should have married him, he simply wasn't suitable material. Recently, she had met Gavin, a much more suitable match and one that she, not her father, had found. Gavin was a barrister just like her brother. He specialised in corporate law and made an awful lot of money. He had no children, nor had he been married before. She had met him through her brother at a law society function and they had instantly got on. She was impressed and he was enchanted.

So what to do about Freddy? She considered and consulted friends who had gone through separation and divorce but was not encouraged by how they described the experience. She talked to Abbey about it, who simply said that she should leave him. After all, they hardly ever saw him – he was simply an embarrassment! No, Jennifer had other ideas – the sort of ideas that would provide a much cleaner break and would leave her with everything. Jenny had decided to persuade her daughter to make false allegations against him that would see him incarcerated for a very long time.

When she judged the time to be right to approach her daughter with the idea, far from any notion of resistance, her plan was instantly endorsed with vindictive enthusiasm.

When they reported to the police to make their statement, Abbey was utterly convincing; the pain, the tears, the embarrassment, and the trauma of the intervening years were all evident. She played the part with relish. The interviewing specialist police officers lapped it up, and they were suitably sympathetic and obviously well motivated to prosecute the perpetrator.

All was set for a Crown Court trial.

Chapter 7

Pony was in emotional turmoil. The pressures of growing up were compounded by her terrible ordeal at the hand of the very man who had been tasked with protecting her. When she was moody, Anton would say that she was unruly and Rebecca would support him. If she was meant to be unruly, she would show them unruly, she thought, and so her behaviour deteriorated at school. The more the abuse continued and the more she felt unable to disclose it, the more she was blamed for her own plight and the more she misbehaved. At school staff were beginning to run out of patience.

When she returned home late one night from a party, dishevelled and smelling of alcohol, she walked straight into a row. Rebecca was blaming her husband for not sufficiently curtailing his daughter's deteriorating behaviour, and for not exercising enough control. Under pressure, Anton decreed an unrealistic series of sanctions to be instantly applied and Pony glazed over and ran upstairs to bed slamming the door.

By the time her mother decided she couldn't leave it any longer and went into her room to rouse her ready for school, she was gone. Looking around the room, a bag had obviously been packed and an exit made through the open bedroom window. Exactly what time that might have been was pure speculation. Rebecca sat on the edge of the bed in tears; *where had it all gone so horribly wrong?* she thought.

When she informed her husband of their daughter's departure, he seemed instantly concerned, but concerned about where that might leave them. He didn't seem so concerned about his daughter or the potential heap of trouble a young girl could get into on the run two weeks before her sixteenth birthday!

Chapter 8

The trial

Not guilty pleas had already been entered to all charges. Freddy had met his barrister briefly before the hearing started and was being prepared for a fall. The barrister had been very clear with him.

'I'm sorry, Mr Wakefield, but you have to understand that in cases such as yours there is no real hard substantive evidence. The case is almost entirely subjective. Whatever did or did not take place between you and your daughter, her account is both plausible and credible...'

'But I didn't do it!' exclaimed Freddy in desperation.

'That may well be true, and I will do my best to represent you, but what I'm trying to prepare you for is the reality of how these cases are dealt with; much will depend on the presentation and character of the respective witnesses, including you. You have a respectable background. You must do all you can to enhance that impression, conduct yourself with dignity and address any questions openly and honestly,' explained the Barrister.

'And that will get the case thrown out?' responded Freddy.

'Possibly, but not necessarily, this is a very emotive area where the sympathises of a jury can vary, but I have to warn you that in most cases their natural sympathy tends towards the victim, the complainant and not towards the defendant.'

Freddy's solicitor tried to reassure him but Freddy was full of trepidation, unease and fear over what was to come. By the time he entered the court room most of the other participants were already present. As he walked in he could instantly sense the animosity in the air, and this was before a word had been spoken.

Once the prosecuting barrister started to outline the details and the circumstances of the case, Freddy's heart began to sink. What was being described was nothing but pure fabrication but oh did it sound so convincing. Freddy was being portrayed as an evil, predatory, cold and callous father; a father who had deliberately and systematically created opportunities to abuse and undermine his daughter over a long period of time, leaving her a physical and emotional wreck.

Shock emanated from the public gallery, tears from his wife and daughter, and grave faces stared out at him from the jury. Freddy's last remaining shreds of confidence were rapidly ebbing away as proceedings unravelled. By the end of the first day he felt drained. His bail had continued to be extended over the whole period of time whilst waiting for the trial. At least he could retreat to his bail address overnight for some respite and reflection. *How had it come to this?* he wondered. Was he really such a bad husband and father as to deserve this level of castigation? His wife could be devious and was very determined but if, as he suspected, she was actually behind these allegations, could she really be so callous? Was his demise really that important to her? Of course he couldn't contact her and hadn't even seen her since his initial police interview. And what had become of his daughter? *What really was her motivation?* he wondered.

If all they wanted was to be free of me, I would have willingly acquiesced, he thought. *Why did they feel that they had to do this?*

As the details of the day's hearing and the whole story of the case from his initial arrest ran over and over through his mind, Freddy felt so very alone and uneasy. He tried desperately hard not to panic, but to instead focus and to avoid feeling sorry for himself. He tried not to think of the prison sentence that would inevitably follow if he was found guilty, then his phone began to ring.

Tentatively he answered.

'Dad, it's Charlie'

Freddy had not heard from his son during the whole affair and didn't even know where he was or what he was doing with his life at that point.

'Charlie... good to hear from you...' he couldn't think of anything else to say initially.

'Dad, I know this is difficult but...'

'Difficult son, difficult! How do you imagine it must feel to be accused of such vile and obnoxious crimes and then to be thrown into the whole world of criminal justice without even a shred of truth in the whole affair?' Freddy replied, finding it hard not to break down.

'I'm sorry, Dad, really I am...'

'Sorry! What does that mean?'

'Well, sorry to hear of your predicament.'

Silence.

'Well I am, Dad. What exactly happened anyway?' Charlie asked, tentatively.

'Charlie – nothing, that's what happened. Nothing at all,' replied Freddy in exasperation.

Silence.

'Well, do you believe me, Freddy?' he asked. It was after all the key question.

'Um, Dad, it's difficult, it's really difficult; I can't say in all honesty what did or did not take place between you two. All I can say is that I never witnessed, heard or suspected anything,' said Charlie sincerely.

'Thank you, son. Thank you.' That was all Freddy could say.

Freddy had not been canvassed as a witness for either side. He had just disclosed, as Freddy suspected, that he didn't really have anything critical to add to the case either way. From Freddy's point of view, Charlie had offered at least a tacit level of support. He wondered what contact, if any, Charlie had with his mother and sister…

Chapter 9

On day two of the trial, the prosecution continued to outline their case before starting to call witnesses. Friends, work colleagues and contacts of one sort or another were displayed to the crowd to speak in glowing terms of the mother and daughter, to the detriment of the father, in the context of their particular knowledge of the Wakefield family. Jennifer's father spoke with passion about his disappointment over his daughter's choice of partner and his absolute shock and horror nevertheless following his granddaughter's revelations. As the day went on, there was no doubt in Freddy's mind where the sympathy of the court lay at that moment and it was clearly not with him.

By day three, the stage was set for the performance of a lifetime by one Miss Abbey Wakefield. After being assisted to her feet and to the witness box, and following a pause of several minutes to allow her to compose herself, the audience waited eagerly in anticipation of hearing the star act and she didn't disappoint. Many of the jury were left in tears, as were many in the public gallery.

Abbey had portrayed a classic pattern of incestuous sexual abuse to a packed house. The details, the deceit, the control and the devastating impact on her physical, emotional and psychological development were all laid bare. She stood up well to cross examination and managed to maintain her composure right up until the final question before leaving the witness box in tears with her head in her hands.

As Freddy looked around the court room, he couldn't possibly draw any conclusion other than that he was doomed. When he returned to his bail address that night he cried. I don't deserve this, he kept telling himself, whilst trying to believe that the court might yet take his side.

The following day, however, saw the opening of the case for the defence and Freddy had to admit that his barrister was devastatingly efficient at setting about demolishing and casting doubt on all the key planks of the prosecution case. After his initial address, he was able to call on a series of credible witnesses who gave testament as to his honesty, integrity and reliability. Each in turn were able to express their absolute shock at the revelations made in public and in more detail in court.

Their presentations were powerful. No doubt some balance and credibility had returned to Freddy's case for the defence and he was able to rest easier that night as a result.

Day five saw Freddy's turn to give his evidence and to face cross examination. He was highly anxious. On balance, he presented himself quite well, but he still felt in a state of turmoil. Feeling angry and let down, he tried desperately hard not to get too emotional and to gain some composure and dignity, as he had been advised to. All he could say was to state clearly to the court that he utterly and completely denied the charges and attempt to convince them all of his innocence.

Under cross examination, he again stood up quite well and managed to stay relatively calm and composed. The prosecutor did not gain any ground or expose or exploit any gaps or cracks in Freddy's submission. The essence of the case remained as it was, as it always was; a daughter's word against that of her father.

The court had hoped to conclude that day but time was running out when the Judge conceded that proceedings would need to continue into the following week and that he would deliver his summary and summing up on Monday morning before inviting the jury to retire and consider their verdict.

The weekend was inevitably very tense for all concerned. Monday morning could not come soon enough for all those directly involved. When it did the court sat silently through the Judge's remarks when he attempted to summarise and outline the case and to instruct the jury on points of law. He reminded them of the high burden of proof required to return a guilty verdict and of the solemn duty and responsibility they were about to embark on.

The jury retired in silence and the court room cleared. It was twelve o'clock. Lunch was usually at one so hopefully a verdict would be reached before the end of the court day. Freddy did not know what to think. He simply had to wait, he told himself. He had to acknowledge that the trial had been well conducted and that a fair opportunity had been afforded to both sides to present their version of events. It was now in the hands of the twelve members of the jury to decide his guilt or innocence and determine the course of the rest of his life.

At this point those associated with either the prosecution or defence sat separately with their respective thoughts whilst the jury considered the evidence. Jennifer wondered whether her daughter's full five star performance had been perhaps a little too staged and could only hope that they had collectively managed to convince the jury that their entirely fabricated story was the truth or close enough to ensure a guilty verdict and a conviction.

From time to time officials entered the respective rooms, raising expectations of a result, but it was not until mid-afternoon before they were invited back into the court to hear the verdict of the jury.

In relation to the charges of three counts of rape and five of sexual assault, on all charges, the jury unanimously returned a verdict of GUILTY.

Relief and shock swept through the court in equal measure as hugs, congratulations and tears were all exchanged. Freddy sat in disbelief and horror at what had happened. How had a jury of what seemed to be made up of reasonable people come to the wrong conclusion? He didn't know – this was after all completely new and unfamiliar territory to him. His counsel could not console him. Freddy sat alone whilst the remainder of the process carried on around him. The Judge, he was reliably informed, summarised the case again and the grounds on which his sentence was to be based. Given a not guilty plea, Freddy was not entitled to any reduction in sentence to allow for acknowledgement of guilt. In the court's eyes, he had deliberately chosen to force a trial, to put all the witnesses and the victim, his daughter after all, to go through the trauma of the full process.

At the end of which, Freddy was informed that he had stood up as instructed and had fully heard his sentence being handed down. In fact, he had no recollection of any of these finer points. By the time he was visited in the cells by the duty probation officer before being taken away to prison to begin his sentence, his mind was a blank with nothing registering after the announcement of the word GUILTY. The probation officer had to remind him that his sentence was in fact fifteen years.

Freddy Wakefield, former successful businessman and model citizen with no previous convictions was now a convicted sex offender due to serve seven and a half years imprisonment and a period of licence in the community. This would be accompanied with lifelong registration on the sex offenders register and a permanent responsibility to keep the authorities informed of his whereabouts and to cooperate with any of their enquiries. From that moment on, life had fundamentally changed and was never going to be the same again.

As the respective counsels cleared their papers and walked down the corridor back to their rooms, they exchanged uncomfortable glances.

'He didn't do it, did he?' commented the prosecuting barrister.

'No, I don't think so,' replied his defence counterpart.

Chapter 10

Whilst concentrating on what he wanted, Anton had brutally ignored the terrible impact of his actions on others. Pony of course was the principle victim, but in their own way both Ricky and Rebecca were victims too. The impact of sexual abuse is widespread and devastating. Ricky lost touch with his sister after she ran away. He genuinely had not been aware of his sister's plight and so, as well as a deep sense of sorrow at her departure, he was left with the guilt of failing to protect her and not knowing what, if anything, he might have contributed to her distress and her decision to run.

After Pony left there seemed no point in Ricky staying in that toxic house any longer, but at fourteen his options were limited. In the short term at least, he felt he had to endure his strange existence in a cold and secretive household he didn't understand.

For Rebecca, inevitably, there was a sense of guilt too. Why had Pony run? *What could I have done differently to help her?* she wondered. And why was her husband seemingly so unconcerned about what might become of their vulnerable young daughter in these circumstances? Did he know more than he was letting on? Or did he have something to hide? All these questions haunted Rebecca, and they had no immediate prospect of resolution.

For Pony, however, her course was set as she embarked on a lifelong path of self destruction, chaos and shame. Confused about what had happened to her and why, strangely at first she blamed herself. She must have done something wrong, she felt. She felt guilty for leaving Ricky in the house but equally knew that she could never tell him why. She felt disappointed that her substitute mother seemed oblivious to her pains and utterly failed to protect her. Most of all, however, her anger, disappointment and resentment were all fairly and squarely directed at Anton.

Anton, the man who the court had appointed to look after her and bring her up; the man who was supposed to nurture her, except that he didn't, he abused her. She also felt pain for her poor mother who knew nothing of these terrible events and who the same courts had decided was unfit to bring up a child and so forced her to surrender her and her brother over to more 'suitable and worthy' parents. Except that they weren't.

For Pony, life drifted from one temporary unsuitable form of accommodation to another, from one abusive relationship to the next and from drugs and self harm to eating disorders, anxiety and depression. Seemingly unable to influence let alone break the pattern of self destruction, Pony's life was a mess spiralling out of control.

The pain, the guilt, the destructive self-denigration haunted her. Pony felt trapped and unable to even consider potential solutions; no, she felt compelled to flounder.

Chapter 11

Two different life stories; two contrasting sets of circumstances, two sets of events that never should have happened, two distinct tragedies, but equally two sides of a wider picture. There were also some similarities.

In neither case did Freddy nor Pony choose the paths their lives embarked on. Both felt powerless to influence events and both were sadly hurt so deeply that hope often seemed impossible.

What might have helped? *How might it have been different?* they both wondered.

Both Freddy and Pony's wishes and aspirations, on the face of it, were quite straight forward; they simply wanted to be heard, to matter, to be of significance. Perhaps most of all, however, what they craved for the most was for THE TRUTH to be acknowledged.

5. With a song and a wave

Author's note

This is a story about the 1st World War. My Grandfather fought with the King's Shropshire Light Infantry at Gallipoli and in France and he survived the war.

He never talked about it, and he died when I was still a child. This is a story I've wanted to write for a while. It's not an attempt at a historically accurate account of his war – I have very little specific information to base it on. It is unashamedly a story, but I hope it reflects the sorts of experiences he and men like him endured and is a romantic tribute to him and all those who fought.

I had an interest in the 1st World War as a youngster and had studied it at school. It's written as if he felt able to describe his experiences openly. As if I had been able to interview him as a teenager about his memories and therefore it represents a conversation we never had.

Chapter 1

My Grandfather was a railwayman, a train driver. He was married and had five children. He lived within walking distance of the railway station. He also ran several allotments and his garden to feed the family, bringing produce back and forth on his bike, whilst liking a pint at his local pub.

I don't remember a great deal about his life directly. When I knew him, he largely sat quietly in his chair – a man of few words.

I never heard him speak of the war. I only heard second hand stories handed down. I wish I had asked him about it, but he died before I was old enough to make any sense of it. Neither is my Dad still alive now, so the opportunity to ask them both has passed, but what if we did manage to have that conversation? Who knows? But might it have been anything like this?

***

Granddad, tell me about life before the war.

It was simple. We lived a simple life. I lived in Bradley in the country with my mother, my stepfather and my brother, George. We kept chickens. We grew much of our own food. My father looked after the cows. I suppose you'd say we lived on a smallholding or a sort of croft. It was basic, with no running water, sanitation or electricity in the cottage. I started work as a shepherd but had an interest in engines and later worked in railway maintenance.

My Dad had a horse and a cart and the horse knew its way into Stafford through the country lanes to collect supplies, and where my Dad used to like to stop for a pint on the way. Going to town would take all day in those days. They were gentle times, at least before 1914.

You volunteered then, Granddad?

Yes son, I did. I felt it was my duty. I'd just started on the railway and, when they asked for volunteers – the Pals Battalions they called them – the railway bosses asked who wanted to join and of course most of us did. There were other lads in our street and lads I'd been to school with. We joined together – The Railway Regiment we were called, all railwaymen from across the country. We soon had enough men to make five Battalions.

Did you know what you were fighting for, Granddad?

No, not really, we just did as we were asked to and were proud to serve our country and the Queen.

Had any of you been to France before?

Lord no, the lads I joined with hadn't been any further than Newport!

What was the training like?

It was tough, I suppose, but it was fun too. We started our training in 1915. We were in a tented camp on Cannock Chase. We were issued with our uniforms and equipment and taught how to use and look after it all and keep it clean. We had regular kit inspections to make sure you had done as you'd been told and had everything ready to go. Then we practised long marches, carrying it all until we were fit enough to march twenty miles a day. We were mostly country lads, so we were used to walking and living outside. It didn't feel real at that stage. It was fun, quite an adventure really. That is until we went to France.

So what happened?

Well, we left our camp with a song and a wave. We were sent down south to the coast to wait for a boat to take us across the sea to France, not really knowing what to expect. At least we were Pals together. I served in the 3rd Battalion.

NCO's had been appointed from the ranks, mostly supervisors of one sort or another on the railways, and the Officers were from the managers or local land owners or owners of the railway company themselves. Some were public school boys. Once in France, there was more training and long marches, taking us ever closer to the front lines. As we got closer, you could hear our artillery firing and the sound of their shells landing someway off in front of us. Suddenly it was serious – this wasn't a game anymore; we were actually going to war to fight for our country. That was about all we knew and perhaps all we needed to know.

When were you actually first deployed, Granddad?

Oh, I'm not exactly sure, son. Sometime in the winter of 1915/6. I remember it was cold and the lads were writing home to send us more woollen socks. I gathered at the time that the build up to war had been slow and that both sides had dug in and formed defensive positions with trenches and would patrol between the lines in what was called 'no man's land'. With all the artillery fire, this was an area of absolute destruction. There were no trees, just great big holes in the ground full of dirty, muddy water. Men could even drown in such places.

Did you see any fighting, Granddad?

Oh yes, lad. There was plenty of that, I can tell you. Rifle fire, bayonet and hand-to-hand fighting, but it was the artillery bombardments that took the most casualties – men being blown to pieces. The casualty rate was alarmingly high and the medical facilities were very basic, at least at first. Lots of casualties were simply considered to be untreatable and left to die on stretchers at the first aid posts. We saw them being buried later – there were also some horrible injuries, men with limbs blown off or awful facial disfigurements.

How did you cope with that?

We simply got on with it, I suppose. We were young; everyone assumed it was never going to be them, at least at first, anyway.

We settled down into a routine and, apart from the cold, it didn't seem too bad. Actually, you quickly became numb towards much of it. A reaction to protect yourself, I suppose. After a while, though, once we realised that this wasn't going to be over quickly, it began to grind away at you. Being brave and daring once or once in a while could be seen to be manageable, but being expected to act like that day after day was daunting. Some days actually could be crushingly boring, but most had their moments when your life could've be on the line. Being young and brave can only take you so far, but even the strongest of characters faltered at times.

Did the army accept that, Granddad?

Individuals might have understood, but officially, no it didn't. The emphasis was on maintenance of morale, which of course was vitally important. Discipline was essential to differentiate between an army and a rabble, but there was a sense of fear; a greater fear of failure than a fear of going forward.

I don't understand.

What drives men to attack in circumstances that, for many of them, will almost certainly see their last moments? Call it patriotism, call it pride, but part of it is fear of the consequences should you refuse or falter.

What were the consequences then, Granddad?

At worst, the firing squad. To keep discipline, the official line was that any malingerers or cowards would need to be dealt with severely to deter others and maintain 'a fighting spirit'.

And was that right, Granddad?

No, not always. There were those who failed in their duty, but I'm sure some of those shot at dawn were already casualties of war and should have been dealt with more sympathetically, but we all knew the rules.

After a sombre moment for reflection, Granddad asked me if I was OK? I nodded. What happened next? I asked.

At one point, a new development took its place on the battlefield. GAS.

I remember the first time I saw the Germans use it. A cloud of yellow and green smoke floated across the landscape towards our positions. At first we had no idea what it was and the initial casualty rates were frighteningly high. We had no defence against it. As the mass use of gas masks took place, we were better prepared, but certainly in the early days the equipment was very basic and could be unreliable. Gas attacks were horrible, leaving awful injuries. Many lads suffered, as I did, with their chests ever after and had breathing difficulties due to lung damage. These, like many other injuries, were of course unseen.

Did we use gas too?

Yes, son, I'm afraid we did. We really shouldn't have done it. It's a horrible weapon and so dangerous, not least because a change in wind direction can so easily result in gassing your own troops.

After that, the atmosphere changed, we became more serious and yet more determined. Something big was brewing, you could sense it. We got the impression that the Generals wanted to break out of the stalemate of the trenches and move forward, to take the Germans on, you might say. Masses of stores and ammunition were being stockpiled. I remember hearing the Company Commander and the Second in Command discussing tactics in the dugout late one night when I was on guard. They seemed to be saying that any big push forward would need lots of men and that, given the limitations of our training so far, they couldn't expect us to do more than simply move forward across no man's land in straight lines towards the enemy. Artillery would be the key, they said, to blow up the German barbed wire and keep their heads down while we moved across open ground, or to completely obliterate their defences before we started. I remember that conversation distinctly.

Then, as winter turned to the spring of 1916, our battalion was moved out of the line to be replaced by some new lads. We were pleased to handover at that point. We were moved back to provide guard to key points on the railway: track junctions, signal boxes, installations of one kind or another, locomotive sheds and ammunition dumps, and guarding prisoners of war. Masses of troops passed us on their way forward to the front; Australians, New Zealanders, Indian troops and South Africans, as well as Scots troops wearing kilts and Battalions from all over Britain. I'd never seen such a concentration of soldiers. Chinese labourers also worked like dogs building roads, repairing trenches and burying the dead. At least where we were you could get to a shop to buy fags and even have the odd pint. Some of the boys also spent their money on the local girls, but I didn't fancy it; queuing for hours for five minutes, no thank you.

All along the front, preparations were being made for something big as we reached the early summer months and, thank God, it got warmer and drier in the trenches, although we were in billets at this point.

So, was this leading to the Battle of the Somme then, Granddad?

Yes lad, I suppose it was. We heard the massive artillery bombardments day and night weeks before the attacks started. Surely no one could survive that sort of punishment. We all assumed that our soldiers would move forward unopposed and take the German trenches. Anyway, you must have heard what happened when the action finally started in July; far from a walk in, as soon as the artillery stopped, lads were telling us that the Germans simply reappeared in their trenches and opened up on our poor men with machine guns. It was carnage, they all said, at least the few that made it back. Thousands of men, whole Battalions mowed down by machine gun fire. Why were we so confident that the enemy would have been destroyed by our artillery? we wondered. Many years afterwards, it came out that apparently many of our shells weren't assembled properly and failed to detonate and that we used the wrong type of shells to destroy the barbed wire and, all too often, simply blew it up into the air only for it to land back again largely intact. Our tactics were wrong, you see, son. But thousands of good men died because of it.

Chapter 2

We stopped for a while. Granddad had tears in his eyes and got up to walk around the garden before coming back to make a cup of tea.

I was keen to learn more and, although he found it painful, I sensed that he also wanted to let the next generation know what it was really like. Tell me of your memories after The Somme then, Granddad.

Yes, afterwards, well from our rear guard position, we saw some of the thousands of bodies being brought back down the line and what seemed like an endless procession of casualties, some walking wounded, many on stretchers or in ambulances. The medical facilities were just completely overwhelmed; it was pitiful seeing men suffer who perhaps could have been saved.

We felt really sad and I suppose a little guilty as, by chance, we had missed most of it. That feeling soon passed as we realised that no doubt our turn would come. Of our five Railway Regiment Battalions, three were directly involved in the battle and all three were decimated. Afterwards, there were so many scatterings of small numbers of soldiers left without a viable unit that many Battalions were disbanded. The remaining troops were reallocated to other regiments to make up their numbers. We were brought back to full strength with men from our other Battalions and several other regiments. We welcomed them, of course, but it was difficult for them to integrate, at least initially. They were still in shock and desperately missed their mates.

Weren't they allowed time to grieve?

No, not really, the impetus was simply to get on with it. The time for thinking about it would come later. It was a dreadful shock, though, to have deployed such vast numbers of troops only to lose so many of them for such minimal gains. Officially, of course, there was an attempt to portray the battle as a great victory but, for the soldiers who were there, we knew that it was not. It had been a disaster, a humiliation.

After that, we kept on fighting nevertheless. After the disappointment of the Somme campaign, I suppose there was a fear that the Germans might gain the upper hand and we didn't want that to happen, or what had all those men died for? We owed it to them, you see, to carry on. So we did, we licked our wounds re-formed our Battalions and looked for new ways to defeat the enemy.

So was it worth it, Granddad?

That's for others to judge, I'm afraid. I can't say, it was a noble attempt but poorly executed; we could have done much better, but you have to be realistic – we didn't know what that was at the time. Mistakes can lead to learning and, if anything, that was the victory on The Somme – in later campaigns we were more effective. Tactics have to evolve you see.

What tends to happen with a new war is that you start fighting it in the same way as the last one. But, of course, things change. We soon learnt that old-fashioned cavalry charges might have tested the enemy in previous campaigns but men on horseback with sabres were no match for modern infantry armed with machine guns. Early exchanges in the war soon proved that.

I see. So what happened after that?

Well, we were sent back into the front line. Routine patrolling continued and raids on enemy trenches to grab the odd prisoner as a source of information and intelligence. Regular artillery exchanges continued and men still got killed and badly injured. Stalemate, really, yes stalemate – that's what happened, if you really want to know.

Chapter 3

At our next meeting, I was keen to continue the story. Granddad sighed as he sat down with a tear in his old eyes.

They were good men, son, good men. After the shock of The Somme, it took some time to readjust. Senior Officers were obviously trying out new tactics and, between us, the men had their ideas too.

You see the power of modern machine guns – I say modern, I mean as they were then – meant that infantry couldn't safely just advance in slow time over open ground. That led to slaughter. We had to think how we could neutralise the enemy for long enough to get close enough to be able to fight them. Artillery was only part of the answer. We did learn in time to use the right shells to destroy wire and to improve the proportion of shells that detonated properly. But we clearly needed something else too. It took time, but as I remember, by about the following year we had started to come up with a solution.

What was that then, Granddad.

Our Battalion was still intact, and we'd had some leave. I'd been injured immediately on return from a shell fragment and had to go back to the UK for treatment. After surgery, I had a period in convalescence, which was good. I was well looked after and didn't particularly want to go back, if I'm honest, but once fit I did return to my unit in France to start a new campaign around the Passendale area in spring 1917. I remember clearly how bad the weather was. By the summer, all we got was rain, rain and more rain. The ground couldn't take anymore and the local heavy clay soil became horribly deep sticky mud. Movement was so difficult by foot, horse or tracked vehicle. Constant rain was like constant bombardment, it got you down, it sapped your strength. Morale was suffering but we fought on nevertheless.

In order to make that ground relatively safe to be able to get close to the enemy, we needed to have 'one foot on the ground'. In other words, not from the artillery but from our own men, we needed to be able to, I suppose, leap frog. To put down our own machine gun fire at close range to keep their heads down and stop them firing at us whilst we moved forward a length at a time and then provided covering fire for the first group to catch up. Do you see what I mean, son? Granddad said, reaching forward to the table next to his chair, the one with his glasses case and a pack of cards.

You see, if my glasses were the first group of soldiers and they fired first at these trenches – he said whilst he placed a pencil along the far edge of the table to be the enemy trenches – then the second group, the pack of cards, could move forward. Then they stopped and fired to let the glasses catch up and go a little beyond and so on – like I said, a sort of leap frog. Do you see what I mean? Then you stood a much better chance of still having enough soldiers to beat them in their trenches when you reached their front line. The problem in the earlier campaigns was that we didn't react quickly enough to combat this and, by walking forward in long straight lines, we simply presented an easy target – too easy.

At the same time, you see the artillery had got better at instigating a creeping barrage.

What's that then, Granddad?

You see you blast the hell out of them to start with but, once your own troops start to move forward, the trick was to keep the bombardment just far enough in front of your own men to protect them and at the same time to keep the enemies heads down. This took skill and practice, but we got better at it.

By then we also had the advantage of air cover. Aircraft were still quite new then, but they could add to the bombardment and provide a picture of what was going on in front of you. You see trenches weren't just built in single lines, they were prepared in depth. That meant that even if you over ran the first line of trenches you could still come under fire from a second line and there might well be a third and a fourth. That was part of the reason why it had become so hard to break out of trench warfare.

Wow Granddad, it must have been so exciting.

Exciting no son, terrifying, but we tried not to think about it. If you believed that what you were doing was right and that your lives wouldn't be wasted, then you just kept going. As winter approached by then in 1917, we hoped that our efforts would bring a swift end to the war.

And did it?

No, not exactly, but the tide was turning in our favour. Once the Americans joined us, even the Germans began to realise that we simply had far more men than they did. In effect, it became just a matter of time and they knew they could no longer possibly defeat us.

And there was one more thing – Tanks. Armoured fighting machines had made a slow start on the western front but the technology and reliability was improving. Infantry crossing open ground felt much better if they had tanks in support. They weren't so vulnerable to machine gun fire, could return fire and move relatively easily. Mind you, they didn't like the terribly rough ground that we often fought over, with massive bomb craters everywhere. If, however, they could ensure reasonable movement forward, they proved to be a great help. Infantry could gather behind them and move forward protected. That in itself gave us a great boost of confidence.

Certainly by this stage in the war, we had learnt some hard but useful lessons and tactics had developed a long way. Passendale however was hard. As I said, the weather was against us and despite our increased experience and improved tactics the casualty rate was still very high.

Guys who had joined us after the Somme campaign were passionate about protecting the soldiers and doing all we could to keep casualties down to a minimum. As before, as Battalions suffered heavy casualties; they were often disbanded and the men transferred to other units. By the end, with all the transfers in and the arrival of conscripted men, our membership kept shifting. I lost count of how many soldiers we had from other regiments, not that it mattered really, it was just difficult trying to keep any sense of continuity.

Did you lose anyone close to you, Granddad?

Oh yes, son, many times. After a while, you learnt not to get too close to anyone, because they might be gone tomorrow. I can't remember anyone I joined with coming through the war like I did.

So how do you deal with that?

You don't really, son. It still hurts now. I miss them all and will always remember them.

Do you do remembrance then, Granddad?

You mean the parades and stuff? All that ceremony? No, that was not for me. That stuff was for the politicians who sat comfortably at home, not for the men who actually fought. That's not to say I didn't think about them, I did all the time. The things they missed, the sacrifice they made, their bad luck and my good fortune, because that was all it was, son. A lottery – one minute a man was alive and talking to you, then next minute he could be dead.

I remember being caught out in the open once in no man's land by a salvo of shells and we took cover in a shell hole, me and my mate. I could feel him next to me and I talked to him for ages until the shells stopped, when I looked across to him to find that I'd just been talking to his arm. God only knows what happened to the rest of him, but he was gone. That was life and death, no pattern to it, no sense, no justification, just slaughter, random slaughter on a massive scale. At the same time, however, we did feel that we had to win, both to preserve our freedom and to end the slaughter as soon as possible. We hadn't managed to end the war in 1917, but the general feeling was one of desperation as we moved into the spring of 1918; we had to end the war before the beginning of another winter. By then, the Germans seemed to have accepted the inevitability of defeat, the fight had largely gone out of them, but we had to press on to ensure the best possible terms come the peace negotiations.

The war had left a terrible scar over Europe and, indeed, much of the world. If we ever stopped long enough to think about it, the growing feeling was 'never again' – this had to be, as was said, 'the war to end all wars'.

By the end, breakthroughs in the line had become common place and German defence and morale were crumbling. By summer 1918, there was a sense that this really was coming to an end.

Chapter 4

I just sat and listened intently as Granddad continued to tell his story.

Finally, when the end came, on 11th of November 1918, it was inevitably something of an anti- climax. We were desperately hoping and wishing for good news, and so keen not to lose more lives in those final days, but sadly men were still dying. I lost another friend two days before the end of the war. He was shot by a sniper when walking past a low part of one of the support trenches. It was a place he had passed so many times before, but that particular occasion, presumably feeling some degree of justifiable complacency, he failed to duck as far as he usually did and some over keen sentry in the German lines took advantage. It just perfectly represented the randomness of death in the trenches and the individual futility. I remember that was really hard to take; what difference did his death make to the eventual outcome of the war? I often wondered. No difference at all, I was sure.

When the announcement came, we almost couldn't believe it. Then the shelling stopped, it was eerie with a strange and novel silence hanging over the trenches. We didn't know whether to cheer, to laugh or to cry – we were all simply exhausted. That I remember was the overwhelming feeling; many of us just lay down where we were and fell asleep. We didn't feel like celebrating, not immediately anyway.

Of course, when we woke things were still largely the same; we were still in uniform, subject to military discipline and still a long way from home. We hadn't dared to think too much about this stage, but when it came, we realised that we all couldn't simply pack up and go home. There was an enormous amount of work to be done. Bodies still to recover, casualties to treat, prisoners to oversee, vast amounts of stores to be repatriated and a huge clean-up operation. The land was scared, littered with the debris of war: armaments, bits of uniform and equipment, rats, latrines and of course body parts everywhere. In time, the trenches would need to be filled in and returned to civilian use, and the scorched landscape replanted.

There was also the legacy of war. The vast numbers of soldiers who had been killed and placed in temporary burial places close to the front would need to be relocated and buried properly. That in itself would be an enormous task.

There were all sorts of parts of vehicles lying around and gun emplacements, miles of barbed wire, heaps of ordinary domestic rubbish and, of course, all the horses. Many were so traumatised that a return to normal life was impossible and they had to be shot and they never left the front lines.

It was clearly going to take ages to sort this mess out, and a long time to demobilise all the troops. In the meantime, everyone had trouble sleeping despite being so tired. It was too quiet, you see. We had all got used to living with constant noise that silence was disturbing. Odd, just another odd thing, I suppose.

So thoughts turned to home, to wives and children, to jobs, to ordinary life and, of course, to remembrance. Holding our discipline was probably harder at this point than almost any other; you just wanted to say bollocks and walk away but you realised that you couldn't. One of the worst things was that men were still dying, not only of wounds but the impact of unexploded ordinance as we started the cleanup. Every day, it seemed that some poor bastard got blown up. That was truly terrible. I also remember some poor Scottish lads who had survived the war were drowned when their ship sunk in bad weather in January 1919 on the return crossing to one of the Scottish islands. How awful was that for the relatives, knowing that their men were virtually in touching distance only to be left with bodies being washed up on the shore?

It was only then that we started to realise that the impact of the war would be far greater than the loss of those killed and the impact on those injured – it would affect us all, and for many years to come. We didn't know then, but many of us would suffer terribly with nightmares, guilt, regret and what you would now call mental health problems. Nobody had heard of 'shell shock' at this stage, let alone stress, but it was nevertheless present. No, the world would never be the same, and certainly neither would our own little individual worlds; we were all changed forever.

Chapter 5

The next time we met, Granddad continued to tell me what had happened as the war ended.

It really felt strange, to be honest with you. By this time, virtually none of us were regular soldiers who had been in the army when the war started. So, for volunteers, the Pals and the conscripts alike, all we knew of army service was our recent experience of the war, therefore still to be in the army in 'peace time' seemed odd. Do you understand what I mean?

I nodded and said that I thought so.

Our whole purpose for being had passed. Not unreasonably, once that had happened, we all just wanted to go home. We were sick of the trenches, the smell of rotting bodies, the rats, the poor food, the weather, you name it; we'd simply had enough. We had done our job.

We had 'won' the war, apparently, although it didn't feel like a victory. We wanted out, but accepted reluctantly that for the moment at least there really was no option but to continue occupying the trenches. So that's what we did, but not for days… it was months actually.

Initially, we never thought for a moment that we wouldn't be home for Christmas, but in fact we didn't make it. It was not until 1st February 1919 that our Battalion formally marched out of our trenches with a song and a wave back to the nearest railway station, where what was left of the 3rd Battalion The Railway Regiment got back onto a train and headed for home.

Home, again of course that was another major adjustment. In fact, it was probably a good thing that we couldn't have gone home straight away. After an experience like that, you needed time to adjust. Oddly, once on the train, at times it felt like we even missed our trenches – they had been home after all for the best part of four long years. Suddenly, this strange existence, which after all most of us had volunteered for and accepted, was now over; we'd won, for what it was worth, and were now going to be demobilised. Demobilised, what a term for handing in your kit, putting a suit on and walking, not marching, out of a barracks armed with no more than a rail warrant home, a few things in a small suitcase and a final payment meant to tide us over until we got our jobs back. Jobs that we were assured were still waiting for us.

And were they, Granddad?

No, of course not. We hadn't realised it, but most of the jobs that we had done before the war that we regarded as jobs only men could do had been done by our wives, girlfriends and daughters while we'd been away, and actually done well for the most part too! There were no jobs to just walk straight back into.

Adjustment was another shock leading men to wonder very quickly quite what they had fought for – and what they had seen friends die for... We wanted to return to the world that we had left, but actually, not surprisingly, that world had changed too. We were not the same, but neither were those we had left behind; the war had changed us all.

It took time, of course, for the economy to return to peace time production. Again, we hadn't realised what it had been like for those left at home; the food shortages, the fear of losing loved ones and, for some, even the fear of invasion. I suppose we just thought that it was only us who were suffering, but that wasn't true – the folks back home suffered too. Some men came back not to a hero's welcome but to find that family members had died, or grown up and left home. Babies that had been left behind were now running about and asking their mum who this man was in their house. They had coped without us because they had to, and now it almost felt that they didn't need us and, in some cases, didn't even want us back.

No son, it was hard, for many it was not the home coming that we expected, for the married men particularly. I was still single at the time, without even a sweetheart waiting for me, but I soon felt that I didn't fit in back with Mum and Dad, which I wasn't expecting.

It seemed for many of us young men that there were so many young women available with not enough men to go round that at least you could more or less take your pick who you fancied, get married and get on with it. It was the missing I felt most sorry for; men who were officially missing and presumed dead, some for years, nevertheless they returned only to find that their wives and sweethearts had found somebody else and they couldn't turn the clock back. There were some really nasty incidents when men came home to this, as you can imagine. I remember a few being charged for violent conduct, even murder in a few cases.

Did they kill the men who had stolen their place, Granddad?

Yes, some of them did, but some killed their wives instead, or even both of them! Jobs were not easy to come by and some fellows walked miles to find work only to be told that there wasn't any. The wounded and the widows at least got their pensions, but if you came back intact there was nothing for lots of men. We actually were lucky as members of the Railway Regiment that the railways did manage to offer most of us jobs back in the industry. I trained to be a train driver –I'd never driven more than a horse and cart!

Yes, adjustment had its problems, but many of us got through it. As you know, I went on to marry and raise five children. Now I have grandchildren, including you!

So what about your thoughts since then, Granddad? Was it all worth it?

The war, you mean? Well, I don't know, not for the poor blighters who didn't come back, and for those who were seriously affected by their experiences and never recovered.

I don't know, son, really I don't. We won; we beat the Germans fair and square on the battlefield. Was that worth the loss of all those lives on all sides? No, I don't think so. Was the world a better place for it? That's more difficult. If we hadn't have fought, would the Germans have stopped advancing on the French coast? No, probably not, and Britain could well have been invaded again for the first time since 1066. Was that worth stopping? Yes, it was.

Did it bring everlasting peace. Well, of course not – that was probably always too much to hope for. It was not the war to end all wars. In my life time, I saw the next generation fight in Europe again, which saddened me deeply. That was not the war to end all wars either, but maybe it did end all the big ones.

I've had my time now, son. I've done my bit. I'm past fighting now, and I have long since fought my last battle. I suppose I just hope that one day humanity will learn that killing each other doesn't really achieve very much, and we'd do much better to work together, but when the enemy threatens your very existence, what do you do? What would you have done, son? I just hope you don't have to fight another war.

With that Granddad stood up blow his nose and wandered off into his garden to check his runner beans and later assured me that they were alright. He never mentioned the war again, at least not in my hearing.

6. This is serious

A story about serious & organised crime

Author's note

In modern times of economic recession, austerity, growing cynicism and a civil service structure struggling to hold us together, crime will flourish. Massive cuts in resources for the police, the courts and criminal justice in general have also had an impact on growing crime rates.

Crime affects us all. At local level, petty crime is now often unreported or not investigated and no action is taken. This is a worrying trend and a threat to social cohesion; it creates widespread public unease but more worrying is the growth in serious and organised crime. As the chances of being detected reduce, and therefore the less likelihood of facing any consequences, organised crime is on the increase. It knows no boundaries, respects no borders and ruthlessly enforces its dominance. From the drugs trade to people trafficking, from the sex industry to fraud, the opportunities to make large amounts of money for little effort with little realistic chance of facing prosecution is a growing threat to world security.

This is no less than the blatant piracy of the modern age.

Chapter 1

Cambridge 2019

The audience applauded as Baz Bahati took to the stage to receive his prize from the Vice Chancellor. The audience enthusiastically celebrated his success. The head of the business school and the business minister shared their smug delight at the living proof of their noble endeavours. Baz had won all the accolades. He was the star student. He had secured the best possible education from humble beginnings and had been assisted by the government's new gifted and talented grant initiative. The pride of the minister, the scheme sought to identify the most talented children from deprived backgrounds and give them 'a leg up' to the top. A glowing future lay ahead of him. His plans to build his own business had been endorsed by many significant academics and business leaders. The good and the great had flocked to be involved in supporting this young man and his honourable aspirations in his pursuit of success.

His parents could scarcely believe that this was their son. His father was a first generation immigrant from India and his mother a second generation settler from Romania. They had met in a resettlement hostel in London and worked incredibly hard to establish a home and a family of their own. Baz, it was soon apparent, was a very bright child. He walked early, he talked in sentences at two and was quite fluent in three languages by the time he started school. They lived in a poor area of East London and Baz attended the local primary school serving an area with children facing multiple levels of deprivation, but nevertheless he did well. He was identified as exceptional straight away by his experienced class teacher who loved the stimulation of teaching a gifted child. He learnt music, took the lead in school multi-faith festivals and astounded his teachers throughout his time at primary school by regularly exceeding educational targets set for his age.

The local secondary school took up the challenge and Baz was soon encouraged to learn lessons well beyond his years. He took GCSE maths at fifteen and passed twelve more GCSEs at sixteen before moving to a successful sixth form college. Baz was lucky to attend schools with inspirational heads and sufficient insightful teachers to recognise the boy's potential and give him the best chance to exploit it.

It came as no surprise to anyone who knew him when Baz passed all the entrance criteria to secure a place at Cambridge University to read maths. With excellent A level results, he was one of the few pupils from his college that made it through to Oxbridge.

Chapter 2

Manchester

Chloe Mcintyre was good at manipulating men; she'd had plenty of practice at it. She could persuade her father to do virtually anything for her and used the same influence over her peers and boyfriends as she grew up. She flirted, offered her favours and threatened to end relationships on a whim. She had no sense of loyalty to men – they were her toys to exploit at will.

When she met Damien Glover, however, things were different. She found his power and charisma intoxicating. Chloe was captivated by him and felt that she had to make a bid for him. Her approach was not subtle but it worked as they spent their first night together in a hotel room in Manchester.

Damien was from Liverpool and had come up through life the hard way. Born into an established criminal family, he was schooled in theft, extortion, sexual assault and robbery from an early age. Encouraged to fight and to join gangs, he soon progressed through the stages of initiation to establish himself as a ruthless drug dealer and racketeer.

Having committed his first murder at fifteen, when he stabbed a rival to death in the street, he soon acquired a following and a reputation. He even managed at that usually tender age to ensure another rival was in the frame and was sentenced to life for the same murder. He didn't need to try hard to find witnesses that were not actually involved but were ready to testify on his behalf. Ridding himself of two rivals was all in a day's work, he used to say.

In his area of Liverpool drug gangs were already well established, with an elaborate mechanism for establishing and enforcing their respective trading boundaries. Prostitution and protection were in the hands of people he had no wish to challenge. No, not worth it, he used to tell his minders. There were easier ways to make money and he set out to demonstrate what he meant.

Damien was selective in choosing his clients. He opted to provide a bespoke top class service that was discrete and secure, supplying the rich and influential with the best cocaine. He wasn't interested in the seedy lower end of the mass market. He built up a customer base of powerful people, including members of the police force and the legal profession who were dependent on his ability to protect their identity.

He also specialised in blackmail. He would carefully recruit first year degree students in northern cities and seek out 'sugar daddies' to support them financially in return for sexual favours. Once the arrangement was established and the evidence collected, Damien would move in to invite these philanthropic individuals to donate large amounts of tax deductable payments to his labyrinth of 'charitable causes' – in other words, his growing criminal empire.

Chloe encouraged Damien to be even more ambitious and to extend his criminal affairs further afield to other northern cities. Over time, he established networks in Lancaster before taking on Newcastle. Conquering Leeds, he argued, might prove to be a bit more difficult and he didn't want to clash with the established Asian gangs, as that could really cause some trouble, he thought. Together, Chloe and Damien formed a formidable team.

After a year, they were celebrating in a swanky uptown wine bar in Manchester city centre, having booked into the same hotel where they first met. The champagne flowed and they reflected on how easy it had been to build up their business and just how profitable it had become. Damien was able to move money into other projects as a sort of insurance if anything ever went wrong. He bought property – popular buy-to-let executive apartments in the city centre with solid reliable levels of return. He set these up properly and hired an accountant to put everything above board, a bent accountant obviously, one who he supplied coke to, but nevertheless official as he saw it.

Chapter 3

Detective Chief Inspector Ray Sutcliffe sat in his office with his Detective Inspector, Mandy Wainwright. They worked well together and had worked together before as Sergeants in the Vice Squad. They had both transferred to the Serious Crime Squad, a newly established unit formed to coordinate knife crime, gang initiatives and organised crime across the North West Region, headed by a young and very ambitious senior officer.

'You know, Mandy, sometimes I wonder about this job. You think it's going well and you're taking down the big boys and then suddenly you find a whole new crime racket that you didn't even know existed.'

'Is that so? Please explain.' she replied.

'One of the city centre Sergeants approached me yesterday and reported that his daughter, who had just started her degree at Manchester University, had spoken to him last night in tears. She said that her and a few of her friends had been approached by this slick creepy bloke in a pub and asked if they needed any financial support to get through their degrees.' Whilst some of her mates showed interest and asked questions, as a copper's daughter, she immediately smelt a rat.

'When they talked about it the following day, they all felt quite unnerved and wondered what the catch would be. Again, his daughter suspected straight away that these 'gracious loans' would be in exchange for something. She wondered about sexual favours, having heard from older girls that such arrangements had become quite common, with many students working in the sex industry in one way or another; men, of course, as well as women.

'The Sergeant mentioned it to me to see if I knew anything about a scam like this in Manchester,' explained the DCI.

'I see. I knew students were struggling these days, and this sort of exploitation could easily be well established, but I'm not aware of any specific players on our patch who are orchestrating this, sir,' responded the D.I.

'No, that's what I thought. No names came to mind. I could immediately identify a string of operators running prostitution rackets but not this angle. I think we need to investigate it, Mandy,' announced the DCI in a determined tone.

Chapter 4

Baz had met Giles at Cambridge. They both had studied maths. Giles Meredith came from the more usual Oxbridge background, via a wealthy upper middle class background, and St Paul's school in London. His family lived in the capital and enjoyed holidays in their ski chalet in the Alps or their lovely old house in the Highlands. Both parents were doctors and had studied at Cambridge too. Indeed, that's where they met. Oddly, on the face of it, having so little in common, Baz and Giles got on really well from their first encounter. They lived next door to each other in college rooms and spent much of their study and free time together.

Rather to his parents' disappointment, Giles had no plans to become a doctor, not of medicine at least. His interest in maths was allied to computer science and particularly the study of artificial intelligence.

Baz was more interested in the power of prediction and probability using mathematical formula. Both young men were exceptionally bright and a little eccentric; not an unusual combination at Oxbridge.

They both progressed well in the demanding and stimulating context of an elite university. From their respective backgrounds and perspectives, they flourished and strove to reach their potential. The concentration of so many bright minds and the quality of academic guidance gave them the opportunity to shine. From small group tutorials to formal debating, from offering to assist younger students to seeking out opportunities beyond Cambridge, they absolutely loved the whole experience. But there was a darker side; both quickly realised how they could exploit their talents in ways that were less than conventional, but potentially very lucrative.

By the time they had completed their studies and both graduated with first class degrees, they were a potential great asset to the jobs market. Baz had decided on a business career but did take up a one year post in a research project linked to Artificial Intelligence, or A.I. Giles was recruited by an investment bank that was very keen to utilise his potential in the field of probability.

They based themselves in London, of course, initially sharing a flat owned by Giles's family right in the centre of the city. The life of the young executive initially suited them both, as they enjoyed the company of other similar aspirants. Initially, fine clothes, wine bars, trendy pubs and eating out offered an obtainable and attractive life style.

Chapter 5

DCI Sutcliffe held an impromptu meeting with his team leaders to seek their collective knowledge on scams in the sex industry working in their area.

'Hi all, thanks for making yourselves available. I just wanted to get you together to pool our knowledge.' He explained about the Sergeant's daughter's story, and how that had sparked off an inquiry in his mind.

'Does anyone have a particular angle on this?' he asked, more in hope than expectation.

'Yes sir, I do,' responded Sgt Jasmine Singh proudly.

'Go on, Jas.'

'Well, as student grants ended and student fees have increased, it's not surprising that many young people have struggled in these circumstances and, sure enough, the criminal fraternity have spotted a rich opportunity here.'

'So how does it work, Jas?'

'Students are invited on social media to attend a recruitment meeting, usually at a classy venue with nibbles and free drinks. The line is recruitment into the hospitality industry – waiting on people, acting as a host or hostess, that sort of thing. They look to sign up the most attractive candidates and invite them to have some photos taken to promote their chances of being hired. Then, armed with the photos, they are distributed to their large list of dubious clients and the young people are invited by text to attend a low-key dinner as hosts. Suitably sexy uniforms are provided and the occasion conducted within reasonable bounds.'

'I see,' nodded the DCI.

'After two or three goes at this at a generous rate of pay, they are invited individually to meet wealthy clients who offer them a deal. The deal usually amounts to a steady reliable weekly payment, sufficient to get them through their studies, in exchange for regular sex. Once drawn into the arrangement, individuals find it hard to manage without the money and, by and large, continue until graduation, when a new bunch of willing volunteers take their place.'

'This is abuse of young women, I take it?' asked the DCI.

'Oh no, sir, both men and women,' replied Jas with authority as the DCI raised his eyebrow.

'So, who is running this type of racket in our patch then, Jas?'

'The two names that come immediately to mind are Damien Glover and Chloe McIntyre. Both relatively new on the scene, but up and coming. This seems to be what they specialise in.'

'Nothing else then? No drugs or other scams?' asked the DCI.

'No, not that we are aware of,' responded Jas.

'That's great, Jas. Well done. You see, folks, where a little initiative can take you?' casting his eye around the team.

'How did you come across all this information ,Jas?'

'Because you tasked me to do it, sir,' she replied as others smiled.

'Did I?' he replied.

'Yes, sir, eighteen months ago you told me to start gathering intelligence and monitoring this area of activity. Don't you remember, sir?'

'Well, that was obviously very far sighted of me,' the DCI explained, laughing at this revelation. 'No, honestly I don't remember setting you this task, but thank goodness I did, eh?' As he smiled, they all shared the joke and appreciated his honesty.

'Things change so fast now. I can't remember what I did last week never mind eighteen months ago! Well done anyway, Jas. Check with our colleagues in the North East, see if this pair's empire extends into their patch, and research what's available on all our computer intelligence systems.'

'Will do, sir.'

After the team had departed Mandy turned to her DCI.

'Good, I thought that was useful. Unusual for you to forget what you'd set in motion, boss?' she ventured.

'Yes, maybe, but the Assistant Chief Constable is pressing us hard on progress with knife crime and gang intelligence – that's where the priority lies at the moment.'

'Yes, that's true. OK, so it's not just old age then, sir?' she asked cheekily.

'Sod off, Inspector. Remember I write your annual appraisal,' was his crisp reply as they smiled and called it a day at eight o'clock.

The ACC, Dai Jones, stopped them as they were leaving to enquire how things were going.

'We're making progress, sir, on your key priorities and we are just looking into a new line of criminal activity.'

'Excellent, well done, keep me informed. I'm just off to meet the Home Secretary. He's pressing hard for extra police resources. It could be in your interests,' remarked the ACC as he dashed off into the waiting car.

Chapter 6

Baz was enjoying his attachment to the research project. It gave him a focus and, of course, an income whilst he was setting up his own business. A.I. represented the future, he argued, and he was not short of people with real money who were more than prepared to invest in him. Their gestures, of course, weren't mere good will. They were hard-headed business decisions with a clear expectation of a good return on their investment. For all his intelligence, Baz was yet to learn the realities of the business world.

After the initial excitement of something new, Giles found that investment banking wasn't as interesting and glamorous as he first thought, or had been led to believe. There were a lot of boring men in grey suits who expected the new junior colleagues to work ridiculous hours, whilst they enjoyed late starts, long lunches and early finishes to catch the train back to the Home Counties. Much of the work actually became really quite repetitive and dull. The working routine had become punishing: very early starts with very late finishes. Life had to be totally subservient to work, with every practical domestic element subcontracted, like laundry, household maintenance and cleaning. Sometimes work ended with a pizza delivery at your desk and a taxi home for a shower, a shave and a clean shirt, then straight back to work for a 'breakfast meeting', grabbing a bacon roll and a coffee on the way. Giles increasingly felt that he never saw the apartment that he supposedly lived in.

He quickly came to the conclusion that this was a con, an illusion. It was not living, it was just an existence, a corporate existence in which he felt that he was being exploited. This was not for him, he decided. Even with the cocaine, it wasn't manageable, let alone enjoyable or even stimulating.

The alternative started modestly, really – just a few bets, just a few calculations – but Giles soon realised that he could create mathematical models that could predict with sixty to seventy percent accuracy a multitude of things from the weather to the FA cup final, from horse racing to share prices. With modest levels of investment, he found that the returns were spectacular. The bank paid him a very generous salary, but this approach was far easier and far more lucrative. Giles found that he was regularly working eighteen to twenty hours a day, maintained by cocaine, which he reasoned was not sustainable. Something had to give and it was clear to him that something was the bank. He resigned. They protested. They had expectations, demanded loyalty and told him he was a fool to walk away from this, but Giles wasn't listening. As far as he was concerned, he had seen through their corporate con and was happy to leave it behind.

Chapter 7

Damien and Chloe were very pleased with their efforts to expand their criminal empire. Moving into Newcastle had proved to be a great success, and their student financing scam was booming. So far, none of the sponsors had refused to kindly donate to their 'charitable causes', which they were pleased about. Abdul Rashid, however, as their enforcer, was not so impressed. Abdul had worked for Turkish internal security, where he had learnt some useful tips about threatening behaviour, torture and ruthless commitment to the cause. Never mind, he thought, his time will come; someone will opt to test his metal at some point and they would find out how he operated.

Under the radar, the high end drug supply business was also doing well, so well that maybe they could try their hand at something else, they considered.

Over the next few years, various ideas were established and tested, some with more success than others. Consistently, however, fraud proved to be the most successful; from selling high end property abroad that didn't exist to wealthy speculators to hacking into individual and company accounts. Assets could then efficiently and ruthlessly be transferred back to themselves, via a long chain of potentially untraceable bogus business accounts.

At first, money, a lavish life style and a shallow inflated sense of self importance sustained their interest. Ambition and greed, however, began to take hold and affect their judgement. Their absolute confidence in their own ability to keep expanding and avoid detection was about to be tested.

Damien wanted to take on Leeds. They didn't need the money but, for him, it was about power and domination and Chloe simply encouraged his delusion. When they moved into the high end drugs market in Leeds, initially all went well, until it wasn't only the authorities that were taking notice.

***

DCI Sutcliffe called another meeting of his team to review and assess progress. After considering initiatives on knife crime and gangs, they turned their attention back to sexual exploitation and their growing interest in the activities of two particular local players.

DCI Sutcliffe had made a case at tasking to use surveillance to monitor and gather intelligence on Damien Glover and Chloe McIntyre. As a tactic, this could be effective in establishing a firm case for prosecution of some of the bigger players. As an expensive resource, however, it needed to be deployed wisely.

Initial investigations soon indicated the sort of involvement in criminal activity that the police had anticipated. It didn't appear that the couple were conscious of being watched, nor even particularly concerned. They didn't seem to attempt to disguise their activities to any significant degree. Deliveries were observed using secure deposit boxes at Manchester railway station. A courier would leave the cocaine in a discrete concealed package in a deposit box and later the customer would access the same box, take the package and leave payment in cash. Sometime later, a difference person would appear and extract the cash. This was a consistent pattern and really quite a slick operation, with junior couriers taking all the risk carrying the drugs, and more senior trusted members of the set up collecting the money. This presumably reduced the risk of the junior courier level creaming off the profits for themselves. No honour amongst thieves, it seemed.

Not unusually, whilst evidence collected could be used to prosecute the lower operatives, so far it failed to directly incriminate the two bigger players the police were targeting. The authorities knew that attempting to establish financial evidence was a much more complex and time-consuming process, but they waited and watched patiently.

When Damien and Chloe were observed taking what appeared to be more than a passing interest in Leeds, police suspicions were aroused. Cooperation was established with their North East regional colleagues and operations were suitably coordinated. The break came when a tip off led to deploying a surveillance team at the right time and place to observe a heated meeting between senior members of the drug dealing fraternity known to the Leeds police and our two ambitious Mancunians.

The scene looked like an angry confrontation with Damien and Chloe and their minders being challenged. The Asian gang took an apparent violent dislike to their attempts to infiltrate the Leeds patch. Strong words were exchanged and it seemed like the Asian gang were more than determined to protect what they saw as their territory.

The DCI took this new information to his ACC.

'So that's the picture, sir, I'm tempted to say let them get on with it and they can eliminate each other.'

'Yes, whilst tempting, as you say, I can't risk open warfare on our city streets. The chances of the innocent getting caught in the cross fire are too great. No, we need to intervene,' replied the ACC calmly.

'What would you suggest, sir?' asked the DCI.

'OK. I have a potential plan. This is highly sensitive and confidential but I am aware that our colleagues in Leeds already have an undercover officer discretely placed in the Asian gang, known as 'The Tigers'. They are ruthless, apparently, but so far our man has managed to maintain a presence and drip feed useful intelligence back to us via his handler. So what I anticipate doing is setting up a joint operation with Leeds to round up a few of these characters before the shooting starts. Leave it with me and I'll put wheels in motion then hand it over to you. Well done, this could be a significant breakthrough.'

Chapter 8

Giles soon found that his talents were eminently suitable for being more than a little mischievous in dealing with some of his contacts in the investment banking world. If he could gain access to their financial information, could he predict who was actually doing better than others? If so, Giles reasoned, would he be able to sell that information? A little research indicated the possibility of exploiting this knowledge. Using his contacts and computer skills, Giles found that yes he could predict with reasonable accuracy which companies were doing well and, hence, were worth investing in and, more pertinently, which companies were about to crash and where it would be wise to move money away from quickly.

At first, he borrowed money to test the theory and was soon in a position to repay the debt and generate a substantial profit. This was gold dust – he anticipated that this sort of knowledge would be worth millions! Very late that evening, Giles disclosed his findings to Baz, who was impressed and could immediately see the potential in this idea. Together, they set about exploiting it.

Giles arranged to meet contacts in the financial world and mentioned over expensive lunches that it was known to him that a certain company was in trouble. He knew that his host, whilst trying not to give anything away, would be interested in either withdrawing any investments immediately or approaching the company as a potential acquisition. Once the seed was planted, he would change the subject and leave the details hanging in the air. Later, he would arrange a further meeting and wait expectantly for his grateful host to thank him for the tip off and to ask to keep him informed. Lunch was then paid for and a generous envelope left on the table with a sweetener, like two tickets to a very expensive corporate box at Wimbledon the following day.

Using this approach, Giles was able to build up a small but highly significant group of contacts to sell his interesting corporate predictions to for large amounts of money. This easily far exceeded his previous earnings from the bank and required far less time and effort. *What could possibly go wrong?* he thought.

Meanwhile, Baz was busy exploring the scope for greater use of AI in all sorts of settings. He found that he could easily write computer programmes to order to facilitate full use of AI in fields as diverse as the car industry and nuclear power generation. On the face of it, this was legitimate business and continued to earn him much acclaim for his success from both the worlds of business and politics. What was not quite so legitimate, however, were his attempts to sell working software to one company and a deliberately flawed alternative to a competitor – of course, at a price to be paid by the dominant player. He assumed, with some justification, that he could sufficiently disguise his 'planned obsolescence' to confuse and distract the company he had deceived and not to attract too much attention towards himself. It wasn't until sometime later that this naive assumption started to unravel.

Initially, things were all going so well for the two aspiring Cambridge graduates and some of their dodgy money could be squirreled away for future security, or so they hoped.

Chapter 9

The joint operation between the two northern serious crime teams was carefully prepared and planned. The objective was to extract the covert officer and place him in close protection for debriefing and reorientation, before implementing a coordinated operation to arrest a significant list of leading players across the north of England, operating in established serious crime groups. Plans were checked and rechecked and assurance provided of their likelihood of success, security and secrecy.

Final details were being put in place the day before the operation was due to go ahead. A comprehensive plan had been established and rehearsed too; secure the safety of the covert officer, minimise the risk of suspicion falling on anyone else, and minimise the wider risk to the general public.

All was in place when some terrible unexpected news broke.

The senior command group set up to oversee the operation and keep ministers informed had received a DVD at police headquarters depicting a gruesome execution of the covert police officer the day before he was due to be extracted from the gang.

'Gentlemen, I don't need to tell you how disappointing this is. One of our brave officers has lost his life in indescribable circumstances and our whole planned operation is now compromised and cannot take place,' announced the ACC gravely and looking very uncomfortable.

A collection of very senior and experienced Superintendents looked on in silence as the implications were disclosed and their significance assessed.

'Now this is personal,' responded one senior officer. 'We have to take these people down. We owe it to our colleague and everyone else concerned.'

Nods of agreement and approval were readily apparent.

'The Chief Constable is briefing the Home Secretary now as we speak. He indicated to me briefly before he left that our attempts to secure extra funding for precisely this type of operation had been successful, just unfortunately too late for this young officer. Our responsibility is to renew our resolve and go after these evil people.'

New plans had to be drawn and old ones revised. No one in the room had any doubt about the wisdom or legitimacy of their actions. One question remained in all their minds however; how did the gang know?

***

Later, the Chief Constable visited DCI Sutcliffe's team.

'I just wanted to say, personally, how sorry I was about the loss of the Leeds officer and the inevitable end of what promised to be a successful operation.'

People nodded their appreciation around the room.

'One of the sad consequences of this type of occurrence is the seeds of doubt and mistrust it places between forces. Not unreasonably, from their point of view, Leeds and the North East area blame us for the failure of the operation. They think that the leak could only have come from us.'

Shock and disappointment resounded across the room, quickly followed by anger. The whole team found this most distressing and very hard to take.

'I can read on your faces what you think of that and I sympathise, this is not necessarily about truth, it's about perception. Realistically, this is likely to affect working relationships for a very long time,' responded the Chief.

Chapter 10

Baz discovered that large corporations didn't only object to people taking them for a ride but they also employed significant numbers of lawyers who were perfectly capable of vindictive retribution. It came as a shock when one day a letter arrived from one such firm threatening court action. Baz's initial reaction was one of disbelief; how *dare* they? He thought they were just fishing but Giles advised him otherwise. In this particular case, it proved to be the start of a long and complex process to retrieve every last drop of recompense possible. This was just the start – then other companies joined in and Baz found that he was losing money just as fast as he had been accumulating it. Maybe this wasn't the simple and easy route to a wealthy and trouble-free existence that he had envisaged...

Giles was more successful in keeping his balance sheet well and truly in his favour, although he did have to watch his step on several occasions when people he had defrauded sought to deal with their grievances outside the law. He couldn't complain, he had to accept; this was the murky world that he had chosen to engage in and bad faith obviously cut both ways. The day he came home to the flat to find it had been completely trashed was a particular low point. It wasn't apparent what, if anything, the people who broke in were looking for, but the flat had been turned over good and proper; everything was no longer useable. There was no choice but to clear it out, increase security and start again. He couldn't really claim on his insurance in the circumstances, and he accepted that he had effectively brought it on himself. No insurance company was going to see this was anything like 'reasonable wear and tear or accidental damage'. He couldn't risk reporting it to the police, so it wasn't officially a crime either. No, the loss was his.

This wasn't an end to it when Giles found himself subject to more direct retribution from what appeared to be a gang of hired thugs. They had chosen their moment and caught him in a dead end with no real prospect of escape, no cameras and no likely police presence. Revenge was short but brutal, resulting in several weeks in hospital and an extended period of recovery. Who would have thought, he contemplated, that suit wearing city bankers would sink so low as this? Or was the attack not directly related? Perhaps local miscreants were jealous and wanted to take him down a peg or two?

On reflection, both Giles and Baz acknowledged that they had some decisions to make: to get out before things got too serious, or to wise up and protect themselves more effectively. Foolishly, at first they opted for the latter. The temptation of easy money proved too great to just give up easily. A sudden run of good luck helped them delude themselves that this really was worth it. The further they got in, the harder it was to change course and withdraw. They were enjoying living the high life and had given little serious thought to where it might take them until they heard about Joe.

Joe was one of their group of friends at university. He had studied law and had become a successful barrister, dealing with probate for the rich and famous. He too had found the temptations of dealing with such large sums of money too difficult to resist. He could readily 'interpret' accounts in his favour or charge unrealistically high fees, but not so high as to incur an argument. He reasoned that 'inverse snobbery' tended to apply, that is a smug sense of self-satisfaction at your ease in meeting extravagantly high fees, simply as a reflection of your own virtue and status. In other words, he fell into the trap of treating his clients with the contempt he felt that they deserved.

Apparently, Joe too had regarded himself as untouchable, until he discovered that in fact he was not. Complaints were made against him and he found that the previously relaxed good fellowship of his long established firm evaporated overnight when he was suddenly dismissed from his post and reported to the law society for professional misconduct. Shame, guilt and a substantial financial liability saw his world crumble before his eyes. He wife's family quickly disowned him, his own family withdraw his name from all wills and he was soon effectively homeless, unemployable and alone. He could no longer even afford his own coke habit and turned to ever cheaper forms of alcohol. His sorry fall from grace ended in a most unpleasant suicide in a grubby little bedsit in Camden.

This was the point when Giles and Baz sat down and shared their fears that this could only realistically end badly.

Chapter 11

Police surveillance on Damien and Chloe continued. The same patterns of behaviour were observed, recorded and logged for potential future use in bringing a case against them. The police were determined, having lost one of their own, to entrap as many of these evil people as possible and bring them to justice.

Unfortunately, as the Chief Constable had predicted, cross-border cooperation with the North East area had largely ceased with their belief that, effectively, the North West had compromised their operation, resulting in the death of their officer. Nevertheless, independently both regional squads were still pursuing similar ends. Sadly, whatever was said to offer reassurance wasn't accepted.

Reports back from surveillance on the safe deposit boxes at Manchester railway station had proved to be interesting. Some of the 'customers' caught on camera collecting their personal drugs supply were not 'the usual players'. It seemed that the sales pitch from the supply end targeted the relatively successful and affluent, people who would very much not want their drug use to be disclosed in public or, indeed, expect to be caught. Some of them were about to receive a nasty surprise. For the surveillance officers, this was all highly amusing, catching people who they felt should have known better.

The banter at the station inevitably followed the events.

'I can't wait to see the face of that bastard defence solicitor when we bring him in. I wonder who would want to defend him?' speculated the team Sergeant.

'Yes, there will be some very embarrassed senior people exposed when this all comes to light, and serves them all bloody right, if you ask me!' replied one of his colleagues.

'Remember when we had that flat searched in London belonging to those other two posh twats?' remarked the Sergeant.

'Yes, that was well worth it mate; we uncovered some really useful intelligence, didn't we, Sgt?'

'Indeed, we did.'

Then suddenly the surveillance team couldn't believe their eyes. The man collecting his drugs from the safe deposit box today was no other than their own ACC Dai Jones! No, they couldn't believe it – their own ACC buying drugs from a criminal gang, surely not?

When this was reported back to base, silence and disbelief spread across the room. No, not one of their own; he couldn't have, surely, felt all the officers on duty.

DCI Sutcliffe was left to review the evidence and try to stay calm, to stay rational. Yes, he was sure it was Dai Jones. He had to take this straight to the Chief Constable. Had Dai, who it had to be acknowledged, was generally well liked and respected by his subordinates, been in league with the criminals all along? Had he been the source of the leak that led to the unmasking of the covert officer and ultimately his terrible death?

The DCI had never felt so nervous approaching a senior officer with the earth shattering news it was his duty to convey. *How will the Chief Constable react?* he wondered.

As he approached his office and spoke to the Chief's staff officer, Ray Sutcliffe tried to brace himself and stay calm.

The staff officer secured his direct passage into the Chief's office that represented the inner sanctum of power.

The Chief sat calmly behind his desk and looked up as the DCI approached him.

'Sir, I have some grave news from the surveillance team. I'm very sorry to have to inform you that the last person to collect cocaine from the safe deposit boxes at Manchester railway station was no other than our own ACC Dai Jones.'

'Indeed, DCI, I know. Sometimes we have to operate outside the normal parameters. You wouldn't have been aware that I had tasked the ACC to access this particular box to confirm the presence of Cocaine, after my own Deputy Chief Constable had been implicated in this case,' responded the Chief Constable.

'He had the unpleasant task of confirming our suspicions about a fellow senior officer.'

'So the DCC not the ACC was the source of the leak then, sir?'

'Sadly yes, it would seem so. Not necessarily deliberately, I must add, but probably more of a misplaced word to the wrong ears.'

'Oh dear.'

'Indeed. Very sad all round really. The DCC has had a chequered career and been close to the edge of acceptable behaviour several times, but we used to protect such people and turn a blind eye. We can't do that in a case like this.'

'What will happen to him, sir?' asked the DCI.

'We won't be able to prove any link to the death of the undercover officer, but serious drug use is not consistent with a senior command position, indeed any position in a modern police force. He may be prosecuted –the best he can hope for is probably dismissal,' responded the Chief.

Ray Sutcliffe turned to leave.

'Ray, this conversation stays in this room, of course. There will be a statement made clarifying the role of Dai Jones and announcing that the DCC will be leaving his post with immediate effect. There will be some promotion opportunities, Ray. Keep your eye out.'

No sooner gone and the force moves on, Ray thought. *Oh well, I suppose it's for the best*. When the official statement was released, it was greeted with much relief in exonerating Dai Jones and equal disappointment and suspicion about the circumstances of the DCC's retirement. In the short term, his post was suspended in a further round of budget cuts, so the anticipated opportunities for staff movement failed to materialise.

Chapter 12

After losing Joe, both Baz and Giles felt that the time was right to move out of London and to start again somewhere new. Giles noticed an advert for new posts being created with a city insurance firm based in Manchester. Baz agreed that it was worth a punt so they decided to move north. Baz was considering returning to academic study and applying to do a masters concentrating on his interest in AI.

Both men started with strong resolve not to return to old habits, but it was hard to avoid temptation, particularly as they were trying to establish a new base in Manchester. They debated long and hard about ways to make money, both legitimate and not so. They decided to return to attempts to create a mathematical model that aimed to predict sporting events. Horse racing, football matches and the like provided ample scope to study form, compare with real time results and start to create a model considering most of the variables that would at least win more than loose.

Giles also found that he could achieve a good level of return by simply moving his money about, spotting the right investments and using off shore tax havens.

Both sets of activity were borderline dubious but probably just about legal, if they were careful.

Giles started working for the city insurance firm and anticipated being able to do well there. He was researching opportunities on his computer one evening and, in the process of moving money between accounts, found that he could hack into a large business account containing millions of dollars and simply transfer funds from that account to his. Moving the money via a lengthy route between different banks provided reasonable reassurance, he felt, of disguising his activities and making them almost impossible to trace. This, of course, was lucrative but clearly took him over the line between legitimate and criminal activity. Initially, he chose not to tell Baz about what he had done.

Baz had submitted his application to Manchester University to start an MSc course. He was excited about the prospects.

***

Giles was aware of fairly widespread drug use within the financial services industry generally and, therefore, was not surprised to hear of such activities happening at work. One of his new colleagues asked him openly over coffee one day where he bought his coke from and offered to introduce him to his supplier, who he assured Giles was both reasonably priced and reliable. Giles was a little surprised by this degree of candour and indeed disappointed as both he and Baz had made real efforts to distance themselves from such activity.

At the time he took little notice and simply excused himself from the conversation but the colleague persisted and wanted to tell him all about the easy availability of hard drugs in the area. In the process, he named names and described easy methods of distribution, including a slick system of exchange using the safe deposit boxes at the local railway station. He confirmed how drops were made to order and left ready for collection in exchange for payment.

The service was good and the risks minimal, he reassured Giles.

Giles tried to be assertive and distance himself from his colleague. His attempts at predicting sporting events were going relatively well. He would place bets in different locations or on line and could achieve a steady success rate and was making a good living from it. He didn't need to use or get involved in dealing drugs.

***

The police operation to entrap Damien and Chloe and their contacts was about to come to fruition. A substantial list of names had been established and enough evidence had been collected that the DCI was confident it would result in some lengthy sentences and make a significant difference in cleaning up the city. Activities in the North East area, as far as Ray could tell, were also progressing well.

A request came to Ray's attention from the Metropolitan Police to assist in their investigations into fraudulent activities. The request was to pull in two men who had recently moved into Ray's area and had form in London, although neither had as yet been prosecuted. Ray could see no good reason why not to assist so called Mandy, his DI, into his office to organise it.

'Yes, sir?'

'Mandy, I have a request from the Met to arrest two men who live in our patch by the names of Giles Glover and Baz Bahati. They have a history of involvement in fraud and the Met have sought our cooperation in assisting them with their investigation.

Just have a check on our systems to see if they are known up here and whether we can add something to the Met's case.'

'Ok sir, urgent or not?'

'No, not particularly, but I'd like to clear this one out of the way before we launch our major operation against our other two friends,' confirmed the DCI.

'Ok sir, then I'll get onto it.'

'Thanks Mandy. Keep me informed.'

Mandy did her research and gathered her troops. There were no indications that either of these two men would resist arrest, or present any undue difficulties. She hadn't got any hard evidence of criminal activity committed by the them in the Manchester area, so on the face of it, this was simply a favour for the Met.

The following morning Mandy and three officers set out to give the two men an early morning call. When the officers arrived, both Giles and Baz were present and asleep in the flat, as expected. They were surprised, of course, and more than a little alarmed at this unexpected intrusion. Nevertheless, they both quickly dressed and left the flat with the officers. On the journey to the station, both men opted to stay silent and offered no resistance.

On arrival, the two men were efficiently processed through the custody suite and directed into separate interview rooms.

The detectives assigned to the investigation proceeded to question them about their various activities in London. Both men seemed surprised by this sudden interjection and quite perturbed. However, not only did they readily describe some of their criminal activities in London, but they also offered their knowledge of the local drug scene, with Giles relaying in detail his conversations with his colleague at work. For the Manchester police, of course, this was a bonus and would help them in their own investigation. It was also perceived as reassuring that the statements from both men, given entirely independently, were almost identical.

Mandy could collate their findings and liaise back with the Met. The two men were released on police bail pending further enquiries.

Walking out of the station unkempt and very late for work, Baz and Giles felt drained. They had to acknowledge that they'd had a good run and were probably lucky not to have been arrested before. They had been given information about local solicitors who could help them and would obviously need to follow that up promptly. They agreed that they had better report to work and the university and make their apologies and excuses. Even at this stage, it felt clear that this was going to end in serious consequences. They were very quiet, perhaps even a little repentant, but most of all they were frightened. They had both consciously opted to adopt a criminal lifestyle and this was the inevitable result. It was going to be painful, inconvenient and probably expensive, but they felt that they could come through it.

Chapter 13

Everything was in place. Staff were geared up and excited. The operation was due to start early the following morning, with a large number of arrests across the city, including both Damien and Chloe. Ray and his team were confident that they had diligently collected sufficient evidence already and this would be the final piece of the jigsaw. Ray had taken the trouble to inform his counterpart in the North East of their intension to strike, which did go some way towards repairing damaged relations.

Security and secrecy had been maintained and all arrests were secured promptly without too much resistance. None of the players were pleased to see the police, of course, but no one opted to try anything stupid. A significant amount of drugs, pornography and some firearms were successfully recovered from the various scenes.

The officers entering Damien and Chloe's flat were somewhat taken by surprise to find four in a bed and an orgy in full progress as they arrived. The two prostitutes involved were disappointed not to be able to finish their act and were at least relieved that they had already received their money. They were invited to leave the premises and did so in a whirl of perfume, skimpy clothing and high heels.

Damien and Chloe did all they could to obstruct the police investigation by remaining silent or offering offensive responses to simple questions. Both demanded the right to have a solicitor present and the officers were not surprised to see who it was that they had nominated to represent them. The representative was from a local firm of solicitors that were suspected of being as bent as many of their clients.

Amongst those arrested were those who would not normally find themselves in such circumstances, having been identified by the surveillance operation. As the police had predicted, this round of arrests was going to cause significant embarrassment. The police strategy was to seek a remand in custody for as many of the players as possible to leave the police free to search their accommodation for more incriminating evidence and to disrupt or destroy their activities.

Fortunately, the courts cooperated and all those presented at court with initial charges were remanded in custody. The North East area had conducted a similar operation and the impact on crime reduction was anticipated to be very significant.

When eventually their cases came to crown court for sentence, there were some lengthy prison terms handed out, which would keep many of them off the streets for many years. That didn't necessarily mean an end to their criminal activity, however. Active engagement in racketeering continued in prison, together with bringing influence and retribution to bear on those who might have betrayed them.

This was not the end of the matter, however. The police had committed themselves to bringing these people to justice. Proving exactly who killed the undercover officer was more complex than they had initially envisaged. No charges were brought for murder, not at least initially, but the hunt for evidence continued. No body had been recovered so the status of being missing and the DVD sent by the gang were the only immediate sources of evidence. More than that would be needed to secure a prosecution. It was therefore with mixed feelings that the Chief Constable offered his congratulations to all the staff involved in the operation.

DCI Sutcliffe could see in the Chief's eyes what was troubling him.

'It's not an end for the family of the officer who was killed, though, is it sir? Nor do we know exactly how he was uncovered.'

'Absolutely Ray, you're right. I'm going to visit his family now,' replied the Chief as he left, knowing his task would not be an easy one.

Efforts continued in the North East to find out exactly what had happened to their man. Sometimes the full facts never really emerged. Without a clear indication of who exactly killed the officer, and who else was present at the time, the only alternative was to bring charges against all of the gang under the ruling of 'joint enterprise.' There were doubts, however, about whether such a strategy would be successful.

Ray saw the Chief Constable return from his difficult visit looking drawn and grey. Ray approached him sympathetically.

'How were they, sir?' he asked.

'As you would expect, I suppose: disappointed and sad, mostly just sad.'

'I'm still reeling about the DCC. I do wonder what really happened there, sir.'

'Yes. There was more to it than I'm able to disclose, Ray. I suspect that blackmail was also part of the picture. It seems that the gang discovered more about his chequered past than was healthy. Who knows what you might disclose under those circumstances? I also suspect that The Tigers already had their doubts about our undercover man. Did we leave him in situ too long? Always fine margins with these types of operations, Ray, and that will stay with me, no doubt.' The Chief replied quietly and confidentially.

***

Whilst in custody, Chloe established a pattern of violent behaviour. She went on to kill another female prisoner in a fight, which resulted in her receiving a life sentence. Her time in custody ended prematurely, however, with her death following a drugs overdose. Damien bided his time and returned to crime on eventual release, but he was soon recalled to prison. After a series of long sentences, he never recovered and died alone in a homeless hostel in Preston.

In due course, Giles and Baz were also to appear in crown court in London for sentencing. The police had taken into account their level of cooperation with their enquiries and consequently their sentences could have been considered to be relatively light in all the circumstances.

Nevertheless, prison was likely to be a most unpleasant experience for both of them, albeit a relatively short one. Much of the money they had made was never recovered. Both went on to complete independent careers becoming writers and campaigners for more open access to education, prison reform and better access to treatment for drug users.

The whole experience left a life time impression. Their full potential would never be realised. All the hopes invested in them by their families and the business and political elite had been dashed. It was the loss of support from their families that hurt the most and that was never going to be fully recovered.

***

As the legal process took its due course, others watched with interest, keen to take over the vacuum left in the local criminal market and pecking order. Yes, in the short term this was a significant aid to breaking up criminal gangs and improving public safety, but the battle for control on the streets would continue.

7. FINDING LOVE

Chapter 1

Brendan Heath was forty one when his wife announced that she was leaving him. It was completely unexpected. It came as a terrible shock.

Not unusually, he noted, she had done her thinking and made her adjustments to the new set of circumstances before she had decided to break the news to him.

The news was delivered as Brendan returned home from a car fair in Paris. The prospect of further amalgamations in the car industry had triggered plans for rationalisation across the European operation and the meeting was designed to share knowledge of potential new models and to promote a hunger for sales. Brendan had enjoyed the event and came home full of enthusiasm for what was to come. There was even the prospect of job opportunities abroad. How exciting could that be?

As he collected his car from the airport car park, Brendan was trying to guess what Stacey's reaction would be to these new prospects. Being a civil servant her job was defiantly UK-based, but maybe she would welcome a change? Maybe this was their chance to start a family? Either way, he anticipated that she would be pleased for him.

So it was with excitement but some uncertainty about the reaction he might receive that Brendan pulled up on his drive, got out of his car and went into the house to share his news.

'Hello, hello Stacey, I'm back!' he shouted with enthusiasm. 'I have some exciting news to share with you!'

As he entered the living room he could immediately tell that Stacey was more sombre; *has someone died?* he wondered.

He looked at her aghast and couldn't help but notice the two suitcases standing next to her. He didn't need to ask, the explanation was coming.

'Brendan it's over, I'm leaving you.' This was the stark message delivered in a flat but serious tone.

He didn't know what to say and just stood there in stunned silence.

'Well, aren't you going to say anything?' she asked.

'Stacey, I was going to tell you all about new opportunities in the car industry and how that might work for us,' he replied limply.

'What?' she said. 'I've just told you that I'm leaving you and that's all that you can say?'

'Well, OK, if you've got to go we can talk about it later. When are you coming back?' he asked innocently.

'No Brendan, that's the point, I'm not coming back. I want a divorce. It's no good, I've tried, I've really tried, but we are just not compatible any more, maybe we never were.'

Brendan collapsed in a heap on the chair, not really knowing what to say.

'Why Stacey, why? Why haven't you mentioned this before? What's suddenly brought this on?' he asked as the doorbell rang and at least broke the tension.

He stuttered and thought he'd better just answer the door. No, he didn't want to help conduct a local market research survey that would only take fifteen minutes!

When he came back into the room, Stacey was standing and holding her two suitcases.

'Perhaps it would better if I just go,' she announced and walked out of the room towards the front door.

'I'll be in touch and collect the rest of my things in due course.'

'Stacey, where are you going?'

'That's not your concern,' she announced as she started to cry and walked through the door and out of his life.

Chapter 2

Brendan just stood in the hall looking out to where Stacey's car had been parked and the dry patch it left on the drive after it had been raining. He didn't know whether to laugh or cry, or quite what to think. *What had suddenly got into her head?* he wondered. Would she simply get it out of her system and come back? Would it be tomorrow, the next day… he really wasn't sure what to think.

At times of crisis, are you the sort of person who would immediately reach out to friends for support, or the sort of person that would prefer to be alone? he asked himself. The answer was obvious – he was the latter. Stacey, he knew, was the former. That was probably where she had gone to now, to one of her friends; would it be Lucy, or Carmel or perhaps April? Of course it would be Carmel, he decided. Should he ring, or leave her alone? Perhaps he should write, or email.

In truth, he didn't know quite what to do. His brother lived in Australia, his mother was dead and he knew his dad would only say something unhelpful like – 'I always said she wasn't the girl for you!' Stacey never wanted children so he couldn't look to them for solace either. He could go to the pub. He laughed, yes go to the pub and be one of those boring people you just don't want to talk to who collar you occasionally and you just know it's going to be 'a life story' job.

No, Brendan went back to the living room and sat down. *What did she say?* he asked himself. She's leaving – did she mean it? He really wasn't sure. Had he really been such a bad husband? Had it been such a bad marriage? Brendan's mind wandered.

He remembered how they first met. It was at University, he was reading Modern European Studies and she was doing languages. They met in their first week at a fresher's party. There were lots of young people and after a while they started to pair off. As the music played he remembered looking across the room and realising that they were the only ones left. He drifted across to her and limply asked if she wanted to dance and she equally limply nodded. They spent that night together, the first time for both of them, because that's what you did. Then they just kept on seeing each other and eventually got married, because again that seemed like the obvious thing to do. Did he really love her? Well, that was a question. *What was love anyway?* he thought.

Maybe, on reflection, it wasn't love, just youthful infatuation. He never seriously thought of being with anyone else, though; he never drifted or actually wanted to, unlike several of their friends he could think of. Had she found someone else? Was that it? He couldn't think of any particular clues recently that might have suggested that. No, she always seemed quite contented, as he felt he was… *at least up until now*. So why leave and why now? That's what bugged him.

Chapter 3

'Carmel, it's so good of you to put me up for a couple days!' Stacey remarked.

'Oh, it's all I could do in the circumstances, Stacey. We've been friends for years, after all,' replied Carmel.

Stacey cried as Carmel made some tea and sat down with her friend to ask the obvious question.

'So what brought this on?'

At that, Stacey started to cry even more. Through the flowing tears, Stacey tried to explain, if only to herself.

'I don't think I ever really loved him, he was just convenient. He is a good man at heart, a little adventurous, but honest and reliable.'

I'd settle for honest and reliable, Carmel thought, especially after some of the men she'd had in her life.

'I just don't want to spend the rest of my life like this. Why should I? I deserve better, don't you think?' she asked rhetorically. 'We have different interests. He spends too much time working away… "doing what?" I sometimes wonder. I want to advance my career too but he keeps talking about children. I never wanted any, I always told him that. His dad used to say that would be a breaking point for us and I think he was right. Oh dear, Carmel, what am I going to do now?' she asked, still in floods of tears.

'Well, you've done it now, girl, haven't you?' said Carmel in a blunt matter of fact way. 'No turning back now, you've left him. You'd better find yourself somewhere to live and a good solicitor. That house must be worth quite a bit; you should do OK out of a divorce settlement.'

'Yes, yes of course, Carmel. You're right, as usual.'

Chapter 4

Brendan woke after a poor night's sleep, the previous day's event still running through his mind. He felt disappointed more than sad, a little ashamed, although he didn't know why, confused and he felt a growing sense of unease.

'Why leave and why now?' were still the big unanswered questions in his mind.

Again, he tried desperately to think: was there any reason to believe there was somebody else? *Surely, she couldn't have just left me?* he kept thinking and *what do I tell people?*

As he got up and went for a shower, he realised that he hadn't even brought his bags in from the car yet. *What was today's agenda?* he asked himself, still not fully awake.

Unpacking the car helped Brendan remember that he had a couple of days off before going back to work at the car dealership where he was the manager. What would people think? He felt embarrassed.

Unusually for him, Brendan couldn't decide what to do first. He didn't want to announce their separation to the world. He supposed he would need to contact a solicitor, but there was plenty of time for all that. He thought of the impact on his pension, the potential positive and negative effect on his career. He wondered how he would feel when he and Stacey met next time… Then he tried to just stop thinking.

He recognised that he would need to get some food in and so decided to do some shopping; yes, a practical task – a distraction. Stacey usually did most of that but he was domestically capable. He set off to the nearest supermarket. The car park was full with young families and bored husbands were being taken out for the weekly reality check. Brendan successfully avoided agonising over which particular variation of baked beans to adorn his trolley with, selecting the basics, then went through the self-service check out and headed back to the car park, which was where he bumped into Clive and Suzy.

Brendan and Clive went back a long way. They still played in a five a side football team together. Brendan liked Clive's wife, Suzy, and had always regarded their marriage as something to look up to.

'Hi Brendan, on your own? Where's Stacey this morning?' enquired Suzy chirpily.

'She's gone,' he blurted out before giving himself time to think.

'Oh, gone where, Brendan? Off with the girls on some jaunt?' responded Suzy with a cheeky smile.

'No Suzy, I mean she's gone. She's left me. I came home from Paris yesterday, all excited to tell her about some new opportunities at work, and she announced that she was leaving me.'

'Oh,' said Clive inadequately. 'I'm really sorry, mate.'

'I don't know what to think,' responded Brendan as he started to get emotional.

'How about you come back to our place for a coffee, Brendan, and we can talk about it properly?' suggested Suzy, being practical.

'That's it, there's nothing more to say.'

'Or would you prefer it if Clive came back with you and you boys could have some time together?' Suzy asked sensitively. 'Perhaps go for a walk or something?'

So, somewhat sheepishly, Clive ended up back at Brendan's as his friend made the coffee. He felt that Suzy was right, but he also didn't fancy the prospect of talking to their two kids, who he was so very fond of, if not more than a little jealous.

They sat down and Brendan had a chance to unload.

All those mixed emotions, those pent up feelings: the hurt, the insult, the blow to his pride and of course the wondering 'why?' Clive listened and tried to absorb it all as the responsive friend. He had to admit that he was surprised, shocked in fact. He hadn't ever thought that there was anything seriously wrong between Brendan and Stacey. They always seemed happy enough, he thought.

They went for the walk, as Suzy had suggested, and called into a country pub for a pint on the way back. Both of them had known other couples who had separated, and perhaps some that didn't that should have done. They knew of men who presented the perfect image at home and were seeing other women in the background. They knew of those who had successfully moved on following separation and those who had never recovered from it. Their conversation helped to put things into perspective.

The following few months were difficult for both Stacey and Brendan. Stacey wanted to move things forward and settle their affairs as amicably as possible. For Brendan, that was all too soon. He needed to go through the attempt, albeit perhaps notional, of trying to get back together. That of course didn't work. He wanted answers; further explanation of what she felt had gone wrong. There wasn't anybody else involved on either side, which in some ways made it more difficult. There was nobody else to blame. For Stacey, it somehow seemed more acceptable and credible to tell her friends and family that she simply had to call time on a dysfunctional relationship. For Brendan, he found it much harder to talk to others about it and felt most uncomfortable about the inevitable speculation and office gossip that followed.

Brendan had never been violent or abusive, which Stacey readily acknowledged, although it didn't make it any easier for him to understand why she felt the need to leave him. At forty, she just felt that she wanted to take her life in a different direction, one that couldn't accommodate Brendan. Most of her friends were sympathetic and understanding and tried to help her to feel OK about simply wanting to assert her independence, but there were the snide comments, the accusations of disloyalty, the double standards and the male condemnation.

When the time came for them to meet and properly discuss separation arrangements, perhaps they were both over the worst. Phone calls and messages between them had helped to address some practical issues, and to establish, at least on the surface, a level of mostly cordial communication.

Brendan had managed to avoid the temptation to simply empty the house of all of Stacey's belongings and leave them in a heap on the street. Even if claiming to be the one spurned, he had no wish to reap revenge and damage or destroy her belongings. No, he was at least more civilised than that. They had managed to agree reasonably between them who would take what from the house and had arranged for Stacey to remove her share in Brendan's absence.

They were due to meet that afternoon at Carmel's house to discuss longer-term arrangements and the potentially contentious issue of the financial settlement. It was also an opportunity for Stacey to finally hand over her keys, as they had decided that Brendan would keep the house and buy her out.

Whilst Carmel's house was hardly 'neutral ground' Brendan could accept that it offered a confidential place to talk and that Carmel would provide the coffee and tissues, if necessary, and would leave them to it. That's how it worked.

There were rubbing points, of course, and at a first meeting not everything was satisfactorily resolved. There remained some significant differences of view on how to apportion their joint assets, but they had sat down together, kept composed and parted with a polite acknowledgement.

Carmel was there to pick up the pieces for Stacey and Brendan was left to lick his own wounds at home. It felt strange coming back to the marital home in these circumstances. Brendan had at least started to redecorate and to make the place more of his own.

Once the solicitors got involved inevitably things got more difficult and attitudes and grievances became more entrenched, but they got through it. The legal process followed and eventually resulted in their successful divorce.

Married, divorced like so many other couples, failures – *was that what it amounted to?* they asked themselves.

Chapter 5

So what now? That was the question for both of them.

Stacey had secured a promotion at work and moved from the Department of Rural Affairs to The Ministry of Transport as a team leader. Her section was responsible for the implementation of HS2 and for drawing up options for the future management of the whole rail network. She had moved to London and, once her share of the equity became available, she was able to rent a modest apartment in a reasonable part of town.

Initially, at least, Stacey was not looking for a new relationship, she was more content on her own, or at least that's what she thought at the time.

Brendan, on the other hand, was definitely looking for love. Now, at forty two, he had tried reliving his youth with nights out at the local bars and night clubs but, unsurprisingly, had found it an unsatisfactory experience. Seemingly out of kilter with the youngsters, and keen to avoid the separated and desperate, he found this was not a good method of finding what he thought he was looking for.

Had he really loved Stacey? he still wondered. He thought probably so, at least initially, surely... He wasn't certain; how do you know after all?

Clive and Suzy had been supportive. Reaction from Brendan's family had, as he expected, varied from casual acceptance to his dad's forthright condemnation of 'that woman.' At work it soon became yesterday's news and people moved on. The opportunity to live and work abroad failed to materialise and Brendan sought promotion nearer to home, taking over responsibility for a larger franchise.

As regards potential partners, Brendan had dated a few women and made some new friends but initially hadn't found anyone who he felt inclined to spend the rest of his life with. He made the financial adjustment to being single and was coping with the practicalities of living on his own. He still felt that he wanted a family but wondered if he was in fact getting too old. He thought about having a dog but decided it would be too much of a tie and probably unfair on the dog! No, for now at least, Brendan Heath, aged forty two, was single and living alone. That was until he discovered internet dating….

'Have you tried internet dating sites, Brendan?' asked Clive. He explained how it worked and that several people he knew swore by them.

'It's how it's done these days, Brendan. You need to get with it!'

Brendan sat down with his computer, feeling a little unsure and mildly embarrassed. He was used to ordering stuff off the internet, but finding a partner – he was sceptical. A little research, however, soon uncovered a vast choice of potentially suitable females. He couldn't believe it! Some sites seemed better than others, and some were perhaps best avoided. Then there was grinder! *No, not for me,* he thought. As he trailed through the options, Brendan couldn't believe how many lonely people there must have been out there!

He read through some of the profiles and thought they must be too good to be true, which of course many of them were. They did include a photo, however, and unless they were touched up – or indeed a picture of somebody else – they must have been genuine, surely? He laughed as he read one pitch where he felt sure that the photo was of Emily Ratajkowski, the model, and not the woman who claimed to be twenty five in the description.

As he looked further, Brendan read a few male pitches to see what sort of things men said about themselves. He couldn't believe his eyes and then laughed out loud when he came across somebody he knew from school – someone who must have been the same age as him, but had described himself as a savvy thirty five year old globetrotter from London, although Brendan knew he had probably never been further south than Bognor Regis! The man said he was a heating systems engineer, but Brendan remembered him as a driver delivery man the last time they had met, albeit he recalled that it had been for a heating engineering company. *What were people thinking of?* he thought.

So it was with more amusement than curiosity that Brendan ventured to meet his first 'blind date.' Well, blind-ish. He had arranged to meet Stephanie that evening in the Bull and Bear pub for an introductory drink. Would he recognise her from the photograph? How might she recognise him?

In the event, as soon as they met they both realised that they knew each other, or at least had met previously on a corporate event. Stephanie worked as a service receptionist at another dealership locally. Well, that was a good start; they had something in common.

They found that they could talk freely and both said that they had enjoyed their first meeting. They went on to see each other regularly for a while until

Brendan wondered whether that was really what he wanted or, indeed… well, what was he was actually looking for? They got on quite well as friends, he felt, but was she the lifelong partner he thought he was looking for? No, probably not, he concluded, and actually when he plucked up enough courage to raise the subject she said that she felt the same, so they broke off contact.

Perhaps he needed to think a little more clearly about what it was that he actually wanted. Brendan had, after all, adjusted quite well to being single and actually quite liked his own company; he didn't miss all the little compromises that go hand in hand with living with somebody else. There was still the family issue, although at approaching forty three, he again wondered if he had left it too late. Part of him still wanted someone special in his life, however, somebody to share things with and to care for. To love and be loved, or was that too much to ask for?

After a few more internet encounters, Brendan decided to leave it for a while. The process felt too clinical and he found many of the self-descriptions to be at the very least somewhat optimistic and exaggerated. It would have been refreshing to read something more honest, like 'I am slightly overweight, going grey, I know I snore and I have a liking for pickled onions and ice cream, but not at the same time!'

Chapter 6

And then there was Lorna.

On one of his shopping trips, he followed a woman with two young children out of the supermarket towards the car park. They happened to have parked next to each other. She was trying to manage the two children, watch the road and unload her shopping, when she temporarily let go of her trolley and it proceeded to roll away towards the road. Without a thought, Brendan rushed forward to stop it and managed to catch it just in time. As he brought it back to her and their eyes met, it felt new, it was something different. She talked very quickly – feeling embarrassed, she tried to do everything at once. Brendan tried to help her put her shopping in the car. Tongue tied, he managed to drop her box of eggs on the floor and she was good enough to laugh about it, and the kids both thought it was great! She settled them into the car and drove off quickly, leaving Brendan just standing there aghast.

It was a while before he happened to see her again. She was with the two children having a picnic in the park as he walked past just taking the air.

'Hello,' he said as he stopped next to them. She looked up and smiled and then her son reminded her.

'Mummy, it's the man who dropped the eggs!' he said, actually quite excited, as his big sister went on to tell the man that actually they did manage to buy some new eggs, so he needn't worry!

They all laughed and, after a while, Brendan sat down to join them. After introductions, they chatted easily and she invited him to join their picnic. It felt so easy, somehow so homely, nothing like the forced unease of his internet experiences.

They smiled and exchanged glances and the kids seemed to respond well to him too. Brendan was both pleased and encouraged and, unbeknown to him at the time, so was Lorna.

When he got home, Brendan felt like a love sick teenager – he couldn't get Lorna out of his mind! He was captivated by her, he liked everything about her. He just wanted to be with her. Should he call? Would that be too much? Might he frighten her away? Brendan had never had feelings like this before and was surprised by the intensity of his own reactions. He remembered having given her his card with his mobile number and email address on it and tried to sound casual as he said simply, 'Here's my card, by the way. If you like give me a call sometime.'

She had smiled and he wasn't sure whether that was a polite rejection or an expression of interest, of course he hoped it was the latter!

***

Back home with the children, Lorna was reflecting on her day. They had enjoyed it and had a lovely time. They had spent time together, played, talked, all the normal things that you do as a family, but of course, still without Daddy and that still felt strange. It was early days, without him, she supposed, but it still hurt so much. The children both missed him terribly. He was gone, lost forever in little more than an instance.

She had tried to make other friends, to force herself to engage with adult company. Her parents had been so supportive since Adam died and they were only too willing to look after the children if she wanted to go out, but really she didn't. She was still off work, it was coming up to a year now and she knew that she would have to make a decision soon. Could she face going back to work? She had her doubts. Certainly the shifts would be difficult. Adam had always been so good at helping look after the kids and taking a full part in all things domestic – indeed, in all ways really. He had been a wonderful husband.

She still cried when she thought back to when they had first heard the diagnosis. After the consultant had said 'inoperable and incurable cancer' nothing else had registered, she had closed off at that point. She was telling her that she was going to lose her husband, the only man that she had ever loved and thought would live forever.

Adam tried to be stoic but it was so hard for him too and absolutely devastating for the children. It was the hardest things he'd ever had to do, he said, to tell your own kids that you are dying. He went downhill so fast, from being fit and active and loving life to being confined first to hospital, then to the hospice, where he only lasted a few precious months before he died eleven months ago, to the day actually, she remembered.

The funeral was so sad. It was very well attended and the vicar summarised his life and their loss so well, but it was still awful. Afterwards, she felt so alone, despite all the offers of help and support that she received. She had tried so hard, particularly for the children, to keep going, to act like all was normal, to maintain a facade. They seemed to cope with it far better than she had expected. They missed their father terribly, of course, but they did seem to accept his death and they talked about him all the time.

Could I ever love anybody else? she had often wondered. No, she thought not. Oh, she had not been short of offers, an attractive woman of thirty seven suddenly alone, but with two children. It obviously wasn't their fault – the 'passion killers' her friend called them. Most men who had showed any interest were quickly put off by the prospect of taking on two young children.

Now she had met Brendan, twice as it happened. She liked him. She certainly hadn't been looking for anyone. She knew nothing of his circumstances. He might be married, for all she knew. Then she remembered the card he had given her. Um, sales manager of a large car dealership, she didn't know how she felt about that. Adam had been a teacher. He taught general science, although he was really a physics specialist.

The children had asked after him several times and they genuinely seemed to like him. Ruby, now aged five, thought that mummy should have a new man and told her so frequently. Oliver, aged three, still laughed at 'the egg man', from when Brendan had dropped their eggs in the super market car park.

Ruby burst into the kitchen to shatter her peaceful and thoughtful moment.

'My brother stinks!' she announced indignantly.

'Oh, what sort of stink?' she replied, although she had guessed really.

'A poo stink, mummy. Boys, they are so horrible!'

'Anyway, its bath time now, honey. We'll soon get him clean again,' mum replied reassuringly.

During bath time, Oliver asked about 'the egg man'.

'When will we see that man again, Mummy?'

'Oh, I don't know that we will, dear,' she replied nonchalantly.

'Oh but we must, Mummy!' Oliver declared loudly and Ruby agreed.

Well, that's it then, she thought.

Chapter 7

After she had put the children to bed, Lorna sat down quietly and looked across at Brendan's card on the table beside her. *Should I ring?* she wondered. After pondering she decided to text.

It was nice to see you again we all enjoyed your company. Lorna.

As his phone pinged, Brendan sat up sharply; *could it be?* he thought.

He stumbled and nearly deleted the text – it had come up as an unknown number. *Lorna! Fantastic*, he thought, and felt so pleased.

What to say? How to sound interested but not too keen, and certainly not desperate?

Hi Lorna, so nice to hear from you, I really enjoyed it to. We must do it again sometime! He added a smiley face.

Was that too much? he asked himself. What if she doesn't reply?

He waited, glued to the screen, willing it to respond. He waited and waited. Then it pinged again.

OK, actually we are going to the zoo tomorrow. Would you like to come along? she asked.

Wow, Brendan had never been to a zoo in his life. *But yes, let's go to the zoo*, he thought. Fortunately, he was off tomorrow anyway and had no particular plans. They made arrangements to meet there, in the car park. Brendan was so excited! Actually, so was Lorna and both her children.

Chapter 8

Brendan woke all excited like a child – a day at the zoo! He began to wonder where the fun had been in his marriage, he couldn't remember ever doing anything like this.

He dressed as quickly as he could and thought he could treat Lorna and the kids to a meal there. Phone, wallet – ready to go!

As he drove towards the meeting point, his thoughts were all about Lorna; the zoo was irrelevant, or was it? No, it was integral, he thought; a real family day out. It was something that he had never done with Stacey, nor could he ever have imagined doing it.

Lorna was frantically trying to organise two kids, a picnic, a change of clothes for both of them, just in case, the tickets, the route, sun cream, plenty of water…

Who would be a mum? she asked herself. Ruby was sensibly putting a few things into a little bag to take with her: a comic, her favourite teddy, a notebook to write down all the animals she might see for her teacher and a biscuit. Oliver was racing round blowing raspberries and trying to wind up his sister when the phone rang and then someone was at the door, all at the same time. Lorna rushed to answer the phone only to be informed again that she had been in a car accident and some smart arse lawyers were so kindly offering to represent her. *I don't think so*, she thought. Ruby went to the door and shouted through the letter box that her mummy was busy and her daddy was dead and the caller went away.

More or less on schedule, Lorna bundled the two kids into her car and set off. Had she got everything? She was absolutely sure that she hadn't. Did she know where she was going? No, not really, but that was nothing new. It would work out alright, she hoped.

Ruby sat quietly and wrote a list of the animals that she would most like to see while her brother told her that all animals poo and that he wanted to see it all.

Brendan stopped at a petrol station to fill up and bought a paper. He noticed that they also sold eggs so he bought half a dozen to replace the ones that he had broken when they first met.

They arrived at the zoo at about the same time and managed to park up near to each other.

Everyone was excited as they rolled out of the cars and collected their things together. Brendan presented the box of eggs to everyone's amusement and Lorna tried to check that she had everything she needed.

Oh, the picnic, she thought, looking round the car, and then remembered that she had packed it all ready and left it safe and sound on the kitchen table! The kids looked disappointed until Brendan offered to treat them all to a McDonalds and became an instant super hero.

'I'm so sorry about the picnic,' Lorna tried to explain.

'Don't worry, it doesn't matter. Let's just enjoy the day!' responded Brendan as they looked into each other's eyes and smiled.

'Right kids, where do you want to go first?' announced Brendan, quickly followed by an apology to Lorna for not consulting her to start with.

They walked off together, laughing and joking as Ruby took Brendan's hand and promised to look after him all day. He melted. Oliver scurried along, picking up used lolly pop sticks as he went and trying to put them down the back of his sister's dress. Lorna calmly kept reminding her dear son that this wasn't a very kind thing to do and that McDonalds only served good children and he seemed to get the message, checking periodically that he was still qualifying as 'good'.

They took in all that was to offer, seeing the lions and tigers, the monkeys, the giraffes and the sea lions all by midday. The children loved it, with Ruby diligently writing down the names of the animals they had seen and Oliver trying to work out how each particular animal did their poo. In fact, they all enjoyed it; for Lorna, this was a glimpse of what family life might have been and for Brendan it was a revelation of what it could be.

As Oliver sought further confirmation of his behaviour status, they approached McDonalds and the adults consulted briefly, readily reaching agreement that all had passed the test and Brendan proudly escorted them all into the restaurant. Brendan wanted to pay and Lorna didn't argue. They sat comfortably outside with a selection of the best fast food can offer and munched away under the eagle eyes of the waiting birds eager to collect the crumbs. They loved it. Lorna realised that it had been too long since they had done this and felt so pleased that they were doing it now. Being with Brendan came so easily to her that she didn't even stop to think what she might be doing or where it might lead. Yes, of course she felt some sense of guilt being without Adam, but she felt that, in the circumstances, he would understand and would want to encourage her not to spend the rest of her life alone.

For Brendan, there was a sense that this was great and just felt right. After finding the elephant enclosure, including mounds of poo, much to Oliver's amusement, they returned to the sea lions for the afternoon feeding demonstration and an ice cream. By the time they reached the cars, the kids were worn out and slept all the way home.

Lorna invited Brendan back to their home to share the picnic that was dutifully waiting where she'd left it. Fortunately, it had been in the shade all day. They'd all had a lovely time and Ruby smiled as she saw mummy kiss Brendan before he left. When Lorna saw the children off to bed, Oliver assured her that he liked 'the egg man' and wanted to see him again soon and Ruby calmly told her mother that he was a very suitable man for her.

Lorna sat quietly downstairs by herself and tried to make sense of things, then decided not to try too hard. She was happy, and so were the children. *What more could I want?* she thought. When she later talked to a friend about it, she agreed and encouraged her to just go with it and not to over analyse. *Strange sometimes how life works out*, she thought.

For Brendan, back in his own house, he felt a bit empty, incomplete and alone again. This just felt right, no questions, no real doubts; this appeared to him, even at such an early stage, to be the sort of relationship that he wanted – what he was looking for? *Was it too good to be true?* he asked himself.

Chapter 9

Stacey was enjoying her new found freedom and her new life in London. She wasn't looking for a replacement relationship. *Why bother?* she thought. Too many of her friends, she felt, had simply dumped one unsatisfactory liaison for another just for sake of appearances and she wasn't prepared to do that. No, what she wanted was a change, something a little more refreshing and exciting, casual even. She wasn't looking for long term commitment.

Stacey found that she was happy to meet men at her convenience and, if she liked their company, to enjoy it for a while before moving on. That way nothing got boring or stale or mundane. There was a greater honesty about it. Why not? If she didn't do it now she never would!

***

Brendan and Lorna continued to see each other and enjoy each other's company. The children seemed to really like Brendan and to benefit from having another adult around. Days easily turned into weekends and, without seeking to force the issue on either side, both of them felt very comfortable with the arrangement.

Over time they were able to share their previous experiences with each other. Lorna managed to tell Brendan more about Adam, the fact that he had died leaving her on her own, and what exactly had happened. Brendan was able to tell her about Stacey, how they had parted and how he was left feeling at the time. It helped them both that they knew, and it was an important test of their honesty towards each other.

There was something, however, for Lorna that she didn't quite know how to tackle and avoided raising the subject. Not sex, that happened quite naturally, and it was actually a refreshing bonus for both of them. No, it was not that, it was the children. How did he honestly feel about them? And, she asked herself, how could she ever trust the children of her marriage to anyone else?

Her parents had kindly suggested that perhaps they needed to spend more time together as just the two of them. They seemed really pleased for her and genuinely liked Brendan. They had offered to have the children more than once to give them the space to be together but Lorna had made excuses and avoided the issue. Maybe she was worried that, if she asked the question, she might not like the answer? *But if he had doubts too, wasn't it better for me to know?* she thought.

At the end of one evening, when the children were in bed and Brendan had already made it clear that he wasn't stopping that night as he needed to be up early and off to work for a special event the following day, she tried to broach the subject.

'Brendan, can I ask you something?'

'Yes, of course, anything you like!'

'Where are we going? I mean, what do you see as the future for us?' she asked tentatively.

'What's brought this on?' he replied as she started to cry and he reached out to comfort her.

'Brendan, I love being with you, you know that, but I suppose it's the children. You wouldn't have wanted it this way, would you?'

'You mean an instant family, as it were?'

'Yes exactly,' she replied.

'Well, actually, whilst I wouldn't have planned things like this, it does really suit me,' he replied, to her surprise.

'You see, I've always wanted a family. I'm not getting any younger, so would it be wise to start one myself now I'm over forty?'

'People do.'

'Yes, but it's more than that; you see, my family's medical history is not good. There are several inherited serious conditions, which fortunately have by passed me, but I was warned as a young adult that there was a high chance of passing on the negative genes should I ever have children.'

Lorna looked surprised as she tried to make sense of this new information.

'That was one of the reasons why Stacey never wanted children. Although, in fairness to her, I don't think she wanted them anyway, even without my family history.'

'What is the condition, Brendan?' she asked.

'It's irrelevant now, Lorna' he replied holding her tight. 'You see, I had the snip many years ago, so I will never father any children now anyway.'

'Oh,' she responded, still trying to take it all in.

'So Lorna, if you are asking me 'would I be prepared to take on your children?', the answer is 'yes' – not just because I can't have any of my own, because it's too risky and I'm too old, but because

Lorna... because, well, I've grown to love them, as I love you.'

She snuggled into him as tears appeared in both their eyes.

'Oh Brendan, what an awful thing to have to bear, and I was worrying over nothing. I know you love them and they love you too, they tell me so all the time.'

'Really? But how do you feel about restarting family life after losing Adam?'

'We already have, haven't we? Obviously, I didn't envisage things this way, but you have brought joy back into my life, Brendan,' she said, sincerely looking deep into his eyes.

'You have too, I didn't know what was missing between Stacey and I, but I'm sure I've found it with you, Lorna. I love you and would marry you tomorrow, but I was unsure how you might answer and feared the risk of rejection.'

'Oh Brendan,' she said, holding his arm so tight, 'you might be surprised!'

He turned towards her – this was the moment. He could not let it go now. She agreed, of course, and begged him to stay over after all; he couldn't leave her now!

Chapter 10

After a wonderful night together the early morning, in contrast, proved to be chaotic. Brendan woke to the unwelcome sound of his alarm. As he started to crash about, he woke Lorna, who wanted to be supportive and to see him off for his important event at work.

Ruby suddenly appeared and asked why Brendan was in such a hurry. It was unusual for Oliver not to be the first visitor to her bedroom in the morning, so Lorna went to just check that he was OK. She walked into his room and everything was unusually quiet. She looked down lovingly at him, but something was wrong. She leaned over him and looked closer; he was all wet – he had been sweating heavily. Feeling his forehead, he had a raging temperature. She couldn't wake him; he seemed limp. She was worried. She called out to Brendan to come immediately.

He arrived, shaved but half dressed.

'It's Oliver, something's wrong, I'm sure!' she cried, starting to feel a sense of panic as she stood there, helplessly staring at him and not knowing what to do.

Brendan immediately sensed her unease and he agreed something was seriously wrong. He checked for a pulse and that Oliver was breathing. He tried to rouse him without success.

'Gosh, he's boiling up, Lorna!'

'What do you think it is? Some sort of fever?' she asked desperately.

'I think it's more serious than that,' he replied whilst starting to remove his pyjamas.

'What are you doing?' she asked.

'Checking for spots, Lorna.'

There were none immediately obvious.

'It's not chicken pox or anything like that, Lorna. The only thing I've ever come across like this is meningitis. I don't know a lot about it, but I do know that early access to treatment is vital. We need to get him to a hospital NOW.'

It was ten past six in the morning.

'Shall I call an ambulance?' she asked.

'No, it would be quicker to take him there ourselves.'

'What about Ruby?'

'Come on, there's no time to argue. We all need to go NOW,' Brendan responded decisively.

'What about your event at work?'

'They'll manage, Lorna. This is more important.'

'I'll make Ruby some breakfast. Would you like an egg?' she asked.

'No, Lorna, honestly we really have to go straight away, as we are.'

'But I'm not even dressed!' The very thought of hospitals raised anxiety for Lorna after losing Adam, but she needed to put her faith in Brendan's judgement.

'Put on a dressing down and let's go,' shouted Brendan whilst wrapping Oliver up in a sheet and, still half-dressed, he bundled them all into the car and set off hastily for the hospital.

Arriving quickly at A&E, they found that the hospital was quiet at that time of day. Brendan helped Lorna out of the car and, whilst carrying Oliver and with Ruby just behind holding tightly on to her teddy, they ran in and up to the desk.

'This is urgent – a suspected case of meningitis. This child needs to be seen immediately,' announced Brendan with such authority that actions fell into place straight away. They were rushed past triage and through to an assessment bay where a doctor appeared from nowhere and checked Oliver over.

'I agree,' announced the young doctor. 'The ambulance crew were right. Thank god they were there!'

Lorna looked at Brendan in disbelief, but there was no point in arguing that there had been no ambulance. They had succeeded in accessing immediate attention.

'Right, there is a test for this. I'll need to draw some spinal fluid from his back. In the meantime, I'll get some antibiotics into him straightaway while we wait for the results.'

The doctor went about her business as other staff joined them to assist. Oliver was quickly wired up to a monitor and antibiotics were pumped intravenously straight into his bloodstream.

Amazingly quickly, the test results came back as positive.

'It's a serious condition, but at least we know what we are dealing with. It's good that you got him here so promptly; time is of the essence with this disease.'

'We came here straight away. Teddy nor I have even had any breakfast and my Daddy's dead!' announced Ruby.

'What exactly do you mean?' asked Lorna, becoming upset as the doctor looked on bemused by Ruby's comments.

'Put simply, the quicker that treatment is applied, the greater the chances of recovery, and the lesser chances of damage and long term consequences,' explained the doctor.

'What sort of consequences? How serious is this?'

'I'm sorry to have to tell you that meningitis can be fatal, although thankfully not in your son's case. It can leave its mark, however, but at this stage let's be optimistic that your son could make a full recovery.'

'And if he doesn't?' asked Lorna.

'There were many different possible implications, I'm afraid, but none of them life threatening. At his age, I remain hopeful that he will be OK. Try not to worry. He'll need to rest now and let the antibiotics do their job. I'll review him repeatedly during the day. I suggest you and your family, including teddy, have some breakfast.'

'Thank you, doctor,' said Brendan, holding Lorna and Ruby close.

Lorna started to laugh as she noticed that they were all still only half-dressed, but that didn't matter. It was about Oliver and he was what was important.

After breakfast and suitable reassurance, they were advised to go home, get dressed and visit Oliver again later. Lorna wasn't sure but acquiesced after some persuasion.

Back at Lorna's home, Ruby went back to bed and Lorna and Brendan collapsed on the sofa.

'Well done, Brendan. You were marvellous. I'm so glad that you stayed and that you were here. I wouldn't have known what to do without you. He will be OK now, won't he?' said Lorna.

'Yes, I hope so. I think we caught it in time.'

'How did you know about meningitis, Brendan?'

'My brother died from it when he was twelve and I was fourteen. None of us had heard of it and we didn't realise the implications. We kept him at home and tried to look after him, but by the time we sought help it was too late and he was dead. These things stick with you,' replied Brendan, trying not to become upset.

'Thank God you were here with us, Brendan,' replied Lorna, holding him tight.

'At the time, I couldn't help my brother, but I'm delighted to have been able to help Oliver,' he replied quietly.

'What about your event at work?' remarked Lorna as she remembered Brendan's plans for the day.

'Well Lorna, the mark of a good manager is that your team can carry on without you and, in this case, I'm sure they would have been more than able to do so. I'll go in tomorrow and thank them all,' he replied philosophically.

She felt so proud of him.

Later, they all returned to the hospital to visit Oliver. The same young doctor was still on duty and looked very tired.

'How are you and how is he?' asked Lorna as a concerned as any parent could be.

'OK. There have been two c sections, a heart failure and a serious road traffic accident since you left, but I'm fine, I think, thank you. Oliver, isn't it? Yes, he's OK. The antibiotics have done their job, the immediate danger is over and he shows all the signs of making a full recovery. He keeps asking for 'the egg man', if that makes any sense? Go in and see him now. He's sitting up in bed.'

Lorna smiled and they headed to where the doctor had pointed to find a single room with a little boy who was only too pleased to see them all.

'Hello mummy,' he muttered quietly, as Lorna kissed him and tried not to cry.

'Look Oliver, I've drawn you a picture,' said Ruby. 'It's of a magic wizard to make you better.' As she hugged her little brother, he thanked her for the picture.

'Mummy, Daddy really wanted me, before he went to heaven... but 'the egg man' saved me, didn't he, mummy? Can he be my new daddy now?' asked Oliver as everyone else wiped tears from their eyes.

'Yes. Yes darling, he can,' replied his mummy reassuringly.

8. TERRORISM ON OUR STREETS

Chapter 1

Britain 2019

John Grange stood by his office window in London looking out across the city. Only one question recurred, going round and round in his head: could he protect the good citizens of the Capital?

He had recently been appointed to head up a new unit in MI5, the government's internal security department. The unit was created to collate and assess intelligence threats against UK cities. A great deal of information was already known, but it was held in so many different places within the intelligence and security community that a need had been identified to bring it all together in one place for one single aim – to prevent terrorist attacks on the streets of Britain.

As John set about selecting his team and started getting to grips with the task, he began to realise just how widespread and complex the web of intelligence had become. Countless organisations had a stake in this. Vital, small pieces of information could so easily be lost in the morass of data with potentially tragic consequences. John became even more determined to narrow his focus. He had been very clearly tasked to concentrate on drawing together the threads of known intelligence and identifying the most likely groups and individuals who had the will and the capacity to inflict significant harm on the UK population via terrorist attacks.

Some of the team members were selected from personal experience, having worked together before, some by reputation and others to simply offer a different perspective. Erin Cruger, for example, was a young woman with useful experience developed during her work with a variety of foreign intelligence agencies across Europe. She spoke seven languages fluently and had a grasp of several others. Harry Stainer was a stalwart and the natural choice as the anchor man to run the office. Manuel Hermandez was born in Bolivia and had extensive knowledge of South America. Daisy Taylor was a computer whiz kid, an Oxford graduate with a first class degree in international relations. She also specialised in the study of the growth of Muslim fundamentalism and the politics of the Middle East and North Africa.

John himself had a military background in the Intelligence Corps and considerable knowledge of the threats posed from both Russia and China.

Chapter 2

When the team first met there was a definite excitement in the air, with all members well motivated to succeed. Each individual had their own particular experience of terrorism and their reasons for wanting to confront it.

Harry set about organising systems and basic routines, assisted by Daisy who started researching existing intelligence systems and operations to establish links between groups and individuals. As team leader, John was able to brief everyone on some key known targets, figures he had been specifically tasked to monitor.

Secrecy, security and trust were vital to success. Each member had been thoroughly vetted for suitability, reliability and loyalty. The team didn't refer to rank or titles, just first names. Information was strictly encrypted and was never taken out of the secured confines of the office. Targets were referred to by number only and each member of the team lived in designated safe accommodation that was monitored 24/7.

This project was deadly serious and had political support from the very top, including the Prime Minister.

***

After a series of terror-related atrocities on home soil, including the London Bridge attack, concern in the intelligence community heightened. John considered how well prepared they really were to counter the threat. There were gaps in their knowledge, which was inevitable, it went with the territory. However, of greater concern was the recurrent failure to make best use of the information that was available.

Information was regarded as the key, but more than that, the ability to make an assessment and draw reasonable conclusions from it was what really mattered. If you know the opposition has access to explosives, for example, that doesn't necessarily mean that they are planning a bombing, just that they have the capacity. *What factors might lead to them taking action?* John pondered. Often the presence of a 'bomber' and a target had some particular reason, a trigger, held in the moment like an anniversary or a particular event that could raise tension. If all these factors are present, risk becomes both high and imminent, John kept reminding himself.

The reality for the security forces is that such sets of circumstances can come and go all the time, often without incident – so how could they tell which threat might be realised? Well, probably they couldn't, most of the time at least, reasoned John. However, you need to be prepared, ready for both the anticipated and of course the unexpected, the wildcard that no intelligence system could reasonably detect. That is why intelligence remains an inexact 'science'; predictions are more than simply guess work, but less than guaranteed, he used to say.

John came from a military family and remembered his father talking about his experiences in Northern Ireland during the troubles. John himself had seen active service in Iraq and Afghanistan. Previous British army campaigns in Aden, Cyprus and Malaya, for example, pointed to lessons about internal security and peacekeeping. Each campaign had its subtle differences, though modern terrorism presented different challenges again; it was not always clear who your enemy was.

Terrorism respected no boundaries or borders and organisations like ISIS had no notions of any limits to the type of tactics they are prepared to use. Terrorism against civilian targets, potentially anywhere in the world, added a whole new dimension, a frightening prospect and a need to be ever vigilant. If the authorities increased the protection of airports, the terrorists could hit railway stations, if they concentrated on shopping centres, schools or even hospitals could be the target. Some incidents would be planned meticulously over a long period of time, with the prospect of an intelligence leak offering a warning, yet others could be spontaneous; they could be conducted by individuals, not groups who suddenly felt that they could contain their anger no longer. That was why his task was potentially so daunting, but John Grange didn't dwell on the difficulties.

Chapter 3

It wasn't long before senior officers in MI5 and their political masters were keen to see results from their new initiative. John always expected to be under pressure, but even he was surprised by its intensity. Who would strike where, when and how, he was constantly being challenged to declare. It was tempting to succumb to the pressure to offer senior officers something, just to keep them satisfied but John knew that would not work. Diligence and patience were his watch words and that was a strategy he intended to stick to.

***

Monitoring a range of possibilities, John and his team were soon fully occupied. Manuel was analysing drug activity associated with South America. Growing tensions between the south and their northern more powerful neighbour were intensifying, with the possibility of a backlash, potentially against any Western target. Manuel was aware of five significant groups in the UK with criminal drug connections leading back to South America and their potential to seek revenge on a Western country and any friend of the USA was obvious. Nothing on his radar suggested an imminent threat, however.

Erin was keeping her eye on far right and nationalist groups. They had the potential for launching multiple attacks against the established authorities in any European state. At any one time, she was actively monitoring groups and individuals who were known to support a violent response to the apparent complacency of the established elite. One particular group caused her the most concern, however.

Based in Germany, a group calling themselves 'The Sons of Allah' was firmly on the radar of the German authorities. Originally based in Turkey, they sought to disrupt Western power from within and further the cause of Muslim influence. Several incidents in West German cities were attributed to this group. Their known members were subject to tracking and information sharing across Europe between intelligence authorities and restrictions on travel for group members was already in place. Unauthorised travel, though, was of course still possible, although the German authorities claimed to be confident in their ability to detect and intercept it. Erin, however, wasn't so sure. *How could they possibly track all the players?* she wondered. She was also keen to establish any links between this group and the Turkish community here in Britain. Some immigrants settling in Nottingham, for example, had family links back to Turkish refugees in Germany. She started to research social media for any evidence of communication between these groups.

Daisy was concentrating on monitoring those British Muslims known to have travelled to Syria to fight for ISIS. They might intend to return to the UK even more radicalised than before and were now experienced in unofficial operations, including some use of very worrying tactics. Some of her players came from Northern English towns and cities, including Bradford, but most hailed from the West Midlands area, especially Birmingham.

Intelligence coming back from Syria was limited, but some of the ISIS fighters had been identified individually as originally British. She established extensive profiles on three of them – numbers 158, 291 and 754. She was preparing a brief to share with the team later that day.

As members gathered that afternoon, Daisy was pleased with her findings. John summarised the wider picture before inviting her to make her presentation.

'Ok Daisy, the stage is yours,' he said, encouraging her to bring them all up to date. Daisy got up and, using the whiteboard, she wrote down the key points as she spoke.

'Thanks John, let me share with you what I've got on these three terrorists – numbers 158, 291 and 754. They are all male, originally from the Birmingham area, and all third generation British Muslim. These seem to be the most ruthless and dangerous of the currently known players.

158

Radicalised in prison. Believed to have been an early supporter of the ISIS cause, he first visited Syria in December 2012. He then disappeared from view in the UK and was later identified as an active ISIS fighter in Mosel in 2015. He was involved in several atrocities, including the beheading of male civilians and the widespread rape of women. No sightings have been reported of him in Syria since 2018. However, officers in West Midlands have recently spotted him back in his home area, and he is associating with like-minded individuals.

He's not an illegal immigrant, but a British citizen and we had no jurisdiction over his activities whilst he was abroad. The Syrian authorities have no plans to request his extradition and official policy would be for the UK not to cooperate anyway. His status is currently unemployed and he spends much of his time in the local mosque. Our sources within the mosque offer no specific further information at present.'

'Thanks Daisy, so he's effectively dormant at present?' posed John.

'Yes John, indeed, but he has potential. We need to consider why he came home…'

291

Again, currently a UK citizen, he travelled to Turkey to work as a 'courier' in 2003 and is believed to have been a significant player in the drugs supply to UK from Afghanistan via Turkey for many years. However, he was first sighted fighting for ISIS in Aleppo in 2016. He has experience in heavy weapons. He is readily identified by significant scarring down the left side of his body from a fire in 2017. He returned to Turkey and then came back to UK, being smuggled in, we believe, together with a drugs consignment in 2018. Officially therefore he is still not a resident in the UK, but he seems to be working in the restaurant trade in various locations across the West Midlands. He is a current concern.

754

The oldest of the group – and possibly 158's father or uncle. He is also a UK citizen and has no record of travelling abroad. His role seems to be in selecting and preparing suitable young people to go to fight for ISIS in Syria.'

'Well done, Daisy – so what conclusion do you draw from that?' asked John calmly.

'Given they are all in Birmingham, it's not inconceivable that they know or are aware of each other, there could be a link, especially given the likely family connection.'

'Anything tangible to back that up?' asked Harry.

'No, not really – but let's see.'

'Any links established with any other associates?' asked Erin.

'Again, not yet, but I'm watching,' concluded Daisy, pleased with the team's reaction. 'I've been tracking social media as a possible source of evidence if there are connections between these groups.'

'Good. OK folks, let's get back to it. Any leads to suggest intended activity in the Birmingham area, I want to know about it,' announced John.

'Hang on a minute,' said Manuel. One of those profiles sounds familiar. 291, the guy with the burns – I have someone like that who has been noted operating within the drug supply to the UK from Mexico. I wonder if it's the same guy...'

'Check it out between you – that could be important!' responded John.

Chapter 4

The man known as 158.

2000.

On leaving school in Birmingham with no job, plans or prospects, 158 accepted an offer from a local drug dealer to run operations for him across the city. He was provided with a smart new mountain bike and offered good money, so he took the 'job'. No application, no interview, correspondence or induction, just a bike, a bag full of packages and an address list. Money would be collected by someone else, he was assured. Simple, well, until he was apprehended that is.

Later, sitting in his cell for twenty hours a day, 158 wondered what this was all about. The young offender institution was brutal, run largely by white men overseeing mostly black prisoners. Most of the kids he talked to came from nothing; they were from nowhere, with no money and fuck all prospects, other than dealing drugs. There was something wrong here.

With any excuse to get out of his cell, 158 signed up to attend the Muslim prayers session on Friday mornings. The Imam was great, he understood, he made sense of the world – he offered them hope. The Imam told the group about British colonial history, of the domination of Black and Asian people, of slavery, abuse and exploitation. He led them to believe that there would never be justice in a white man's world; that Christians were all evil and that Allah was the only true God.

The more he attended, the more he believed the message and the more he felt affinity with his Muslim brothers. Other prisoners shared stories of white oppression and the more he knew the more he felt that, for him, there was only one true course to take: retaliation, to take revenge. 158 learnt to listen, he learnt to repeat the message and he learnt to hate.

When a man met him outside the prison gate on immediate release, 158 knew that he was with a true friend. The man offered to help him go abroad – to take the fight to the oppressor, work towards an Islamic world and to defeat the infidels. Together with extreme propaganda on the dark web,158 endorsed the narrative.

By the time he arrived in Syria and things weren't quite as they seemed or what he expected, he was experiencing the early seeds of doubt, but it was made very clear to him that there was no turning back. Allah would not forgive him and in this world retribution would be swift and brutal. 158 saw the consequences of attempts to question or to refuse to cooperate. He was there and that was where he belonged, like it or not, for better or worse. If he thought life was hard in the training camp, he was deluded; much worse was to come. The experience of fighting the Assad regime was beyond anything he could have imagined, the level of sheer brutality, the casualty rate, the impact on local civilians, the level of destruction… it was all near impossible to bear.

It was also unrelenting, never ending, day after day the same unless you were killed. He often wondered if that was preferable to carrying on…

There were other aspects that distressed and disgusted him too. The propaganda war was almost as bad as the conflict it supported, with its twisted interpretations, selective presentation and outright lies. Both sides engaged in this, he acknowledged, but the pious, self righteous and indignant line from the West he found repugnant. There were many incidents, but one in particular haunted him – the bombing of a school.

The West had the advantage of scale; they had a vast force, professional armies and overwhelming resources. Mass bombing was an obvious tactic, but it was indiscriminate. The phrase 'collateral damage' did no justice to the innocents who lost their lives. On this one occasion, a school was in the wrong place and was hit and destroyed completely. If the West were the moral superiors, as they claimed, why didn't they simply admit they'd made a mistake rather than attempt to blame ISIS or the very people who were killed?

Whilst the war was terrible, the bitterness, the resentment and the deeply ingrained hate continued to grow inside him. At times it seemed too much to bear. If it was not for his dear friend who he knew from a child, 158 believed he wouldn't have made it. The support and comradeship of a friend made the difference for both of them; although they rarely actually fought together, they were together in spirit.

Yes, his friend was very important to him, a friend the West referred to as 291.

Despite the concerns, the contradictions and the horror, 158 tried to continue to believe he was on the right side, that he was fighting for something worth fighting for.

**

When 158 eventually returned to Britain, still as a British citizen, he found the transition difficult. Whilst he was glad to be away from Syria, he felt uncomfortable leaving the fight uncompleted. He also felt unwanted and out of step with life in Britain. The media only ever portrayed ISIS as bad. There was no acknowledgement that an independent Islamic state was a legitimate aspiration for many Muslims. Also, all those who had chosen to fight in Syria were regarded as having somehow been persuaded against their will, but that wasn't entirely true either. No, he felt isolated. He was neither comfortable with the reality of ISIS nor did he feel fully accepted in Britain. Whether through ISIS or not, he still felt that an independent Islamic state was worth fighting for.

291felt even more angry. He was keen to reap revenge on the surrogate homeland that denied his heritage and assumed the right to demand his loyalty.

Both looked for answers to these dilemmas and the only person offering solutions was 754. He promised them the opportunity to have their justice and revenge and to strike a blow for Muslim freedom. He promised them that Allah would approve of their actions and reward them in the next life – that they would be heroes.

Chapter 5

Britain 2019

Manuel's research identified that 291 was indeed the man responsible for securing deals in Mexico to smuggle drugs back to the UK. This man had significant contacts and it seemed he was far more than just a foot soldier.

Both Erin and John instinctively felt that there was more to know about 754. What was his relationship to the other two players? How far was he involved in the planning aspect of any terrorist intentions? And, most importantly, who else might be involved that they didn't yet know about?

John was due to attend a meeting with his superior later that day, who would no doubt be expecting to hear of some progress. John was always careful what he relayed up the chain because he knew that his superior would read between the lines – she was very astute after all. John was always aware of the pressure on teams to be able to reveal a breakthrough of some sort, and the tendency for information to be inflated at each stage it was reported, with the consequent risk of it being over interpreted. It was not quite 'Chinese whispers' but the slightest hint of intelligence could so easily be talked up to represent unequivocal fact. The Justification for invading Iraq had been based on such a premise, with its 'sexed up dossier' that later was found to be wanting.

Intelligence was always incomplete, reflected John, and it was important to remember that. There was the risk of seeing what you wanted to see, of making loose ends fit, even if they didn't. John was stoic at resisting the easy criticisms levelled by the hindsight brigade when things went wrong and that gave his team confidence. There was no need to jump the gun yet. Solid reliable intelligence with good analysis and reasonable conclusions was his business. He was not drawn to wild speculation.

Harry, working quietly in the background, received a report from West Midlands Police siting concerns about radicalising activity centred round several of the local mosques. One man's 'radicalisation' could be another man's 'religious teachings' at the margins. *However, using culture to incite hatred or to recruit impressionable young people to inflict serious harm on random innocent members of the public, had no place in any religion*, he thought.

Harry studied the report in detail, trying to assimilate what it told him, but inevitably it led to further questions. There were enough indications of people in the UK who were potentially willing to commit terrorist atrocities, but the key questions of where, when and by what means remained unknown.

Harry checked his information systems to look for any other updates on available intelligence from a wide variety of sources and one report caught his eye. It was an analysis of the common links between all the vehicle-related terrorist attacks over the last two years. Hiring a van was easy and using it as a weapon was effective from the terrorist's point of view. It was unpredictable, presented a moving target and could potentially strike anywhere and anytime. The various incidents weren't directly related, let alone coordinated, but were there any patterns, any clues that might help detect or prevent any future similar attacks?

Harry was deep in thought, systematically working his way through various possibilities and different scenarios that could occur. *If that was still the likely method, then what might be the target?* he wondered.

In London the attack on the bridge was a high profile site, but was it spontaneous or was it deliberately selected as the target? Harry wasn't clear which. Trying to see things from the terrorist's point of view, if the target area was Birmingham, and that of course was a major assumption, what would they go for? What would represent a fundamental attack on Western democracy? The council building in the central square? One of the museums? A church? A military establishment? The list could go on. *There was no certainty, which is the nature of the game*, he reminded himself.

John walked through the building. He reached the secure meeting room to join the select few participants in this particular forum. His boss would be in the chair, a senior military representative and other members of both MI5 and MI6 would all be present.

John presented a concise summary of the current intelligence picture from his team's perspective and the others nodded in agreement. There were several indications that all seemed to confirm a reasonable conclusion that the risk to the UK of a serious terrorist attack remained high. Nothing more specific, nothing more certain than that.

John felt instinctively that the next incident would not be in the capital. He favoured Birmingham as the target, but he accepted that it could easily be Leeds,

Manchester or Liverpool, or any other major city. The kudos lay with the cities, he felt sure. They considered what anniversaries were due, or any other reason to favour any particular date or any particular place. No firm conclusion was reached as the meeting ended.

Chapter 6

A call was reported to Harry. A manager of several car hire outlets in West Midlands had rung the police to report a man making enquiries at several different places about car hire. It was strange that he seemed so interested in the carrying capacity of the cars and several staff had asked him what he intended to carry and he became very defensive and left. It was reported as unusual and suspicious.

Carrying capacity, Harry wondered, *was that an indication of wanting to transport something heavy?* A bomb possibly packed in something metal to cause maximum damage and or injury? He asked for the cooperation of the police to pick him up; they had quite a comprehensive description.

The police response was less than enthusiastic.

'We can't just arrest somebody for making enquiries about car hire,' said the control room operator.

'Can you at least stop him and see how he reacts – is he calm or does he panic? If you can get a DNA sample, that would help; a single hair will do,' responded the MI5 duty officer, but he wasn't hopeful.

A message was passed to all patrol cars in the area and one driver did notice a man walking along the pavement that looked like the description they'd been given. He pulled over next to him as his mate wound down the window. The guy acted cool but the experienced officer could detect some anxiety. He engaged him in conversation and asked if he'd seen a fictitious child who had been reported missing and the man said he hadn't. The officer thanked him for his cooperation and, as he turned to walk away, he noticed a fine hair blowing in the wind attached to his wing mirror, where the man had leaned over to talk to him. He retrieved it as they'd been instructed to and they drove on.

When this was reported back to Harry, he was inclined to go along with the officer's intuition. In due course, the hair revealed an interesting result. There was a significant match with 158, who had provided a DNA sample whilst under arrest prior to going to prison. It seemed likely that they were brothers or at least cousins. There was still the suspicion that 754 was related to one or both of them. Now it seemed likely, if anything, that he was a link between the two of them, a father or uncle possibly, Harry speculated.

Then came a break; the car hire manager was able to report that the driving licence the man was using when enquiring about cars was suspicious – he suspected it was forged. The police had asked how he might know and the manager said that they dealt with quite a lot of possibly forged licences and, if they hired a vehicle in those circumstances, they didn't always get the car back, so they noted it. Right, thought Harry, the police can arrest him on that.

Things moved quickly as the arrest was made, the suspicious nature of his car hire enquires and his potential relationship to significant others was pointed out to him and the man started to crack. It didn't take long for the investigating officers to get a pretty firm indication from the guy that he had been tasked with finding a car capable of carrying a heavy bomb. He claimed to know no more – no idea of what use, where or when, might be intended, but it was a strong indication that the threat related to a bombing.

When 754 heard that his runner had been intercepted by the police, he was not impressed. The man was immediately brought to him and his answers provided no reassurance.

Earlier that day, the same guy was spotted being driven around Stafford in a Mitsubishi 4x4 visiting the County Show Ground, Shugborough and County Hospital, before showing an interest in Weston Park on his way to Wolverhampton and back to Birmingham.

Harry drew together the available shreds of information. They had a potential terrorist cell, a method, a means of delivery but still no indication of when or exactly where. The tour around Stafford could indicate a preference for a tourist or large public destination. Maybe this was a dry run? He couldn't be sure. He wanted to interview the man again to see if they could gain any further clarification and asked the police to pick him up.

Chapter 7

Several weeks later.

Sam Cartwright was proudly driving his newly acquired Land Rover into Wolverhampton. Sam was a fire fighter. He was off duty today and enjoying a spin in his new vehicle. He had always had a fascination with Land Rovers and felt so proud now to finally own one. He drove along the Cannock road towards the city centre. Traffic was light and it was a lovely late afternoon. His bluetooth phone rang – it was fire station control.

'Sam, there's a report of a major fire at the Wanderers ground; we're calling all available staff to come in. Crews have been called from all surrounding counties. This is a genuine emergency, can you respond?'

'Yes of course, but I'm just driving past the Wanderers ground now and I can assure you there is no sign of any serious fire here!' he responded.

Harry heard the response. *So what's this?* he thought, *a faint to draw the emergency services in the wrong direction, so the danger would be on the other side of the region?*

'What's happening across West Midlands tonight then?' he asked.

Erin looked up the options quickly.

'There's a major event at Coventry Cathedral tonight, boss.'

'That will be it then – it's such an iconic site for us that it's where they will want to strike. Put out an emergency warning on all networks, Daisy. We need to get people there in numbers.'

Cars raced across the city.

'Who's attending, Daisy?' asked John urgently.

'The French President, amongst others.'

'That's it, the link – the French treatment of Muslims has been very contentious, particularly in Paris. There were riots there last week. He's the target, but with one hit potentially they could cause major damage!' responded John as he left to make a call.

'What time does the event start, Daisy?' asked Harry.

'Seven o'clock.'

'Then we've got two hours.'

The whole team were fully alert as the realisation of what they faced unfolded, assuming of course that John was right and Coventry Cathedral was the target…

'Try again to get the police to pull in that guy they interviewed earlier. He might know more than he disclosed.'

Daisy made the call.

John came back into the room.

'On what we've got, the response from No10 is that they are not prepared to cancel the event at the Cathedral at this short notice. Even if they did, there would still be large crowds present who would offer a target for the terrorists. We can't mount a full armed response operation in time, so we will have to do what we can. The West Midlands Police anti-terrorist branch are in command now and have deployed officers already. We've played our part. Now all we can do is wait,' said John with a heavy heart.

Chapter 8

Six o'clock

Road blocks and traffic restrictions were in place across Coventry. A police helicopter was in the air. Local hospitals had been alerted. The authorities wanted to be as prepared as possible without making an open announcement and risk causing mass panic.

Firearms officers were deployed on nearby roof tops with comprehensive views all round the Cathedral.

The French President had been informed and his personal guard were on high alert. He was due to land soon by helicopter. The landing site was changed at the last minute, just in case.

The Mayor of the city, the Dean of the Cathedral and a long list of dignitaries were either already in place or on their way. There comes a point when cancelling an event becomes unrealistic. The operational commander took the view that to try to evacuate such large numbers of people at such short notice was likely to cause even more problems. There were no indications of a bomb already having been placed in the area. He put his faith in being able to intercept the possible would be bomber. They knew some of the likely players and that the vehicle involved would need to be strong enough the carry any device. Wherever it set off from, it would have to use the local road network and he was confident that would be its demise.

Just before landing, the French contingent changed their minds and decided not to land after all. That was one less piece of the jigsaw at least, responded the operational commander.

Harry wanted to press the police again on any progress with interviewing the man they had previously identified.

'Have they found him yet, Daisy?' he asked.

'Yes, they have, but he won't be any use to us, boss,' she replied.

'Why ever not?'

'Because he's dead. His body was found fifteen minutes ago. He'd been executed, shot in the head and dumped in a skip outside an industrial estate near Oldbury.'

'Killed by his own people presumably? Either for saying too much, or to ensure he said no more,' Harry speculated. 'That's a shame,' he added. 'Now that source of information is no longer available to us. We must try harder. We need greater clarity around where and when they might strike.'

***

In the meantime, Sam Cartwright was driving past Wolverhampton via West Bromwich on his way back home in Birmingham. His colleagues at fire service central control were still trying to sort out the chaos created by mounting a major alert in response to a false alarm. Crews from surrounding counties had already set off and had to be stood down and told to return to base. All the local off-duty staff who had rushed into work were also sent home.

By fifteen minutes before seven, no interception of any suspicious vehicles had been reported. The crowds were gathered around the Cathedral and tensions were high in the various control rooms and operational command centres across the West Midlands. Traffic levels were reported as normal and the road blocks and other restrictions were operating fully. All officers were on high alert as the clock ticked down towards the hour.

'How long is the event scheduled to last, Daisy?'

'It's due to be all over by ten, Harry.'

'They might not be targeting the start of the event, it could be anytime between now and ten,' John reminded them.

It was just nearly seven o'clock as Sam approached The Hawthorns – West Bromwich Albion's football ground. A match was still due to kick off at seven thirty as he pulled up at traffic lights next to a white transit van. Sam glanced across at two men of Asian origin, both of whom he instantly thought looked shifty.

The lights had only just turned red and both vehicles had to wait for some time. It seemed like ages as the two men in the van appeared to get more and more anxious and agitated. Amber, green, both vehicles moved off. Sam could see a long queue of supporters lined up on the pavement waiting to enter the ground. Then everything happened so fast.

As he got nearer to the queue of people, Sam noticed the white van again coming up next to him and starting to pass him on the inside. *What was he doing?* he thought. *You can't pass me on that lane.* Then the thought struck him –the recent terrorist attacks, the use of a white van, the TV images of a vehicle ploughing into a crowded place and killing innocent civilians. The look of determination on the men's faces – *was that what they intended doing?* he wondered.

The traffic stopped again at the next set of lights and Sam found himself behind two vehicles and the van again in the same lane. As they started to move forward, suddenly the white van darted to the left, cutting across the traffic and heading towards the crowd. There was no time to think, reactions needed to be instinctive. Sam thrust his Land Rover down into second gear and roared forward as fast as he could to cut off the van before it reached the crowd. By which time, other drivers had become alert to the fact that something wasn't right.

Calls started coming into the police control room. A patrol car was close enough to head straight away to the football ground and arrived at the scene just in time to see a Land Rover intercept a white van dangerously close to the line of waiting fans. There was a loud crash as the two vehicles collided. The Land Rover's low centre of gravity and sturdy construction, relative to the transit, meant it hit the van hard in the side and toppled it over. It skidded nosily across the road and back into the line of traffic. It stopped suddenly as a heavy lorry was the first vehicle to face it sliding along. The loud crash of metal, alongside the smell of tyres and brakes, filled the air as the lorry pulled up and the queue of supporters dispersed in a panic in all directions. Thankfully, nobody had been hit, but fear was clearly in the air.

Sam stopped his Land Rover and got out to survey the damage. Although he was obviously pleased to have stopped the van, he was devastated to see the mess that his actions had made of the side of his pride and joy. People from the crowd came over to thank and congratulate him as they saw the two dishevelled and stunned men emerge from the wreckage of the van in time to meet two burly police officers.

It was only just starting to dawn on Sam what a difference his swift action might have made and he was warmed by the genuine affection he received from the supporters, who wrapped him in 'baggies' scarves and adorned his head with a suitable supporter's hat. The officers efficiently steered the two men away into a waiting car whilst others started to coordinate the wider emergency response. The road would need to be cleared and, although there were no obvious signs of injury, ambulances were called to be on hand.

Chapter 9

Eight O'clock.

Back at MI5, John and his team were eagerly following events and praised the brave intervention of the fire fighter. The potential terrorist incident at The Hawthorns thankfully had been avoided, but was that an end to it or was it merely a further distraction designed to draw attention away from the main incident in Coventry? They still didn't know.

At the Cathedral, the event was going ahead as planned with large crowds gathered to hear the service. The authorities had to hold their nerve. None of the public at that time would be aware of the potential danger they faced, or might have faced. The armed police officers were still in place and a discrete but significant force was available on the ground as well as the helicopter overhead.

As the eyes of our guardians watched intently, the arrangements for the event at the Cathedral unfolded as planned. Both the dignitaries inside the building and the large crowd outside were all still potentially vulnerable. They watched and they waited.

Routine reports continued to be logged. Then, an alert; a man was spotted carrying a medium-sized rucksack on his back. He appeared to be Asian, and he looked nervous. He was apparently alone and walking towards the Cathedral and would potentially mingle with the crowd within minutes. Was he a suicide bomber? Immediate actions followed as police officers on the ground rushed to intercept the young man.

As they approached him, he began to run and the officers gave chase, bringing him down quickly. The rucksack was ripped from his back to reveal several books, a jotting pad, a pencil case and the remnants of a packed lunch. On enquiry, it rapidly transpired that the young man was a perfectly innocent and legitimate student returning to his accommodation from the University library. When asked for an explanation of why he looked so nervous and why he ran, he simply stated that he always felt nervous at the sight of the police and, of course, he ran when they started to follow him.

Then came a report from officers on the outskirts of the city; a road block on the A45 towards Coventry had intercepted another white van, not a car as first thought, and it had been stopped. It was suspiciously low on its axles. Two men in the cab had been apprehended and were readily identified as 158 and 291.

A thorough search of the van revealed a suspicious consignment before the two terrorists could react and possibly activate the device they were carrying in the back. It was clearly an improvised explosive device capable of causing serious harm. It was later estimated to comprise of fifty pounds of semtex explosive packed into a beer keg. The rest of the van was filled with further kegs packed with nails and other metal fragments.

If this had gone off, it had the potential to be one of the worst terrorist atrocities on UK soil ever; tens if not hundreds of people could have been killed or seriously injured. The members of the emergency services at the scene were shocked by the scale and callousness of the incident. Most of the passers-by and other road users would remain oblivious to their lucky escape until, of course, they saw the news reports later.

THE AFTERMATH

After the initial clearing up, operations had been completed, including the arrest of 754, the authorities could breathe a sigh of relief and reflect on lessons learnt.

For the politicians, there were great claims of insight, wisdom and stoic decision making of Churchillian proportions in the face of extreme provocation. For the intelligence and police community, the relief was more heartfelt. They acknowledged that they had been lucky on this occasion and it might not always go their way. The processes set up to counter precisely this type of threat had worked effectively. Despite the inherent scale of communication and coordination required, cooperation was deemed to have been effective. Information had been carefully logged, assessed and analysed. Nothing had been assumed, nothing had been inflated and nothing pertinent had been ignored.

Although, as ever, attempts at prediction were of limited success, enough was known to surmise the 'who', some of the 'how', eventually part of the 'where' and later on the 'when'. Thankfully, this had proved to be enough.

There was no room for complacency, however. After all, only two of the four terrorists were known to them, suggesting that there were still a significant number of unknown activists who were still operating and posing a threat.

Further action was also needed in relation to social media. Open access to the internet and the availability of the dark web challenged the principle of a free society. It was felt that greater restrictions were necessary on the type of material posted on the net, in the interests of public safety.

The terrorists' attempts to throw them off the scent had been challenging, particularly the deliberate distraction at the Wanderers ground. Calling in extra forces then discharging them home would have undoubtedly caused confusion if they had been needed to be recalled again later, in the event of a successful attack at The Hawthorns.

Counter measures such as were deployed, however, were reactive, to secure longer term stability more was needed. Whatever made those young men so disaffected needed to be addressed. How they were allowed to travel to Syria had to be questioned and, likewise, why there wasn't a better, more systematic vetting process in place for their return needed to be challenged.

Attempts at inclusion and cohesion, however, needed to be tempered with realism. The notion that some things were too sensitive to challenge had to be questioned and reassessed, to the extent that the idea that some British mosques were being used as a centre for terrorist recruitment needed addressing, without fear or favour.

The challenge to the world to accommodate difference and live in harmony, it seemed, remained a distant dream. There was still a long way to go.

At least Sam was rewarded for his efforts and his bravery as Wolverhampton Wanderers, West Bromwich Albion and Coventry City offered to jointly fund the repairs to his Land Rover, with the work being completed at the plant in Coventry. Many of the workers assigned to the project had, in fact, been present at either the matches or the service involved and were only too happy to help – a small but significant gesture of kindness that stood in contrast to hate.

9. Ruth's story – swimming against the tide

Chapter 1

Ruth had known Eddie since she was a child. They grew up together living in difficult circumstances on a crumbling housing estate on the wrong side of town.

Their parents struggled to hold things together and experienced periods of separation. They were often unemployed or just managing in a series of insecure and short-term low-paid jobs. The only people doing well on the estate it seemed were the drug dealers, but in exchange for apparent endless wealth their lives were brutal, dangerous and often short.

Education was disrupted through eviction, constant changes of address, apathy and the general chaos of an unstructured, dysfunctional life style.

For Ruth, the regular arrival of mum's new partners, the promise of better things to come followed by the crushing disappointment of failure was the constant grinding reality of modern poverty.

She did at least manage to avoid a descent into drug abuse, teenage pregnancy or drifting into the world of criminal sanctions, institutionalisation and despair. She had an energetic nature, a relaxed attitude of acceptance and an ability, despite all the hurdles, to identify the good side of most situations.

In short, from an early age, Ruth decided to be a survivor and not allow herself to be defined as a victim.

Chapter 2

Ruth had seen various family members and people she had met along the way fall foul of chaos and deprivation. She was sorry, but didn't dwell on it. It only served to harden her resolve to avoid the same fate. Eddie, however, was not so fortunate. He fell for the illusion of the excitement and the status of crime from a young age and graduated through the levels of state intervention, from school welfare, through youth courts to probation and youth custody. Ruth still felt what she readily acknowledged was a kind of fatal attraction to Eddie for all his faults. He had represented one of the few constants in her life and for that she was prepared to forgive him almost anything. He was probably the only person she had ever loved.

Eddie was due for his latest release on licence from custody. He had given his parents' address as his release address but had no intension of staying there. He wanted to be with Ruth, but accepted that her tenancy was hers and that suited them both. Was she looking forward to his return? She wasn't sure. Ruth had managed to build the basics of a home from scratch with nothing. She bought from charity shops and collected things from skips. Work was always intermittent and the benefit system had never coped well with that. She got by – just. She must have been the only single woman in her block without a child, nor did she have a dog. She was self reliant and proud.

Eddie arrived at her flat late on the day of his release having called in to see his mum, reported to probation and been to the pub with a few mates. There was a tradition of buying drinks for those known locally who were just released from prison and by the time he reached Ruth he was the worse for wear. She smelt the booze on him as she opened the door and told him 'to piss off and come back tomorrow.'

He slept on a mate's sofa, shuffled back round to Mum's in the morning for a shower. He presented himself, clean and tidy, at Ruth's door with some flowers he had just nicked from the garden of a house down the road. This time she smiled and invited him in, accepting the flowers whilst not admitting she recognised where they'd come from.

'Right Eddie, let's get a few things straight – if you're staying, give us your discharge grant now and get down to the job centre today. No 'my mate will offer me a few hours doing something dodgy and we'll get by'. No we won't. You need to be working. Did they teach you anything in that prison then, Eddie?'

'Yes, lots of things. You see, there's this scam where you can make…'

'No Eddie, did they teach you anything that will help you get a proper job?' Ruth enquired with distant hope.

'Um, sweeping the floor, clearing the rubbish off the wing, scrubbing the toilets, that sort of thing.'

'Yeah, that's not going to get you nowhere, is it? Didn't you do no education or nuffing?'

'Yeah, a bit but the woman did my head in so I sacked it.'

'Where do you see yourself in five years time, Eddie?'

'On the Costa Brava with you, darling, and with a beer in my hand!' he replied, with his usual brash and misplaced confidence.

Chapter 3

Eddie did manage to get a job with a local project that specialised in helping ex-offenders. They offered initial paid employment and move on opportunities to better jobs if you proved yourself. He got through his licence without recall to prison and even stayed out of trouble, at least for a while.

Ruth became pregnant and Eddie bought her a puppy. Their change in circumstances seemed to motivate Eddie and Ruth was pleased initially, until she began to wonder how his earnings had suddenly taken off.

'Hi Ruth, I've managed to get some more stuff for the baby!' Eddie announced as he crashed into the flat.

'Eddie, where is all this stuff coming from?' she enquired.

'What do you mean, aren't you pleased?'

'It's not nicked, is it Eddie?'

'No, more like borrowed from mates, like – mates who owe me a favour.'

'You mean they've nicked it and you're now in debt to them?' Ruth speculated before rushing to the sink to throw up.

'You alright, girl?' he asked.

'Yes Eddie. I'm pregnant, remember?'

'I didn't think it was a beer gut!'

The door bell rang and a mate of Eddie's warned him to make himself scarce as 'the Afghan boys' were about. Eddie shot out of the flat and down the back stairs, leaving Ruth wondering. She knew 'the Afghan boys', they all did. They were ruthless local drug dealers and racketeers – bad news in other words. If Eddie was mixed up with them then that spelt trouble, she thought.

Ruth answered the door and stood her ground.

'Where's Eddie?' they asked.

'Don't know, and he doesn't do that stuff. I don't want you here,' Ruth responded.

'We weren't asking for an invitation. Looks like you're going to need a little side line.'

She assured them that she was not interested and shut the door. Later that day, when Eddie sneaked back in, Ruth challenged him about any association with the drug dealers. He denied it, of course, but she knew he was lying. She just hoped that he wasn't in too deep already.

Chapter 4

Tensions mounted between Ruth and Eddie, with her desperately wanting and hoping that he would become responsible and him dismissing her concerns as unnecessary worry. Ruth wanted to move to a better flat before the baby was due and hoped that Eddie could take the next step on from the project towards more reliable employment.

He had done well learning skills in bicycle repair and the project had offered him several contacts in that field. There was the potential of securing him stable and reasonably secure employment. Ruth tried to persuade him to take it. Eddie reassured her that he would; he accepted that with a baby coming along he had to move on from his previous lifestyle and accept the reality of employment rather than the haphazard and hollow reassurance of the criminal world. Ruth felt so relieved to hear it and dared to hope for a better future.

Eddie took the job and they moved into a bigger flat before the baby was born. They all struggled with the adjustment of accommodating Aaron at first and, at times, both Ruth and Eddie wondered what they had really done, although they never shared those feelings.

Eddie did try to settle into a more conventional routine but the novelty soon wore off and he was getting more and more irritable, agitated and, if he was honest, bored. A criminal lifestyle could be dangerous and unpredictable, but at least that offered a measure of excitement beyond the mundane. He was still dabbling in this and that, but it wasn't the same. Then a chance came up to take a risk. He became aware of a lucrative scam that the Afghan boys were running and worked out how they collected their money. He reasoned that they had already made plenty of it so they wouldn't miss a bit. Eddie set out to collect on their behalf, not thinking it through or anticipating the dangers of getting involved with this gang, let alone trying to pull this off.

When he moved in on the collection point the holdall was waiting. He simply collected it and left. He walked a short distance before hiding behind a wall to check its contents. The bag was full of bundled used twenty pound notes. More money than he had ever seen. His eyes bulged and his pace raced as he quickly zipped it back up again and continued at pace to return to the flat. Ruth was still asleep in bed. Aaron was just waking so Eddie set about his morning routine, leaving the holdall on the hall floor.

Later that day at work, he returned to the project for a review of his progress. The place was buzzing with rumours. The lad who had alerted him to the scam was apparently aware that a collection on behalf of the Afghan boys had been 'intercepted' and that they were furious. Wild speculation followed about the likely retribution to be handed down to the idiot who had chosen to try to scam the scammers! Eddie tried not to listen, but as the day progressed he became increasingly alarmed and concerned for his own safety. He panicked. He ran. He didn't dare return to the flat so instead he jumped a train to get away as quickly as possible.

Back in the flat, Ruth had taken over Aaron's supervision as Eddie had left for work. The boy was six months old now and doing well. Ruth was still finding it hard but was coping. She was in the kitchen when they arrived looking for Eddie. There were shouts, the door was smashed in and a line of officers entered the flat. The last thing Ruth was expecting was a raid by the police.

She challenged their authority for this intrusion as they quickly searched for Eddie and confirmed what she was telling them; he was not there. As Ruth protested her innocence, one of the officers noticed the holdall and opened it. Ruth was arrested for handling stolen goods. Her protests about having no knowledge of the holdall fell on deaf ears as she was led away screaming, 'What about the baby?' Social Services were called and arrived promptly to secure the child and take him to foster parents as an immediate response.

Chapter 5

The police had been watching the Afghan boys and were aware of their latest scam. They weren't aware of Eddie's exact involvement but knew that he was on the fringe of things. His was therefore one of the addresses identified for a raid to seek stolen goods or drugs. Ruth had been caught red handed with £10,000 of stolen money in her possession and, as the tenant of the property, was guilty of handling stolen goods. She was interviewed and charged, produced before a court the following morning and remanded in custody awaiting committal to crown court.

Sentenced to five years, Ruth sat on her prison bed and cried. All her efforts to overcome adversity, all her misplaced faith in Eddie, all her hopes for Aaron, all were in tatters as it seemed she had lost them all. She had no involvement in the stolen cash – she hadn't even been aware that the holdall was in her flat. She assumed Eddie had brought it home, but she didn't even know that.

Neither her solicitor nor her barrister offered much comfort or took much notice about her pleas of innocence. The evidence as far as they were concerned was clear and unequivocal – stolen money had been recovered by the police in her possession. It was as simple as that.

The probation officer in court was at least a little more sympathetic to her plight and understanding of the implications for her. Ruth had wanted to fight her corner and went to crown court intending to plead not guilty, but her barrister had advised her in no uncertain terms that her chances of winning were virtually non-existent and if she persisted with a trial it would only result in a longer sentence, and the probation officer had agreed. This can't be right, she still felt, that just because someone dumps some dodgy money in your flat you end up with five years, but that was simply how it was.

Once she had got over the initial shock and sense of injustice, Ruth concentrated her energy on frantic negotiations with her family and social services to place her son with her mother or her half sister whilst she was inside. It took time but her persistence paid off when eventually the authorities agreed that her mother was a suitable person to offer the child a home and, after six months in foster care, Aaron was moved back to his family. He was too young to understand what had happened to his mother and, initially at least, the family were reluctant to take him to visit her. Ruth had to endure the separation and Aaron had to live with the disruption and deceit.

The RSPA had taken away the dog and the council recovered the flat. What few possessions were salvaged by the family remained at her mother's. On eventual release, Ruth would have to start again and fight to have Aaron returned to her. Another terrible blow and consequence of this crazy situation, she discovered.

Chapter 6

Eddie arrived at the door of one of his half brothers'
some considerable distance from home. His brother
let him in without enthusiasm and agreed that he
could stay for a while, but there was no spare room,
so Eddie would have to sleep on the sofa. Fortunately
for him, the bicycle shop he was working at was a
chain and they were able to offer him an alternative
placement and a transfer to a different shop, one that
was conveniently close to his brothers.

Eddie had tried to explain to his family over the
phone what had happened and he was genuinely
shocked and horrified to learn what had happened to
Ruth and Aaron, let alone the dog. He didn't expect
them to either believe him or offer any sympathy. He
was out in the cold as far as they were concerned.
Eddie assumed that he had blown it with Ruth and
didn't see the point in trying to make amends; he felt
he knew her well enough to know that was not going
to be possible and he couldn't blame her. He managed
to get a room in a hostel and moved out of his
brother's. Whilst Eddie had tried to do his best for
Aaron, he didn't feel that he was able to look after
him now, on his own. He was pleased when he heard
that Ruth's mum had been allowed to have the child.
He did speak to Aaron on the phone, but he didn't
dare to visit.

It was sometime later, whilst working in the shop,
that Eddie became aware of a customer. One of the
other staff had offered to help the man but Eddie had
heard the response that it was him he was looking for.

'Hi Eddie,' said the man of Asian appearance. 'I hope you didn't think we'd forgotten you! It was so kind of one of the others to let us know that you'd moved up here and were now working in this shop. Well, we are so pleased to have found you.'

Eddie looked up in horror as he immediately recognised the man as one of 'the Afghan boys'.

Chapter 7

Neither Eddie's family nor Ruth were ever sure what exactly had happened to Eddie, but it seemed that he had effectively disappeared. He didn't return to the hostel one day nor report for work the following day. The police didn't seem interested and no trace of him was forthcoming. Ruth speculated that the gang wouldn't have let it go once they knew that Eddie had taken their money. All she could hope for was that retribution had been swift. She tried not to dwell on it, but he had been her man and the father of her child after all, and she still loved him.

Ruth tried to make something of the opportunities available in prison. She brushed up her basic education, having missed so much at school. She worked in the hairdressing salon, learning basic skills of cutting and styling hair. This was the sort of work she could do outside, she reasoned, and still be able to look after Aaron. Ruth learnt quickly how to survive in prison, to watch your back, not get too close to anyone and steer well clear of those who obviously represented trouble. Neither did she side with 'the enemy', she had no wish to be a source of information to staff. Ruth simply wanted to get through her sentence as quickly as possible and get home to be with Aaron.

It wasn't too long before she became eligible for home leave and could spend short periods of time back home with her mum and her son. The excitement of going and the pain of leaving were intense but nevertheless worth holding on to, to help her get through her sentence.

When the time came for her release at the half way point, Aaron was just three. Ruth would spend time on licence in the community, supervised by the probation service, and she would remain on trust for the rest of her sentence.

The day came – the few possessions that she had with her were all returned from prison stores and she walked through the gate with her discharge grant, some money that she'd earned on a work out scheme from the prison in a local hairdressers, and her rail ticket. She waited eagerly at the bus stop and was able to ring home and speak to both her mum and Aaron and reassure them that she was coming home. Aaron was so excited. He still had little understanding about what had happened, but had got used to the routine of mum's regular visits without too much upset. It was the adults who suffered the emotional turmoil of separation, for the child the impact was less visible, although it was no doubt still there.

Aaron didn't ask after his father. Little was said at home about Eddie and, of course, little was actually known for certain, although the family felt it was obvious that the gang were behind his apparent disappearance.

Chapter 8

Adjustment – resettlement was its official title – whatever it was it was difficult, that was for sure. Ruth was not used to living back with her mother and had to rebuild her relationship with Aaron and try to be sensitive about taking back primary caring responsibilities from her mother. Ruth still missed Eddie. She hadn't seen him or heard from him since he had left for work that day. After all that had happened, she had not had any opportunity to say goodbye. She wasn't even sure whether he was still alive, although she felt it most likely that he wasn't. A body had never been found and the police missing person's file was still open, although inactive. In truth, officially nobody really cared. Eddie remained just lost and unaccounted for with no likely prospect of resolution. That was the most difficult thing to live with. It was an experience familiar to the generation who had lived through the war; the status of 'missing, presumed killed' left the same unknowns and uncertainties. Relatives who shared that experience tried to offer Ruth some understanding, but it was still hard.

After a period of reflection and sadness that she assumed was what people referred to as 'grieving', Ruth tried to move on and concentrate on rebuilding her life with Aaron. She started work as a hairdresser and secured the tenancy of a new flat. There was little left of her old life but family and friends were generous in helping her re-establish herself.

Then there was Phil. He came into the shop one day and enquired if they cut men's hair too and, before the proprietor could respond that they didn't, Ruth had invited the man to sit in her chair and was already in conversation with him about what he was looking for. There followed a really quite old-fashioned period of what you might call courtship, with Phil turning up with flowers and gifts and offering to spoil her whenever he could.

Aaron readily took to Phil and really liked him. He knew something of his dad from family conversations, but he never mentioned him himself. Phil was a potential substitute, a man to play a father-like role in his life. Phil said that he had not been married, nor did he have children. He had experienced relationships but they had all ended prematurely, either at his instigation or by the partner triggering separation. He tended to blame them for the failure.

Phil was vague about what he did, but seemed to be comfortably off and had a small house of his own. He was a little older than Ruth and had only moved into the area relatively recently. Ruth and Phil enjoyed spending time together and he was persuasive in advancing the idea of moving in together. He suggested that she should give up her flat and move into his house. After a while Ruth agreed to take up his offer and set about making the transition. Initially there was, of course, a sort of 'honeymoon period' when things were all new and exciting. Phil seemed to be able to win Aaron over, and the boy would readily stick up for Phil, sometimes leaving Ruth feeling a little isolated. Phil liked things his way. He was charming, confident and always persuasive.

He liked to plan things for them. He liked to take a lead. He liked them to be together. Aaron responded to the sense of security, but Ruth didn't always feel comfortable. At work her colleagues recognised that she wasn't as spontaneous and cheerful as she used to be, that she didn't go on nights out with the girls anymore, that yes she even seemed a little withdrawn. If anyone asked her about it, Ruth would make excuses and change the subject. She felt happy with Phil, she thought.

He wanted her to meet with his friends and not hers. He was protective to the point of almost paranoia. He even liked to dictate what she should or should not wear. Ruth wondered, was he jealous? Did he fear losing her? Did he even think that she might have someone else? She really wasn't sure; instinct was telling her to be careful, although she was trying hard not to listen.

She did sometimes wonder what really had happened in his previous relationships. Where had he lived before? And what exactly did he do at work? Ruth began to realise that she really didn't know much about this man she had chosen to live with and to give up her independence for. This made her feel uneasy. He could sense it and that made his behaviour worse. He would question her in detail about her movements throughout the day, who she had spoken to and what money she had spent. Ruth didn't like it, but was unsure how to react and to respond. There were even times when she still missed Eddie. Yes, he was unreliable, a bit of a dreamer and a chancer, but at least she felt like she knew him, better in fact than perhaps he knew himself. Yes, she was sure of it; she still missed Eddie.

Where is he? she wondered. Ruth was determined to find some answers, for Eddie's sake as much as hers. She made enquiries with the police again and with charities that dealt with missing persons, but nothing tangible was forthcoming. She was still no nearer knowing what had happened to Eddie when he left her suddenly that day and she ended up in prison.

It was risky, Ruth acknowledged to herself, but she was increasingly feeling that there was no other way to satisfy her search for the truth. She set out to trace any of the lads who would have known Eddie at the time he was at the project. Surely at least one of them would know something about his disappearance, she hoped.

It took a while but eventually she tracked down an Indian lad the group nicknamed George – she remembered they couldn't pronounce his real name. He still looked the same. He recognised her as she approached him in another bike shop in the next town to where he and Eddie had attended the project.

'I didn't know you were interested in bikes?' he asked as they smiled and remembered better times. After a while George guessed, 'It's Eddie, isn't it? You're hoping to find out what happened.'

'Yes,' Ruth replied meekly.

'Look Ruth, perhaps it's better that you don't know?'

'So, does that mean that you know what really happened to him then George?'

'No Ruth, it doesn't. I just mean that too many questions can only lead to trouble. All I know is that, at about the time you were arrested, the word was that Eddie had helped himself to that holdall, not knowing exactly how much was in it, but that once the gang found him, he would be in serious trouble.'

'Do you mean they killed him?'

'Shh Ruth, these are dangerous words. I honestly don't know for sure, but I think so. That's all I'm saying. Please Ruth just drop it, will you? It will only lead to more trouble.'

Ruth left not sure whether she had the answer she was seeking, but she felt more reassured that her suspicions were probably right. *Should I approach the police again?* she thought. After all this was a potential murder enquiry. Probably not – no, she had no evidence and they probably wouldn't take her seriously anyway. No, she thought, George was right – she should drop it.

Chapter 9

'Where the hell have you been?' demanded Phil as Ruth returned to his house looking drained and later than expected too. A row broke out. Things were said that probably were best left unsaid. Accusations were made and doubts and fears exposed. There was no turning back. It was time to go.

Whilst he stormed off to have a shower, Ruth quickly collected some things, woke Aaron and told that they were leaving. He was confused but obeyed his mother's instructions and prepared to go. They left silently and ran through the night back to the only place that realistically they could go.

Her phone was ringing constantly and announcing the receipt of serial text messages. She ignored them all. As they moved through the streets towards her mother's house, Ruth looked out for Phil's car. She feared that he would set out to find them. Lights flashed and yes it was his car that raced past them as they hid behind a fence.

The next few days were very difficult. Aaron needed to move schools again. Ruth was being plagued by ever more extreme and abusive texts and phone messages. Whilst she felt assured that she'd made the right decision to leave Phil, Ruth was fearful of just how far he might go in trying to get them back. She'd been a fool. She'd tried to convince herself that all was well with their relationship, when she knew that it wasn't. Well, it was too late for regrets now – she had to stay strong and move on again. She had rebuilt her life before and could do it again. Yes, Ruth kept telling herself, she'd be OK.

This time, Ruth was determined to build up enough of a saving pot to pay the deposit on a small terrace house of her own. She didn't want to return again to the rental market. She stayed at her mother's for a year whilst she worked hard and saved. The hairdressing shop was doing well. She never saw Phil again, not in the shop, not around the local area. *Perhaps he'd moved on too*, she thought.

A franchise came up and Ruth decided to take the opportunity. She wanted to go to the next level and own her own business. Between help from her mum and the bank, it proved to be possible. Things seemed better this time between her and her mum and Ruth decided to postpone any moves to her own property for a while longer. In fact, mum seemed to genuinely appreciate them being around as she got older and she wasn't putting any pressure on Ruth to move. Aaron liked his Gran and, whilst she was no father substitute, she was at least a stable influence in his life. Thank goodness she had not had any children with Phil, Ruth often considered. That really would have been a bad move!

It was not long after that time that she met Alan. He was a good deal older than Ruth, but seemed to be a genuine, stable guy who was looking for some comfort in his life after his wife had died young from cancer. He owned his own home and was even quite wealthy, certainly by the standards Ruth was used to! More of a 'sugar daddy' perhaps, as some of her friends commented. Aaron was guarded at first, but he did grow to like him as a sort of half-dad, half-granddad figure.

It wasn't long before he actually asked her to marry him. Ruth was rather bowled over, after her luck with men, that someone was actually offering marriage, with all its relative stability and security. She wasn't sure that she loved him, but she knew that she liked him a lot and felt it was a good offer, so she agreed. A bride at last, albeit unexpectedly.

This necessitated another house move, another school for Aaron. At least Alan's house wasn't too far from her mum's. Mum liked him too, which helped. The hair dressing franchise was going well. Business was brisk and Ruth enjoyed the challenge and the extra responsibility of being her own boss. After all that happened with Eddie and then Phil, this was a welcome more successful and stable period in her life. Ruth was blossoming and her relationship with Alan was good. Refreshingly, he proved by and large to be the man he purported to be.

All was well until one day when one of the Afghan boys walked into the shop. Ruth recognised him instantly, although it had been a long time since their last encounter.

'Hello Ruth, I hear that you are doing well here, I'm pleased for you.' He announced. There was no one else in the shop – the other hairdresser had finished early that day in order to attend an event at her daughter's school.

'So well, that perhaps it's time that you paid back a little of what you owe, Ruth. Remember the holdall, a very bad business. Yes, very bad. You paid a very high price, unfortunately, but not to us. The police took the money, proceeds of crime they call it, a licence to steal more like. But you still owe us, you see. I think a thousand a month would be reasonable until it's paid off, don't you?' the man said.

'What? But I can't afford that!' Ruth exclaimed.

'Well, it would be a shame if your business faltered, wouldn't it? If suddenly all your customers decided that it really wasn't in their best interests to come to you, after a little gentle persuasion that is.'

'You wouldn't.'

'Now come on, you don't believe that. Put it the other way. I'll help you. Some of the customers who currently go to other hairdressers might just suddenly want to come to you. Your business could boom! You could even find yourself in a position to pay me back sooner!'

Ruth paused to consider, but she knew that there wasn't really a choice. If she didn't agree, her business was dead, or even worse potentially, she contemplated. She wanted to ask the man about Eddie, but she didn't dared to.

'So ten months at a thousand a month is it then?'

'Oh no, my dear, you see there's the interest too. I'm not a greedy man, so let's say fifteen months. A very fair offer, I'd say. Many in my position would insist on twenty, or even more. I'm a realist Ruth, that's how I've been successful for so long.' And with that he turned and left, leaving her yet again in tears and in pieces.

Chapter 10

She had to get through this. She couldn't tell Alan as it would break his heart; he didn't come from this type of world. He wouldn't understand it. No, she simply had to find the money every month and get these people off her back. At least the man had been right; suddenly her turnover nearly doubled as a succession of new customers flooded in. She was able to hire two new hairdressers and had four chairs all busy for most of the time, six days a week. Other businesses asked about the key to her success, but she just claimed it was hard work. She managed to keep the truth from Alan, although he worried that she was working too hard.

The payments were made, the time rolled on. No words were exchanged, but the agreement was clear. After fifteen long months, a large overdraft, a build up of credit cards and help from her mum, Ruth had fulfilled her 'contract'. On the day of the last payment, she feared that the man would simply 'suggest' that, as the arrangement had gone so well, it may as well continue, but in fact he didn't. Neither did all the new customers return to their previous arrangements.

Life was sweet; Aaron was growing up and had decided that he wanted to be a Royal Marine. He was fit and very sporty so she felt that he would fit in well.

And then of course things changed. Ruth came home late one day from the shop to find that Alan had died sitting in his favourite chair. He'd had a massive heart attack apparently, a sudden but peaceful death.

She was sad but also grateful for the time that they had together. After the funeral, Ruth learnt that she was about to be become a relatively wealthy woman. Alan, in fact, had substantial savings, all of which would now come to her. He had no children or other surviving relatives.

Burying Alan in a strange way also seemed like burying the memory of Eddie and all her past life with it. Aaron joined the Marine's and passed the selection and training course. Ruth was able to sell the franchise of her hairdressing business at a good price, and Alan's old house too. She had decided to move away. Far away from all that the area represented to her. She would open a bed and breakfast business by the sea and start again.

As Ruth left the shop for the last time, a familiar man walked through the door and introduced himself to the new owner. He didn't even acknowledge Ruth. She walked away.

10. Revenge

Chapter 1

Suffocation was Darren's abiding memory of his childhood. That was until it ended so suddenly.

***

Darren was taken from his mother and twin brother Jason at birth in the 1970's. Social services already had an established case for such drastic action having taken his mother's four previous children into care too.

Darren was placed in foster care with a highly respected couple with a long record of service as foster parents. Jason was placed elsewhere and the twins had no contact or knowledge of each their through their entire childhood. Nor did Darren have any contact or knowledge of his other siblings for many years. No, he was isolated in a rural placement in Shropshire. His foster parents had two of their own children who saw it as their role to bully and dominate incomers. Other foster children came and went but Darren remained with little oversight or assessment from the very authority that had seen fit to remove him.

Mr and Mrs Abingdon were well-meaning people but religion had overtaken their lives and clouded their judgement. Biblical teachings were to be strictly adhered to and respected without question in their house. Mrs Abingdon was trained as a primary school teacher and was consistently praised by the local authority for her initiative in offering home tuition to all her children, which was regarded as innovative at the time. This may have been convenient, certainly for the Abingdons, but it resulted in further isolation and exclusion for the children.

Childhood was mostly a miserable experience for Darren. On the surface he was well cared for – fed, clothed and inducted into life with a comprehensive and strict routine – but there was no love and precious little attachment or nurturing; notions not known to Darren, by the nature of his tender years, and compounded by his isolation. Mr Abingdon worked a small holding on their modest estate two miles up a track and seven miles from the nearest tiny village settlement. There were no neighbours and few visitors.

Darren endured daily religious teachings and prayer to some vague unknown person he was assured was called 'God'. He helped on the farm, as did all the other foster children as part of their 'education'. The Abingdons' own children frequently left the farm to go on all sorts of trips. The outside world could have been forgiven for believing that they were the only children living with Mr and Mrs Abingdon. It was only their own children who later were allowed to attend outside school.

Darren struggled to form relationships and learnt not to trust the Abingdons' own offspring, and not to get too close to his fellow foster children as they could be here today and gone tomorrow with no explanation or opportunity to say goodbye. 'God's good grace,' was often cited as the justification for these moves, whatever exactly that meant. Darren was never sure.

Chapter 2

Through the 1980's, as he spent more and more miserable time with the Abingdons, Darren's sense of resentment only increased. *Was my real mum really that bad that she couldn't look after me?* he wondered. Who else might be in his real family? He didn't know that either. However bad it might have been, could it have been worse that this God-driven hell?

Not only did he dislike the Abingdons, with their sickly-sweet self-satisfied answer for everything, but he was really getting to resent the double standards applied when it came to the treatment he and his fellow foster children received in comparison to that graciously bestowed on their own obnoxious offspring.

Incident after incident illustrated the absolute sense of unfairness that this represented and boy didn't Abigail and Quinton know how to rub it in! Everything from birthdays to Christmas were organised to two entirely different standards and formats. If any visitors were expected, Darren and the others always seemed to find themselves deployed in the fields as far away as possible from the house, as if they weren't even meant to exist. They certainly didn't feel wanted.

If it was wet, Abigail and Quinton would always be allocated some simple, easy, cosy task inside while 'the fosters' tramped off to work regardless. When they went on one of their trips, Abigail and Quinton would do their best to tell them all about it – Darren felt sure it was deliberately done to make them feel jealous. He was determined not to let his feelings show, however, as he would listen intently and walk away disinterested. He wondered what actually lay beyond the farm boundaries, what existed past the end of the long drive. When other children came, they would have all sorts of tales to tell of their experiences from physical and sexual abuse to near starvation, cold, fear and sheer depravity. Some also talked of sweets and toys and clothes and nice things, however – even holidays!

The more Darren repressed his feelings and pushed away thoughts about the world beyond, in a strange way, he became dangerously accustomed to the strict and stark regime he was subjected to. It was, after all, for him 'normal'. That was one weetabix with milk for breakfast and one slice of white toast with margarine with a mug of tea with no sugar. Two half sandwiches of usually cheese or sliced tinned ham, a biscuit, an apple and some water for lunch and some variation on 'wholesome stew' for tea.

Formal schooling became more and more infrequent as he got older. He knew his numbers and could read and write a little but beyond that it was as if it had been decided that he was not worthy of any greater learning, that somehow it might be 'wasted on him' and that God had no need for him to know more. He was constantly reminded that for his 'place in God's world' that was all he would need and that practical skills and experience around the farm were more suitable for him. One day he overheard Mrs Abingdon explaining to the social worker that 'for a boy like Darren, too much education was a waste of time; he simply was not motivated and lacked the capacity to learn.' Apparently, that was it, he thought.

Religious teachings were constant, 'God's will' was used to justify anything, bible stories, hymns and Sunday services dominated his life.

One particular incident stuck out in his memory. He must have been about ten, he thought, *yes, that was right*. Soon after his tenth birthday some damage had been done to one of the flower beds in the main garden when he was the only 'foster' at that time. When he came back from the fields that day, after working hard on dredging the brook that ran through the farm, a real commotion was in full swing. Abigail was crying and Mrs Abingdon was shouting at the top of her voice something about 'wilful damage to her favourite flower bed!' Quinton was looking guilty and, even as he approached the scene, Darren could see the same light soil on his shoes as in the area that had been disturbed. Mr Abingdon had just arrived and was berating everyone and expressing his fear for God's great retribution at such a wanton act of sheer vandalism.

As soon as Darren appeared, already covered in mud, wet and filthy, Quinton looked up and immediately cried, 'It must have been him – look at him, covered in mud!'

Mr Abingdon looked aghast at the lad and back to the disrupted flower bed, across to his grieving wife and sobbing daughter before declaring out loud, 'This act cannot go unpunished. God could not allow it. The guilty must pay; full recompense and remorse must be extracted from the miserable sinner who has shamed us all by defiling this beautiful garden! You, you boy,' he said, turning to Darren. 'Are you responsible for this carnage?' he demanded.

'What? I've been in the fields all day, as well you know. I haven't even been here!' replied Darren indignantly.

'So you deny it and add to your sin?' announced Mr Abingdon, seeking nods of support from his audience.

'Deny what?'

'You must have caused this mess, who else could it possibly be?' exclaimed Quinton loudly.

Darren just looked up with a sense of fatalism. Of course, it had to be him; he hadn't realised, after all, that it was always him. It was always his fault. He hung his head in reluctant acceptance of the inevitability of the process that was about to take place and of course he was right.

Much moral indignation followed and many threats of Godly disapproval and risks of damnation played out before Darren found himself setting about repairing the damage, sorting out the mess and anticipating an early night with a cold tea eaten on his own in his bedroom.

Chapter 3

It was a couple of years later that Darren felt sufficiently intrigued to explore a little. He discovered that the house was quiet after midnight when one night he woke about that time with a stomach ache and couldn't get back off to sleep. So in the end he got up and got dressed. *What now?* he thought. Well, he could hardly go anywhere overtly, so he decided to climb out of his bedroom window and sneak across the roof of the extension, down the wall and off towards the track leading away from the farm. It was really quite exciting at night and he felt a real sense of adventure daring to go forth beyond the farm, a place where he had effectively been imprisoned for as long as he could remember. Darren had only left the farm on very few occasions that he could recall. Once, in response to a toothache, he remembered going to see the emergency dentist to have it removed, which was hardly a great adventure after years of waiting.

Then there was the time the whole family were going out for the day, which had caused such consternation as they agonised over what to do with 'him'; they could hardly leave him on his own all day on the housekeeper's day off and so, with considerable reluctance, they eventually decided to allow 'him' to come too. As long as he kept quiet and stayed in the car most of the day while they did 'other things'. Darren remembered eagerly agreeing to the conditions as he felt desperate to see what there was beyond the track. He had loved the day just glaring out of the car window at different people, buildings, places, cars, everything in fact. He didn't care where they took him – it was just 'out' as far as he was concerned.

At night, as he walked carefully along the track, Darren tried to remember things from that day but he couldn't really. It was too long ago and, of course, it had been light then and now it was not. As his eyes adjusted to the dark he reached the end of the track and wondered what lay beyond. There was a road with no cars around at that time, but buildings and a few lights were dotted around the area.

At that stage Darren felt quite content to just sit on a bench by the road and look out to the world beyond the track.

After several such expeditions, Darren started to ask if Mr and Mrs Abingdon would allow him to 'go out' sometimes. They seemed surprised at such a request, even resentful of the implication that life was not sufficiently fulfilling here at the farm for the boy. He was only 'a foster', after all. They tutted at his gross ingratitude.

One day when his social worker came to visit, after she had spent a considerable amount of time talking to the Abingdons, the young woman came to see him, with Mrs Abingdon present, of course. She seemed more than content to answer all the questions for him, explaining that the boy was 'shy, you see'. Darren mentioned that he had asked to be allowed out and the social worker agreed that this would be helpful for him. Mrs Abingdon was at pains to explain that, of course, his normal activities on the farm were far and away sufficient for a young boy of his age and such limited ability and the social worker seemed to accept all that she said without question. She had explained earlier that no other foster parents would want the boy and that, with God's will, they were prepared to keep him, but that the authorities mustn't expect too much of him, given all that he was and where he had come from.

Darren didn't really know what the social worker was for. He hadn't seen many of them over the years since first arriving at the farm. They were there to check that he was behaving as expected and working hard enough and taking in his religious studies. *Yes, that would be what they were for*, he decided.

It was only a few days after that when Mrs Abingdon explained to him that he was to start going once a week to the local shop to collect some groceries. She would ring through her order as usual but, instead of collecting them in the car, Darren was to set off on a bicycle to collect them, every Tuesday at around two o'clock before the day's bible classes. Darren was already familiar with several bikes that were kept in one of the farm sheds. Sometimes too he had even ridden the quad bike.

So a pattern emerged of going to collect Mrs Abingdon's order every Tuesday, come rain or shine. In fact, he looked forward to it. The bike he selected for the job was an old one with a basket on the front and a rack on the back sufficient to carry the goods home.

The grocer, he discovered, had a daughter of about his age who sometimes was in the shop when he called. She became the first person that Darren had known consistently apart from other 'fosters' and the Abingdon family. Mandy quite liked him, although he was a little strange. He didn't say much, she thought, but dutifully collected the order and went on his way, returning for his bible class, he always said. 'Why doesn't he go to school?' she would ask her mother, who told her to mind her own business.

Over time, Darren continued his expeditions to the shop and, in fact, began running other errands for Mrs Abingdon too. Sometime he would see Mandy walking back to school after lunch. He wondered what her life was really like…

A new boy arrived at the farm, 'a foster' called Jack. He was around Darren's age but much more streetwise. He came from Telford. Jack had told him that his dad was 'inside' and his mum was on drugs so there was no food in the house and it was filthy, so the social had taken him away. Did he mind, Darren had asked him.

'No, not really mate, anything would be better than that shit,' he had said as Darren wondered how long that perception might last. Jack came with two full suitcases with some nice clothes, an early mobile phone and a small compact disc player. In fact, he had two and gave one to Darren and taught him how to use it. He said that he had nicked it from some drunk at a bus stop while his mates had distracted the guy.

Jack did seem to appreciate the sense of order and routine at the farm, including regular meals, but the religious element just made him laugh. He had the confidence to question and challenge the regime, which was not on the agenda at all!

The boys got on well, much to Mrs Abington's disappointment and disapproval. Jack nicknamed Darren 'The Farm Boy', which he supposed was at least one step up from being just 'a foster.'

When Jack was allowed to go to the grocers with Darren, he taught him how to steal sweets from the shop while nobody was looking. Jack was exciting, Darren thought, but he didn't stay for long.

There followed a succession of Jacks over the coming years, often for short stays, always with stories to tell of girls and fags and booze and stuff. They always made Darren unsettled and more curious to learn more about the world beyond the track, a world that the Abingdons were attempting to 'save' him from.

Darren and some of the boys built a den in some woods just off the road between the farm and the grocers, where they kept things that they had nicked from the shop or things that the other boys brought with them that they didn't want the Abingdons to know about. The den became a sanctuary, a special place. Darren provided the continuity so really it was his den.

Chapter 4

Darren was fifteen when he finally cracked, when the pain, injustice and contradictions inherent in his imposed lifestyle simply became too much to take anymore. All the years of being cast as a second class citizen, all the false accusations, the blame, the moral indignation and yes the religious bigotry all collided at one time.

It was a hot summer. The corn had grown well that year, more than sufficient for their own needs to feed and bed down their few lambs, pigs and chickens. There was a local consortium that jointly owned a combine harvester and that day was the Abingdons' turn for the machine and operator to visit their farm. Mr Abingdon was in a high state of anxiety, hoping that God would reward his efforts and shine his good grace of approval on the day's events. The offspring, of course, were not available to help, as ever, having found some new unconvincingly urgent need to be elsewhere. As such, as usual, much of the weight of responsibility and the sheer physical effort of the hard work to come would inevitably fall on Darren's shoulders. He was angry. Resentment and hatred ran through his mind as he prepared for what he knew would be a long hard day.

The combine harvester arrived early, as expected and much to Mr Abingdon's delight, and soon it served to reinforce his sense of self righteousness and smug self importance. It was evident that this year's harvest was set to be a bumper one, and again that only served to inflate Mr Abingdon's view of his own worthy and respectable status. He paraded up and down the field, watching both the grain and the bales appear from the harvester.

Darren was tasked with cutting a corner of the field by hand that the machine couldn't access. The scythe assigned to the task was clearly too big and too heavy for a slender youth of fifteen to handle, but that was the tool that he had to use and would be integral in the judgements made later about his work. He set about his task as best he could by systematically dividing the allotted area into several smaller sections. He could see that this was going to take some time.

In previous years, this corner of the field had been largely unproductive, and often was not harvested at all. A local farm hand used to help if required, but this year Mr Abingdon was adamant that he would not be needed and that Darren had to fulfil the task to earn his keep. When Darren had tentatively tried to express some reservations about the realistic limitations of this plan, he was quickly subdued by eager demands and expectations, coupled with assurance that God would, of course, be on his side and would not be impressed by his expressions of doubt.

This was always a mixed blessing, he felt. The implication was that any failure to meet expectations would be inevitably down to him, as even with God's able assistance he could still fail. Darren desperately did not want to fail again. He wanted to succeed on that day, despite the odds being stacked against him, not to please Mr Abingdon, but for his own sense of satisfaction.

Darren went about his task with conviction. The rhythm of the scythe became almost hypnotic as he moved along his chosen routes to cover the ground and extract as much produce as possible. He had started in earnest at six o'clock in the morning and by midday he was feeling very thirsty, hungry and exhausted. He longed for his miserable two half sandwiches, the biscuit and the apple, not allowing himself to hope for even a moment that today's lunch might be a little more generous in the circumstances. He had long since drained the bottle of water that he had brought with him and was feeling parched.

When lunch did eventually arrive, it was exactly as expected; basic, consistent, boring and wholly inadequate for a growing youth doing hard physical work. Darren shrugged his shoulders and carried on. By three o'clock in the afternoon it was getting really hot. *Too hot to work*, he thought. He had just about finished when he noticed the combine harvester drive away. *He couldn't have completed the whole field in that time*, he thought.

Feeling really pleased with his efforts, Darren noticed both Mr and Mrs Abingdon walking across the field towards him, and they looked animated. *Could my efforts finally be recognised?* he wondered, as they came closer towards him. Mrs Abingdon looked up and, with a cursory glance across the area Darren had been working on, she immediately launched into a diatribe of brutal and most undeserved criticism.

'Is this all you have managed?' she screamed at him. 'You idle, useless child. You were always useless. I don't know why we keep you!'

Whilst this was not the reaction he had hoped for, Darren had to admit that he wasn't surprised, but this time he felt really hurt, far more hurt than usual. To accuse him of idleness after what he had just done was outrageous, as was the accusation of being 'useless', he thought. After all, they wouldn't manage the farm now without him. It was a charge she would have been more justified in levelling at her own two hideously spoiled and objectionable little brats!

As she continued to berate him, Darren closed off his mind and simply stopped listening. Pure anger was growing inside him as Mr Abingdon added, 'You've let us down again. You must have been able to see that the harvester has finished for the day and there is still part of the field to cut, yet you've just sat here on your idle backside!'

What have you done to contribute to proceedings? Darren thought, but he did not utter a sound. After what he'd done, how hard he'd worked, how could they possibly expect him to go on and complete the rest of the main field on his own? No, he resolved he wouldn't do it. He felt a strange sense of release, of being unshackled. He would take no more of this; his patience and tolerance had finally been exhausted. Darren cracked.

He felt the scythe in his hands, recognised its power and potential as a weapon and stepped forward, lifting the implement before him and swung it outwards towards Mrs Abingdon. It struck her across the throat and neck, inflicting an instantly fatal wound, and she dropped to the ground at her husband's feet. Shocked and stunned, Mr Abingdon just stood there, rooted to the ground in disbelief as he saw the scythe swing towards him too, before he fell and blacked out. It was a scene of carnage, an explosion of anger, a sight of utter destruction.

Darren felt strangely calm, self satisfied and contented. A good job, he thought as he dropped the weapon and turned to walk away; away from the life of abuse, exploitation and emotional neglect that had been his lot for far too long. He walked straight across the field without looking back and out onto the farm track that he barely knew. It was the track that led to the outside, to what others might call the rest of the world but to him was still largely an undiscovered place.

Darren went to the only place he really knew, to his den in the woods, where he sat quietly. So he had killed them both, he thought, feeling more a sense of relief than any sense of fear or regret. He felt nothing for them, only that they had deserved to die. Yes, he had no doubt about that.

Chapter 5

Absolute indignation was in the air as Abigail and Quinton waited impatiently for at least one of their parents to arrive at the school gates to drive them home, but no one came. Other parents came and went as usual but not theirs. Their lives had been so ordered, so predictable, that this was an eventuality that left them dumbfounded. *Where could they possibly be?* they wondered.

Eventually, one of the other parents, noting their evident distress, offered them a lift, intending to drop them off at the top of the farm track. Used to a full door to door service this seemed grossly unfair and inadequate but, at the end of the day, it was preferable to no lift at all so, reluctantly and with no hint of appreciation, 'the offspring' got into the car and sulked.

On reaching the track, they both somehow still expected something to happen to rescue them and save them the indignity of the long walk to the farm, but on this occasion it didn't.

In silence, they walked down the track towards the farm, eventually reaching their destination – only to find both parents' cars still parked in front of the house.

'How could they have forgotten?' shouted Abigail with real venom.

'I know. Just wait till we catch up with them, I can tell you!' responded Quinton as they marched into the house.

No one was there. How odd, they thought, still only feeling anger at being let down and not an inch of concern for anyone else.

'Where are they?' demanded Abigail, as if the house would reply.

'They must still be in the field. I bet that useless 'foster' has let them down again. Maybe they are still harvesting? He simply has to go this time.'

There was no sound of work or activity as they moved through the house and out into the garden and towards the fields. A strange sense of calm was in the air, until they caught the smell of something unpleasant on the gentle summer breeze. As they approached the scene that Darren had left behind him, nothing could have prepared them for what they were about to encounter. It was still so soon after the event that nothing had disturbed the scene.

Horror overcame them both as they confronted the reality on the bare ground in front of them. Even with no experience to draw on, it was obvious to them both that it was too late to save their mother as Quinton howled and Abigail cried out. Mrs Abingdon by now was totally still, frozen in a large pool of her own blood. The blood stained scythe lay on the ground nearby and no further explanation seemed to be required.

'The foster!' cried Quinton. 'It must have been him. Where is he? I'll kill him now!'

Abigail looked on towards her father, who was by now propped up against a tree stump and covered in blood. As she approached him, she could sense him moaning and spluttering and trying hard to breath. Thank fully he was still alive, but barely, she concluded. For once their respective thoughts were concentrated on the needs of others as they responded as quickly as they could. Abigail knelt down by her father and held his hand and tried to talk to him whilst Quinton lifted his phone and dialled the emergency services. The ambulance, paramedics and the police all arrived together very quickly in response to his call.

They worked rapidly to save Mr Abingdon, checking his breathing and pulse, applying a drip and attempting to stop any further bleeding. He was seriously injured and had lost a significant amount of blood, but was still alive. As they rushed him off to hospital, the offspring were assured that his chances of survival were good. They decided that Abigail should go with him in the ambulance and that Quinton should stay at the farm to assist the police. He was determined to find Darren.

'I'm sorry to have to ask you questions at a time like this,' the police officer said sympathetically to Quinton, 'but have you any idea what might have happened here?'

'Abigail and I were at school as usual and today we knew that the local consortium combine harvester was due to visit to bring in this year's harvest, which was expected to be a good yield. Darren, our foster child, was going to help. Apart from the harvester driver, he would have been the only other person present here all day. It must have been him,' Quinton replied, starting to break down.

'The ungrateful little wretch!' he cried. 'After all that we have done for him; taken him into our family, embraced him as our own, and then this. This is how he repays us!'

'Where is this Darren likely to be now, sir?' asked the officer.

'He hardly ever leaves the farm. He's not very bright. He doesn't know the local area. He can't be far from here.'

'Is he usually violent? How would you expect him to react to us?' asked the officer, keen to not only find the lad but to minimise the risk to his team.

'As I said, he can't be far away. Maybe he's still on the farm. I really don't know how he might react, the little shit, but you make sure you catch him!' responded Quinton.

The police officers spread out to search the farm and coordinated with control to deploy patrols around the outer area. Darren had to be apprehended quickly.

'Who else does he know around here, sir? Who might have seen him or have an idea where he might go?'

'The only other person he mentions who he sees with any regularity is Mandy at the grocer's.'

Back on his radio, the officer advised control of this lead and asked for someone to speak to this Mandy.

A local patrol responded and picked up the call before heading to the shop quickly. No obvious sign of the lad had been discovered on the farm itself so far.

When the officers arrived at the shop, Mandy was filling up the potatoes in the vegetable rack outside the front.

'Mandy, I assume?' checked the officer.

'Yes, can I help you?'

'Do you know Darren from the farm?' she asked the girl.

'Yes.'

'I'm sorry to have to tell you that a serious incident occurred at the farm today and we urgently need to find this boy. Have you any idea where he might go if he thought he might be in trouble?' the WPC asked sensitively.

'Yes actually, apart from the farm itself, the only other place he ever talks about is his 'den'. I don't think it's far from here, somewhere in the woods between here and the farm track, I imagine. I don't know if that might help?'

'Ok. Thank you, it's a start anyway,' replied the officer, reporting back straight away to her colleague and to control to tell them of this latest development.

'Is there anything else, Mandy, that you can tell us about Darren?'

'Yes, well, only that he's a bit odd really.'

The officers were quickly dispatched to search for the woods and the den. They drove slowly back towards the farm and approached some woodland on the right that stretched as far as the entrance to the farm track.

'There, that has to be it!'

'Ok, I'll pull over and we can go and have a look.'

The two officers got out of the car and walked along the fence line marking the edge of the wood until they found a gap in the wire where the fence had been damaged. It looked like that had been the case for some time. They followed the track from there cautiously into the woods, conscious that time was of the essence and they needed to find this child. Still, at the same time, they were not sure what to expect and, at that point, had no back up.

As they pushed through bramble and nettles, it wasn't long before they could see what was obviously some sort of den.

'There, that looks like it, wouldn't you say?'

'Yes. OK, let's take a look.'

The officers carefully walked up to the den and followed it round to an entrance facing into the wood and away from the road. It was a small enclosure, but just big enough for the two officers to make their way inside to find a teenage boy sitting calmly using a log as a stool.

'Darren?' asked the WPC.

'Yes, how do you know?' he responded naively.

'We understand that there was an incident at the farm today, Darren. Do you know what happened there?'

'Yes, I killed the Abingdons,' he replied.

'Are you sure, Darren?'

'Yes, quite sure. I struck them both with a scythe.'

'OK, well you'd better come with us then, son,' stated the PC firmly.

'Can I go back home now?' asked Darren naively.

'No son, you won't be going back to the farm.'

'No, not the farm. I mean back home. Can I go back to my mum now?'

Chapter 6

Mrs Abingdon had been confirmed dead at the scene but Mr Abingdon was recovering well after surgery. The prognosis for him was good. Being struck by the scythe across his clothing had saved him from a worse fate and his wounds were relatively minor. No organs had been damaged, but he had lost a lot of blood. Had he not been found when he was, he would no doubt have died later that day.

Abigail and Quinton were comforted by friends and an aunt came to stay from London. They were still in shock and struggling to come to terms with the day's events. 'How? Why?' they asked themselves. Yes Darren was a little odd, but this? They struggled to perceive how events had come to this point. They were at least relieved to know that their father would be alright, but they had lost their dear mother forever.

Darren was interviewed formally by the police in the presence of a social worker. He readily and honestly described in full what had happened and how and why he had attacked the Abingdons.

'I have to inform you that Mrs Abingdon is dead and that Mr Abingdon was seriously injured,' said the investigating officer sombrely.

'Oh, isn't Mr Abingdon dead too?' asked Darren.

'No, he survived.'

'Oh, but I meant to kill him too,' admitted Darren readily, with clear disappointment at hearing of his apparent lack of success.

It wasn't long before the officer was able to inform Darren that he was to be charged with murder and attempted murder.

'Oh,' was all he replied. 'They were horrible people, you know.'

Outside the interview room, the two officers conferred while the social worker tried to explain to Darren what was going on and the consequences for him.

'That's the oddest murder interview I've ever conducted!' said the Inspector.

'Yes, strange. The lad seemed so calm and, well, so honest, as if he really didn't understand what he'd done,' replied the Sergeant.

'Yes, I think he understood alright, but he doesn't seem to have any concept of the consequences. I've no doubt that he fully intended to kill them both – this was no accident. This was clearly murder and he'll go down for a very long time.'

Which subsequently, of course, was exactly what happened.

***

Darren arrived at the local youth secure unit. He was still too young for prison, but that would surely await him later. A 'life sentence' for one so young is indeterminate, with any prospect of eventual release being left for the consideration of the parole board in the years to come.

This, of course, was all an entirely new experience for Darren. He was used to confinement in a way but not like this, with so many locks and bars and doors and very little access to outside space, which he was used to. The food was no worse than at the farm, and there were some things to occupy his time, but for the most part life was boring. At least the religious indoctrination was over, though, much to his relief.

A series of assessments were undertaken to reveal various facets of Darren's character and development and to start the long journey of investigating how and why he had come to kill.

By the late 1990's initial impressions from the varied staff group, including psychologists, social workers and teachers, were interesting. Darren remained unusually very open about his actions in attacking the Abingdons. He seemed to have little or no sense of regret or remorse, but regarded his actions as reasonable and proportionate in the circumstances. He did not appear to be vindictive or sadistic, he did not intend to cause undue suffering, but he clearly did fully intend to kill both his foster parents, after what he saw as years of exploitation and abuse.

Something had clearly gone wrong in this case. The level of supervision of Darren as a foster child was woefully inadequate; he had caused little trouble and concern, but it was hard to avoid the conclusion that his development had been marred by his experience. Too little stimulation had been provided and the assumptions by the Abingdons of his 'limited ability' were never properly challenged. Whilst his general educational attainment was low, he was in fact of only just below average intelligence. There were no obvious signs of illness, or mental health issues.

No real attempts had been made to explore the possibility of adoption and the performance of the Abingdons as foster parents raised some serious questions. De-registration or action against them was never pursued, even following the immediate resignation of Mr Abingdon in the aftermath of recovering from his injuries at the hand of Darren.

The experience of relative isolation, differential treatment and religious indoctrination had all clearly left their mark. Darren had a distorted sense of justice, a poor sense of empathy and understanding of others, poor attachment and difficulties forming relationships. Also his limited experience of the world would not hold him in good stead and would only be likely to be further compounded by experience in custody. Darren had been consistently denied access to the outside world, had little experience of it through interaction, books or television, had no access to the internet. His world stretched no further than a mile or so from the end of the farm track. In many ways he was an educational void, but he had a deep feeling of hurt. Cynicism and the impact of religious bigotry had left him with a very distorted and jaundiced view of the world.

As for Darren himself, he still did not really seem to comprehend what he had done and the consequences for everyone involved, nor did he appear to have any concept of what life was going to be like for him now, with the prospect of many years in institutions.

His response to the incident and his immediate actions afterwards were so honestly simplistic. When asked why he went to the den, he simply replied, 'Where else would I go?'

'What were you waiting for?' he had been asked.

'I was waiting for her, of course,' he replied.

'Who? Mandy?'

'No, my mum of course. I always believed that at some point she would come and fetch me and take me home.'

'Do you still believe that now, Darren?'

'No, probably not…'

A case conference was due to be held to discuss Darren's progress and plans for his future. Supervision would remain with social services initially, then pass to the youth offending service and onwards to the probation service when he reached adulthood. He would continue to be held in secure accommodation until transferring to a young offender institution and onwards to adult prison.

The chair asked the social worker to explain more about the management of Darren's case during his time at the farm.

'Darren, as you know, was removed at birth and never knew his own family. He was placed with the Abingdons initially and seemed to settle and presented no real problems, so he remained there.'

'Hardly a glowing example of active case management though, was it?'

'No, I'm new to the case and am not going to try to defend what happened – or more to the point what didn't happen. Put simply, as a service under pressure to manage its number of cases, Darren was allowed to effectively slip under the radar for too many years. The Abingdons were too readily believed that Darren was of limited ability and would not be suitable or easy to place for adoption. With their open ended offer to keep him, the placement was at best convenient,' the social worker explained.

'Convenient for whom?' posed the chair.

'Yes, indeed. Convenient for the Abingdons, I suppose. Obviously as a source of cheap labour, if nothing else.'

'And that was acceptable?' queried the chair, becoming increasingly concerned about what had happened to this boy.

'Look, as I said, I'm not here to defend poor practice, but I suppose it was seen as good enough, or perhaps more accurately as not bad enough to justify moving him. He came from chaos and was at least looked after.'

The chair was far from convinced, but saw no point in lambasting the poor social worker who was not directly responsible.

'Ok, we need to move on, but I will take up the wider issues with your management later, but I thank you for your candour and accept that you were not involved at the time. So, moving on; there are no issues here of further charges or appeals – and there is no dispute about culpability. Darren readily and freely admits what he did. He will no doubt go on to complete appropriate offence-related work later in his sentence but for now our more immediate priority is to establish more about his family background and what makes him tick. I understand that he has no knowledge of a twin brother or of other siblings?'

'No, that's true, unfortunately, but that is something that I can address and I intend to impart that information to him today while I'm here.'

The meeting broke up at that point and the social worker went off to speak to Darren directly.

It proved to be a difficult conversation, leaving Darren distraught and in tears. He was pleased to hear that his mother was still alive and disappointed to hear that his father was not known to social services, but he was overwhelmed by the news that he had a twin brother and other brothers and sisters. 'Why had I never been told?' he cried. 'Could I ever meet them?' he asked. He wanted to know more about them. The social worker not unreasonably concluded that the only place to start was at the beginning, so she committed to starting a life story book with him.

At about the same time, much to Darren's joy and amazement, he received a letter from his twin brother, Jason! He was doing alright, he said, was working and had not been in trouble, and he was asking to visit him at some point. It was some years later when eventually they did meet and Darren felt a real sense of belonging, they both did. It felt so special.

Chapter 7

In 2001, just before Darren moved from youth custody to the adult estate, he had been held at HMYOI Swinfen Hall in Lichfield. Swinfen Hall had a long-established good record of dealing with serious young offenders. In all the circumstances Darren had done quite well there. There was always the concern from the authorities relating to the impact of moving a young prisoner into the adult estate. They were sheltered to some extent, but fully exposed to all ages of adult prisoner, the risks of contamination and manipulation by a far more experienced group were real. This was not just liberal thinking but a real concern based on the likelihoods of escalation of risk and, as such, at this point in a young offenders career, the question was at least asked whether consideration by the parole board for early release was at all realistic.

In Darren's case, unfortunately for him, on balance the collective view from the authorities was that it wasn't. He had completed a good deal of useful and relevant work but there remained doubt about his true insight into his behaviour and therefore his likely ability to control any violent urges that he may encounter in later life. There had also been an incident in custody.

Darren was sharing a cell and, not unusually, his pad mate had been moved to a different part of the prison. When his replacement casually strutted in that same afternoon, and Darren had looked up to make his first statement of intent about who ruled this pad, he couldn't believe his eyes.

'Farmer boy!' cried Jack as he bounced into the small shared cell.

'Jack, well, how are you? Where have you been all this time?' asked Darren.

The prison officer noted that obviously the young prisoners knew each other, which from experience could be either a good or a bad thing – usually a bad thing, though, he thought.

The boys immediately set off talking about their time at the farm and what had happened to them all since. Jack said that he was incredibly impressed and proud of Darren when he had heard that he had killed those two awful foster parents! Darren had to remind him that actually Mr Abingdon had survived, but he had certainly seen to his Mrs. They joked and laughed, genuinely really pleased to meet up again. Jack had always been in trouble and this was just another sentence as far as he was concerned. He didn't even want to discuss the actual offence, it didn't matter to him. All that did matter was his date of release and that was coming up soon.

The incident occurred a month or so later when the prison authorities decided to move Jack out of the shared cell prior to his release. Darren was incensed and struggled to control his temper. When the officer arrived to take Jack, Darren flew at him with both arms swinging wildly in an attempt to stop him being taken from him. The following day, when on report to the governor, Darren tried to explain that he simply couldn't bear to lose his friend again so soon after finding him. They didn't seem to want to understand how important this bond was to him and that, when so much had been taken away from him, this was just too much, and so he had been prepared to fight for it.

That was the obvious concern and swung the balance in the decision making process against supporting Darren in any bid to the parole board for early release. It was felt that, given any emotionally charged situation, Darren would struggle to control himself and could resort to violence. That clearly was not deemed to be consistent with being regarded as safe to be released.

The prison authorities eventually decided that, in all the circumstances when Darren moved to the adult estate, he would be placed in HMP Haverigg, a small category C prison in Cumbria, with a view to a subsequent move to category D and open conditions as soon as possible thereafter. This was to deliberately attempt to avoid the worst excesses of contamination whilst in the adult estate.

Jason did eventually manage to visit his brother at Swinfen Hall before he was moved to Haverigg.

Chapter 8

Jack was released as planned with no further direct contact with Darren, although they did manage to pass a few messages before release. Jack did as he promised and wrote to Darren from outside, promising to keep in touch. He even offered to help him if he ever needed it.

Darren made the transition between establishments better than the authorities expected. At Haverigg he turned out to be a relative star in the garden department, where he could put his knowledge and experience of working at the farm to good effect. He received consistently good reports for his work and his willingness to help others. These were both encouraging trends.

He had completed most of the work expected of him in his sentence plan and was feeling quite hopeful about the future. He had taken some basic qualifications in gardening too, as well as improving his general education.

Darren was very pleased with himself when the parole board agreed to the prison's recommendation that he be moved on to open conditions and was allocated a place at Sudbury open prison in Derbyshire. This was potentially the last lap before release and a return to a world that actually he had never really entered in the first place. His brother had offered to help him and might even be able to offer him accommodation with him and his wife, at least at first. Jason also felt confident about the potential for finding gardening work for his brother in the local area.

Darren liked Sudbury, if it is possible to like a prison at all. Most of the prisoners were either low risk offenders or more serious offenders coming towards the end of their sentences and actively preparing for release. Largely, the days of grand posturing and bravado were in the past for most of these men and they looked forward to regaining some control over their own lives. Yes, people still did silly things, like return back drunk from home leave, steal from their employers in the community and try to deal in drugs in the prison, but they were the minority.

After about a year in Sudbury, Darren was working outside in the community in a commercial nursery, growing and supplying trees and shrubs to local garden centres, gardening and landscaping firms and the big DIY stores. He enjoyed the work and was good at it. Things were going well for him.

He started having short periods of home leave at his brother's house and the proposed release address in Newport in Shropshire. These short term licences were a privilege and an opportunity to demonstrate trust and a capacity to live in the community. He said he did well managing to navigate the transport arrangements and the transition back and forth between the prison and his brother's. It was managed without incident. Darren had never been a drinker or into drugs and was actually quite fit and healthy, which would help, but there were still significant gaps in his life experience. The element of doubt about his ability to control his temper and emotions would likely remain a potential concern for some time, but his recent behaviour had been good.

***

It was not long after that time that news broke of a serious incident in the community. In fact, he read it in a newspaper in the prison library. The police had been called to an isolated farm in Shropshire to investigate the suspicious death of a Mr Abingdon.

'Could it be? Was it possible?' he said to one of the prison officers. When the connection was exposed, and the police rang the prison to check that Darren was still in custody, the system reacted quickly and all outside work and temporary release was suspended until it could be verified that Darren was not involved.

The Shropshire police investigation included some of the same officers who had dealt with the original case of the murder and attempted murder of the Abingdons.

'Just look at the facts: who would want to kill Mr Abingdon? Number one candidate is our Darren. He was stabbed to death. It's got him written all over it, but the prison are adamant that he was fully present and accounted for on the day in question. In fact, the day before and the day after, as he was assigned back to the prison garden department. We can't argue with that, but it seems too much of a coincidence to me. How has the little bugger done it?'

'You're too cynical, sir, The facts speak for themselves; he didn't do it. We have to look elsewhere for the murderer this time,' replied his steady old Sergeant.

When interrogated about it in the prison, Darren expressed disbelief that they could even suspect him and that he would jeopardise his whole future at this stage in his sentence for an old fool like Abingdon!

The CID team looked at alternative possibilities. Could it have been one of his children? There was some evidence to suggest a degree of friction between them. Quinton was known to have tried to persuade his father on several occasions to sell the farm. He was hoping for an advance on any potential inheritance. Abigail supported him and was also known to favour selling up. They both still lived locally, too. However, they both appeared to have solid alibis.

The Inspector asked the prison if Darren had any other contacts or associates he was still in touch with and the name Jack came to light. Was it possible, the DI wondered, that Darren had somehow arranged the murder by proxy?

No other obvious explanations emerged and forensic evidence at the scene was limited. It seemed that the killer had been careful not to leave a trace.

But the question remained: how had this happened and who was responsible? Who had killed Mr Abingdon? And why?

Chapter 9

As the police made further enquiries, some interesting facts emerged. The rock solid alibis supplied by the Abingdon children were actually a little shaky on further examination. Also, the financial aspect of their affairs revealed some questionable business dealings and depleted assets. There was a suggestion that actually they had already gambled and lost the family fortune, such as it was, so the pathetic attempts to persuade father to sell up had already been overtaken by events. Even if he had granted them the money, they had effectively already spent it. Was a motive for the murder perhaps a desire to release the full inheritance, assuming of course that the will was in their favour? Suddenly, the case against the Abingdon offspring was looking stronger.

What about Jack and the murder by proxy theory? *How likely was that now?* the police considered.

The DI sat down with his Sergeant to review the detail again in relation to Darren.

'So our Darren goes off on home leave again on the Monday. He is due to return on Wednesday evening, which he does according to the prison authorities, and the murder takes place on the Thursday – a cast iron alibi, or is it? That brother, a twin isn't he? What do we know about him? And have you checked all the CCTV in the town around that time?' he asks his trusty Sergeant.

'Ok sir, I'll get on it.'

More messages arrived from the Abingdon offspring implicating Darren, and more reassurance from the prison that he was in situ for the whole duration of the murder – a conundrum, a complete contradiction.

Then a breakthrough; the Sergeant had found something. Darren's brother was not only a twin but an identical twin – was a switch possible? Was that how he did it? Jason, he discovered, was also a gardener, making him the perfect substitute.

'The cheeky bugger. So at some point the brother returns to the prison in Darren's place and nobody notices while he is still free to commit the perfect or not so perfect murder. Was that it?' posed the DI.

'I think you might be right, sir. I have CCTV footage from the local railway station at Uttoxeter showing both brothers on the platform together on the Wednesday, the evening before the murder. Then Jason leaves the station to get on the bus to the prison whilst Darren gets back on the train to Stafford on his way to Newport.'

'That's it, that's the switch, that's how he did it. Posting his brother to the prison left him free to murder Mr Abingdon the next day. Check the CCTV footage for the following day, let's see if they switched back again.'

Sure enough, the evidence was there of the two brothers meeting briefly at Uttoxeter railway station, again on the Thursday evening, after the murder had taken place, to complete the switch. They shook hands and Jason got back on the train to Newport and Darren got on the bus to return to the prison.

'So, by Thursday evening the plan was complete and Darren was back at Sudbury. Nobody had noticed the switch with his twin brother, leaving him with the apparently perfect alibi. 'Not a bad plan, really, but not good enough – got the little bastard!' exclaimed the DI with more than a little satisfaction.

Further good news came from the crime scene where officers had managed to recover the murder weapon. The knife that had been used to kill Mr Abingdon was taken from one of the farm buildings, it seemed, and used against him. It had been discarded carelessly in a hedge row on the farm not far from where the incident had taken place. It would be up to forensics now to put the icing on the cake, if they could identify a match with Darren.

It was time to go and visit Darren to take the smile off his face. By now he had been returned to the secure prison estate as a reasonable precaution and was being held on a temporary basis in HMP Dovegate near Uttoxeter.

The investigating officers set off confident about the prospect of a good day to come. Dovegate, as a category B prison, offered a much greater level of security than Sudbury. That was no criticism of Sudbury, their roles were completely different. Reception at Dovegate involved a comprehensive search and security process, despite the officer's obvious identity. They left their mobile phones in the gate lodge as normal and entered the prison with nothing more than the clothes they stood up in. They were taken to a designated interview room where Darren was soon produced to meet them.

Despite the passage of time, all involved immediately recognised each other and even smiled, apparently all being quite pleased to be reunited. After the usual preliminaries Darren opened the serious conversation.

'I've heard, obviously. Abingdon is confirmed dead this time. I can't say I'm sorry.'

'It was a good plan, Darren, but like many a good plan it was not faultless. We know how you did it; the switch with your twin brother. We have CCTV evidence of the two of you affecting the switch at the railway station, both before and after the murder. We are also awaiting forensic evidence to link you with the murder weapon,' replied the DI with some satisfaction.

'Oh, well done,' replied Darren, a little surprised.

'I'll save you the trouble. I have nothing to hide gentlemen, just as I didn't when I killed the Abingdon bitch. I was gutted when they told me that Mr Abingdon had survived my first attempt to kill him. It's been a burning sore every since, but I've learnt to be patient – the prison authorities have kindly taught me that. I knew that one day I would reach open conditions and have an opportunity like this to complete the task, all the sweeter in some ways after all these years. Yes, gentlemen, I killed Mr Abingdon at the farm on Thursday. I saw the look of horror and surprise in his eyes as I approached him with one of his own knives from his workshop. I recognised it as one I had used myself when I was there.'

This was not what the officers were expecting, leaving them almost disappointed. They had expected a bit more of a fight than this, but had to content themselves with a quick and comprehensive confession. Always the best form of evidence, they had to acknowledge.

'Why Darren? After what you said about not blowing your chances of release at this stage in your sentence, you realise now that you'll probably never be released?' asked the Sergeant.

'Indeed, you're right, but actually I don't want to be. After all they put me through, it's worth it to know that I got my revenge. I could never cope with the real world, despite the laudable attempts by the authorities to help me, which actually I do appreciate. No, after all those years of enforced isolation and now the long years in prison, I am in no fit state to suddenly become an independent free citizen. When this is over, I will never kill again. I present no further risk to anyone, but I do not seek release. My life is not recoverable from the damage done at that farm, aided and abetted by the very authorities that were meant to protect me. Well, they failed. How does that feel, do you think?'

The officers didn't know quite what to say and almost felt sorry for him. There was a sense of course that Darren was right – the system had let him down as they knew it let many down, but at the end of the day that doesn't justify murder. No, Darren must now pay the price, they thought, still with some satisfaction.

They parted politely, knowing that they probably would never meet again. Darren would return to his cell and they could go home to sleep in their own beds that night. In stunned silence, the two officers followed the escort back to the gate as if ready to leave.

'Hang on a minute, Sgt,' said the DI as he paused and stopped the escort.

'Something's not right here,' there was still a nagging doubt.

'What did he say? WHEN this is OVER, I'll never kill again. So it's not over, it's not complete for him. Who else is at risk?' posed the DI.

'The offspring, boss, Darren never made any secret of his hatred and animosity towards Abigail and Quinton, not without some justification it would seem. Does he intend to somehow harm them too? Surely he couldn't hope to pull off this stunt again?' responded his faithful Sergeant.

'No, it has to be a different approach this time. Come on, we need to establish where they both are to secure their safety. We need to get back in touch with base NOW. Come on, to the gate please, mate, as quickly as possible.'

The escorting officer nodded and the two police officers were quickly processed through security and reunited with their phones. On leaving the prison, they immediately switched them back on to face a barrage of messages.

As they accessed the first missed call from the station, they stood aghast to hear the message.

'Sir, you need to return here ASAP. There has been a further incident at the farm. Abigail and Quinton Abington have been found dead, poisoned most likely, and the farm is a blaze. The fire service is already at the scene and trying to bring it under control.'

Postscript 2015

It transpired that Darren had rung the farm whilst out of prison and spoken to the house keeper. He had claimed to be from the solicitor's office and had asked to leave a message for Abigail and Quinton to meet them at the farm on Thursday afternoon at two to hear an initial outline of their father's will. He knew how desperate they would be to hear the details, having already spent most of the money, and that they would certainly attend and ensure the house was empty for such a meeting. The house keeper would be ordered home early.

How to kill them? He had given that considerable thought. He would have liked to have done it directly, to see them suffer, but had concluded that it was too risky. He also wanted to destroy the farmhouse, to wipe this miserable place off the face of the earth. Trying to set a remote fire would no doubt be difficult, given the time lapse involved but not impossible, he had concluded. A second more reliable method of dispatch, however, would be needed as a backup. He settled on poison, reasoning that the offspring would undoubtedly be present for the meeting that he had contrived and in a buoyant mood anticipating a celebration. So if he was to leave a carafe of their favourite wine in the room, suitably laced with poison, knowing that they would be the only ones in the house, he felt confident that they would drink it to toast their anticipated success.

They had taken the bate and Darren's crude attempt at setting a fire delayed with a time switch hadn't worked out exactly as he had planned, but it was enough to start a slow smoulder in a pile of straw to eventually ignite and set off the large amount of farm petrol left in place to accelerate the blaze. Despite the fire service's best attempts, the house was effectively destroyed. No one else was caught in the blaze, which had been responsibly reported by Mandy. The house it was found had not been adequately insured and Mr Abingdon had, in fact, built up considerable debts, so after his death and the fire, there were in fact little to no family assets remaining for the Abingdon children, even if they had survived.

Lightning Source UK Ltd.
Milton Keynes UK
UKHW011950020322
399468UK00001B/37

9 781800 317895